C000020305

THE LAST P.

Rich Hawkins lives in Salisbury, England, with his wife and daughter. He has several short stories published in various anthologies. 'The Last Plague' is his debut novel.

THE LAST PLAGUE

RICH HAWKINS

This Edition Published 2014 by Crowded
Quarantine Publications
The moral right of the author has been asserted

A CIP catalogue record for this book
is available from the British Library

ISBN: 978-0-9928838-3-6

Crowded Quarantine Publications
34 Cheviot Road
Wolverhampton
West Midlands
WV2 2HD

ACKNOWLEDGEMENTS

Thanks and gratitude to my family and friends, present and absent; my old mates from the good old days (you know who you all are). Cheers to Matt Darst for his beta-reading talents and literary wisdom, Paul M. Feeney for the kind words, Adam and Zoe Millard for having faith in me, David Moody, Wayne Simmons, Adam Baker and Conrad Williams for inspiring me, everyone in the Facebook groups Moody's Survivors and the Wayne Simmons Fan Page, all the other writers I've come to know online, and everyone who's ever supported me and my writing.

My humble appreciation to you all.

To Sara, Willow and Molly,
Who keep me sane amidst the madness.

PROLOGUE

Her name was Florence, and she did not cry when the end of the world came. She didn't scream when Mr. Stewart from next door stumbled into the garden with something pulsing and wet erupting from his throat.

In the distance a plane fell from the sky and vanished beyond the curve of the earth. She heard the explosion just before the black smoke stained the horizon. She imagined fire and metal and people burning in their seats. She imagined bodies obliterated by impact with the earth.

Mr. Stewart fell down, writhing on the front lawn, spluttering a yolky fluid from his mouth. His bones pushed against his skin. He arched his back and his insides cracked and popped like something chewed by a slavering mouth.

Florence watched him with fascination, her feet planted on the garden path. The smell of cut grass in the air. She did not run away.

Mr. Stewart stopped moving.

Florence's father grabbed her by the arm and dragged her into the house. Her mother was waiting for them in the kitchen. Smudged make-up and running eyeliner. Pale skin like boiled tripe.

Mum put down her mobile phone. "Couldn't get through to my parents. Couldn't get through to anyone."

"What about the television?" Dad asked.

"Bad news."

Florence held her mother's hand. Mum offered a weak smile through glistening tears.

"What do we do?" Mum's voice was strained.

Mr. Stewart was screaming outside. He didn't sound human.

Dad picked up a carving knife. "Lock the doors."

CHAPTER ONE

Two days earlier.

The battered and dirt-speckled Vauxhall Corsa was an intestinal worm in the guts of the Kent countryside.

Frank Hooper's bones shook as the car lurched over a pothole. The road's surface was scarred and uneven, dusted with gravel and dirt. The shadows of trees loomed across the road, stretching from one side to the other, onyx and creeping with the sun behind them.

His back was aching. Driving was bad for his posture. His throat and mouth were dry, like he had been chewing cotton wool. He yawned. A dull pain throbbed at the top of his skull.

"We're nearly there," said Joel, studying the map beside him. "I think."

"Glad you're certain about that," Frank said.

"You're the one who turned off the sat-nav."

"It sounded like my mother."

"I like your mother's voice," said Ralph, from the back seat. "Especially when she talks dirty."

"You're obsessed with older women," said Magnus, across from Ralph.

"I've got a problem," said Ralph. "Always fancied Captain Janeway."

"Who?"

"She's from *Star Trek: Voyager*," Joel said.

"I'd rather have Princess Leia," Frank said.

"She hasn't aged as well as Janeway," said Ralph.

"Good point," said Joel.

"Fucking nerds," said Magnus.

"I didn't say I liked *Star Trek*," said Ralph. "I just said I liked Captain Janeway."

"Captain Janeway is a woman, right?" asked Magnus.

Ralph grunted. "Funny."

Frank glanced at Joel. "Look at the map. Find out where we are."

Joel gave him a mock salute. "Yes, sir."

"No need to be sarcastic."

"Sorry. Right. Okay. I think we're heading in the right direction."

"You think?"

"We just went through Wishford. The house is somewhere around here."

"That sounds reassuring."

"Now you're being sarcastic. It's not very far. Keep an eye out."

Frank's grip on the steering wheel tightened. He slowed his breathing, exhaled through his nose, and his hands loosened upon the wheel until he relaxed again and the throbbing in his head faded a little.

Ralph laughed. He was a short stocky man with a crew cut, eating a packet of crisps which rustled every time he reached his ape-like hand inside. The floor around his feet was sprinkled with bits of food. Frank glanced back to see Ralph brushing crumbs from his lap. Frank sighed, didn't bother to scold him. There was no point.

"You two are like an old married couple," Ralph said.

"They've been like that since school," said Magnus. He was shaven-headed; an attempt to hide male-pattern baldness, a hereditary condition in his family. Thick-rimmed glasses framed his grey eyes. An oversized jacket and cargo pants shrouded his meagre, wiry figure.

"So are you both sharing a room, when we get there?" Ralph asked.

Frank laughed.

"Very funny, Ralph," said Joel. "You should be on TV."

"They wouldn't let the ugly fucker on television," Magnus said.

"Piss off," said Ralph. "There are many women who can't resist the bearded and portly look."

"Depends how drunk you get them," said Frank.

"Very true, Francis."

"Don't be too hard on yourself," Joel said. "There are plenty of ugly, sober women out there that'll sleep with you. A lot of desperate women out there." He winked at Ralph.

"I don't need your sympathy, Joel – you're the poor sod getting married next month."

"Says the bloke who's got his right hand for a girlfriend."

"Left hand actually. Well, both, to be honest."

"Have they got names?" asked Frank.

"Yeah," said Ralph. "Magnus's missus and Joel's missus."

The four men laughed. Magnus tried to twist Ralph's ear between his thumb and forefinger, but Ralph batted away his hand and slapped him on the back of the head.

"Wanker," said Magnus.

Ralph grinned. "Love you too."

They passed a small farm with a grey-walled, crumbling barn. A tractor was parked at the front of the farmhouse.

Ralph finished the crisps and scrunched the packet into a ball.

"Where you thinking of putting that?" Frank eyed him from the rear-view mirror.

Ralph made an innocent face. "Somewhere…"

"Put it in your pocket; if you can't do that, put it up your arse. You've already made enough mess."

"Wouldn't putting it up my arse make more mess?"

"Ralph, don't be facetious," Frank said.

"No need to use the long words, college boy."

"Just do it, mate."

"Okay." Ralph put away the empty packet, then picked up a paper bag of cookies from the seat. He nibbled on one, and crumbs fell down the front of his Metallica t-shirt, over his curved belly and onto his thighs.

"Sorry," Ralph said, mashed up cookie in his mouth.

Joel turned to Frank. "See? That's what you get when you let a monkey in your car."

Ralph gently kicked the back of Joel's seat, and he jumped.

"Don't shit yourself, mate."

"Prick."

"Stop arguing, girls," said Frank.

Joel looked down at the map. "Uh, I think I've worked it out.

"This should be good," said Ralph.

Joel ignored him. "Keep following this road for another few miles then turn onto a smaller road, which will take us to the house."

"Good," Frank said. "I need a beer."

"Same here."

Frank guided the car around a tight bend. The sun was falling and the chill in the air touched his skin. His headache was almost gone now. He spared a glance away from the road and saw the fields open up on either side. Some were filled with the distinctive yellow of rapeseed, stark against the land's dull greens and browns.

"Reminds me of Somerset," said Magnus, staring out of the window.

"Yeah," said Ralph.

"You sound disappointed," Magnus said. "Would you have preferred to go up north?"

Ralph grunted. "You must be joking. Last time I went up north a transvestite tried to fondle me."

* * *

Narrow country roads. Almost sundown. The light was fading.

14

"Do you hear that?" asked Joel.

Frank changed gear. "Hear what?"

"Rumbling."

"Could be my stomach," Ralph said.

A military truck shot around the bend, filling most of the narrow road and momentarily blocking the low sun. Its shadow fell across the car, engine growling like a large, angry animal.

Frank turned the wheel sharply, bringing the Corsa to a stop at the side of the road, skidding on the grass. The truck's massive wheels passed inches from Frank's window, swiped the wing-mirror and kicked up bits of gravel and dust against the car. Ugly angles of dark green metal smeared with dried mud. The stink of diesel and oil filled its wake as it disappeared down the road.

Frank looked at the wing-mirror lying on the road.

"Fucking squaddies," Ralph said.

Another army truck blared past them and crushed what remained of the severed wing-mirror.

Frank scratched the side of his head. "Shit."

Magnus looked back down the road. "Wonder where they're heading."

"They were in a hurry," Joel said.

Frank felt his chest tighten. He fumbled for his asthma inhaler and sucked on it, breathing deeply. His breathing evened out. A rush of relief.

"You want me to drive?" Joel asked.

Frank put away the inhaler. "Let's get going. Try to reach the cottage before late afternoon."

He put the car back in gear and left the mirror's remains on the road.

CHAPTER TWO

J oel pointed ahead and to the left. "There's the turning."

Frank slowed the car and changed gear to negotiate the entrance to the side road. It was more of a dirt track than a road, and the car trembled upon small craters, dips and bumps.

"There it is," said Joel, folding the map, pleased with himself. "Been a while since I've been here."

The cottage was flanked by grasslands, gentle slopes and open fields. A sentinel shape against the clouding sky. Wild flowers were small blooms of colour. The dirt track widened into a gravel driveway. Frank stopped the car at the front of the house. He turned off the engine, savoured the silence. He undid his seatbelt and sat back in his seat.

"Finally."

"Looks like a nice place," said Magnus.

"And we're staying here for free," Joel said.

"Nice one," said Ralph.

Frank glanced at the plastic stump where the wing-mirror had been. He scowled, exhaled. He'd get it fixed when he returned home.

The cottage was a relic from the early years of the last century. An arched flagstone roof. Brick walls painted white. A wooden arch over the front door. Tulips idled in flowerbeds either side of the front door, under the downstairs windows.

Wind-chimes trembled in the breeze.

The cottage reminded Frank of the house he grew up in. He felt a strange pang of childhood nostalgia; of innocent days before the shadow of adulthood: taxes, dead-end jobs, banks, high blood pressure…

…Children. A child.

He pushed that last one away.

"Sorry about the wing-mirror," said Joel.

He looked at Joel. "These things happen."

The four men got out.

Frank leaned against the car, resting his arms on its roof.

Ralph yawned and arched his back, stretching towards the sky like a mad priest; tattoos on each arm, curlicues of black stretching down to his wrists. He bent over, barely able to touch his toes, grunting and grimacing like he was performing amazing feats of contortion. His hairy arse crack peeked above the waist of his jeans.

"Talk about the dark side of the moon," Joel said.

Ralph straightened, raised his middle finger.

Frank opened the boot and started unloading their bags.

"Careful with that one," said Ralph when he saw Frank place his holdall on the ground. "My booze is in there."

Magnus was talking on his mobile, his face flustered. "Yes, dear, I'll call you later, don't worry. What was that? No, I won't get too drunk. No, there isn't going to be a stripper. Joel didn't want one." He paused, listened. "What? No, I don't care if we have a stripper, it doesn't bother me." Magnus noticed the others watching him and shook his head.

Ralph meowed and made a whipping noise.

"Yes, dear, I won't forget to call you later. Look, I've got to go now, okay? Okay then. Bye."

"You might as well have brought your missus with you," said Ralph.

"Is everything alright?" said Frank.

They were supposed to have arrived at the cottage yesterday evening, but Debbie had made Magnus stay an extra night to help look after their sons.

Magnus slipped the mobile into his jacket. "Same old shit. Nothing new."

"Come on, mate," said Ralph. "Grow some balls. It's Joel's stag weekend."

Magnus glared at him. "You know the boys are ill. You know what Debbie's like." He turned away.

"Leave it," Frank told Ralph. "It's not his fault."

Ralph shook his head.

After the bags had been unloaded Frank locked the car. Joel produced a key from his jeans.

"So your Uncle Jasper owns a few cottages like this one?" asked Frank.

Joel swirled the key-ring around one finger. "He owns several holiday cottages up and down the country. He does okay."

"Alright for some," said Ralph, scratching his beard. He picked up his tattered holdall and slung it over his shoulder.

Joel unlocked the door, opened it, and stepped inside. Magnus followed him.

"What do you reckon?" Ralph asked. "Good place for a piss up?"

Frank patted him on the shoulder. "You told me once that anywhere is good for a piss up as long as you've got booze and good company."

"Did I?"

"Yeah, but you won't remember because you were drunk when you said it."

"I do have my moments of wisdom."

"Occasionally."

Ralph grinned. They listened to the wind dance around the eaves.

Frank lifted his bag.

Ralph said, "Listen, mate, I know the last year's been shit for you and Catherine…"

"I don't need pity."

"I know, but I see the anger and frustration in your eyes sometimes. I don't blame you for feeling that way. I can't even begin to imagine what you've both been through."

"I'm fine, Ralph. Really."

"I'm just saying, boss, that if you need someone to talk to, don't feel embarrassed to ask."

"You're just a big softy, aren't you?"

Ralph glanced around like he was about to impart a secret. "Just don't tell anyone, mate. I've got a reputation to protect. Shall we go inside?"

"Good idea."

CHAPTER THREE

Frank put the pizzas in the oven. Joel emptied bags of crisps and snacks into large bowls.

"Have you booked a stripper?" asked Joel. "I specifically said no strippers. I said no strippers."

"Joel, I didn't order a stripper."

"Are you sure?"

"Of course I'm sure."

"Do you know if Ralph did? That's the sort of thing he'd do."

"Ralph hasn't booked a stripper."

"I haven't done what?" Ralph walked into the kitchen, sipping a bottle of German beer. He had changed into a Cradle of Filth t-shirt.

Frank looked from Joel to Ralph. "You didn't order a stripper for tonight, did you?"

Ralph gasped in mock surprise. "Sir, I am offended. Order a stripper? On Joel's stag night? Who'd have thought of such an idea?"

Frank folded his arms. "Did you?"

Ralph smiled. "I didn't order a stripper. Wish I had done, though."

"Good," said Joel. "Where's Magnus?"

Ralph took a gulp of beer. "He's in the living room playing on the Xbox. Poor bloke needs a break from that wife of his. She sent him a text a minute ago saying he was neglecting his *marital duties*."

Frank shook his head. "Bloody hell, that's harsh."

"Is she back on medication?" Joel asked.

"She should be."

"She's always had problems, even before she married Magnus," said Ralph. "Everyone knows she's crazy."

"She's bipolar, not crazy," said Frank.

"Not to mention she weighs about twenty stone."

Frank opened two beers, handed one to Joel.

Ralph scratched his beard. "Did you bring any toilet roll?"

* * *

They downed a round of shots, grimacing as the vodka burned in their throats. Frank welcomed the buzz from the alcohol. He had sent a text to Catherine; a simple message of affection. He touched his wedding ring with his thumb; it had dulled slightly over six years.

Being the groom, Joel would have the master bedroom with its king-sized bed; the others had to pull straws for the remaining two bedrooms.

Ralph pulled the short straw.

"Unlucky, mate," said Magnus, smirking.

"Yeah, bad luck, bud." Frank swigged a beer.

Ralph shrugged. "Doesn't matter. I'll take the sofa. Slept in worse places."

* * *

They formed a circle in the living room. More shots of vodka.

Frank raised his glass. "To Joel: may he be a brave man in the years ahead. May he have the strength to fight the good fight."

"May he rest in peace," said Ralph.

"May the Lord have mercy on his soul," said Magnus.

"Amen," they said together, heads bowed.

Then they laughed.

They downed their shots. Joel was last to finish. He patted his chest, screwed up his face.

Frank handed out the beers. Ralph offered cigars, and only Frank refused one, due to his asthma.

Joel swayed on his feet as he lit his cigar. "How many years have we been friends for?"

"Don't get soppy, mate," said Ralph. "You always do this when you're drunk."

"I'm not drunk," Joel protested.

Magnus laughed. His cigar plumed a tiny streak of smoke.

"Let him speak," said Frank.

"We've been friends since playgroup. How old were we then? Four? Five?"

"More or less," said Frank.

Joel smiled with the idiotic charm of inebriation. "And we were mates all the way through school."

"The Fearsome Four," said Frank.

"Yeah, four idiots," said Magnus.

Ralph studied his cigar. "We left school sixteen years ago. Fucking hell. Seems like such a long time ago. Dumb, spotty teenagers."

"But look at us now," Joel said. "Older and a little wiser. My best man, Frank, and my two ushers. We've got responsibilities…"

"Apart from Ralph," said Frank.

Ralph glowered. "I've got responsibilities."

"You live with your parents," said Magnus.

"It's cheap. Mum does my laundry. Fuck off."

"Like I was saying," said Joel. "We've all got responsibilities and commitments, but we've still remained close."

"Gay," said Ralph, shaking his head.

"Fair point," said Frank.

Magnus laughed.

Joel raised his bottle. "Cheers, lads."

"Cheers."

They drank.

Frank looked down the neck of his beer bottle. "Where did the time go?"

"Not down there," Magnus said.

"Tell me about it," said Ralph. He looked at the floor. "You remember when we used to go out clubbing every weekend? I miss those days. I miss the nights when we would go out and anything was possible."

"Great nights," Frank said.

"They certainly were," said Magnus.

Joel finished his beer. "When you reach a certain age, clubbing loses its appeal. Seems a little desperate somehow. That's why I wanted to spend the weekend here. I didn't want to go to a nightclub or a big city. I know it's a bit crap, but I wanted to be here with my real, oldest friends."

"Joel's going gay again," muttered Ralph. "He'll be wearing a gimp suit and stilettos any minute now."

"We're certainly getting old," Frank said. "I've started to wear cardigans at home. I'm growing man-boobs."

"How do you think I feel then?" said Ralph, patting his stomach.

"That's because you eat too much, not old age," said Magnus, adjusting his glasses. "Anyway, you think you're got it bad? My pubes are going grey."

"And you've got the muscle tone of a crack addict," said Ralph.

Joel laughed.

"That is bad," said Frank.

"Better wiry than curvy," Magnus said.

Ralph shrugged, downed his beer until it was empty. "Fuck it. Put on the DVD. I want to drink until my eyes fall out."

CHAPTER FOUR

Hours passed in a haze of alcoholic fog. They watched *Star Wars IV: A New Hope*, laughing at Joel's attempts to critique every iconic scene. He was a big Harrison Ford fan, and Han Solo was his favourite character.

Ralph kept calling him 'Hand Solo' and making a masturbation gesture with one hand.

Magnus said he preferred the Ewoks. Joel argued with Ralph when Ralph said horror was a superior genre to science fiction. Magnus performed his party trick of balancing a pen on his nose while Ralph poured beer down his throat. He managed to keep it balanced until Ralph swapped the beer for whiskey.

They played *Guitar Hero* on the Xbox. Magnus was surprisingly good, hitting each note perfectly, despite being steaming drunk.

Frank downed enough shots to numb his extremities. He laughed when Joel began slurring his words. He laughed when Ralph tried to light his own farts and only succeeded in burning his arse. He laughed for no reason.

Then there was a knock at the door.

Joel froze with a bottle at his mouth. "Who's that?"

"What's the time?" said Ralph, scratching his head.

Frank checked his watch. "Almost midnight."

Magnus burped, gagged a little. His eyes were watery.

"We expecting any visitors?" said Joel. The last word came out as 'vishitors'.

Ralph looked at Magnus. They both grinned. Ralph turned to Frank and winked.

Frank stifled a laugh.

Joel looked puzzled. Glazed eyes.

"I'll see who it is," said Ralph. He struggled to rise from the sofa. He stumbled into the hallway, giggling like a schoolboy high on sugar. His shoulder grazed the wall, knocking askew a framed painting of a riverside cottage.

Magnus looked at Joel. "I'm sorry, mate. It was Ralph's idea."

Joel's face went slack. "What was…?"

Frank heard the front door open. Voices. Ralph laughed. The front door slammed.

Ralph appeared, trying to keep a straight face as he swigged from his beer. He carried a wooden kitchen chair in his other hand.

"What's the chair for?" said Joel.

"What do you think?"

"Did you...?" Frank asked.

Ralph nodded. "I certainly did, boss." He moved some empty bottles out of the way and placed the chair in the centre of the room.

Joel looked at the chair, puzzled.

A female police officer entered the room, followed by a tall, wide-shouldered man wearing a leather jacket, with a greasy side-parting and a neck like a shaven bear. The man nodded a curt greeting and stood in the corner of the room, arms folded.

"Oh shit," said Joel. His voice was uneven and boyish.

The woman looked to be in her late forties, dyed blonde hair and too much make-up. Eyeliner coated on like paint and blood-red lipstick. Her breasts were almost bursting through her uniform. Crow's feet and poor skin under fake tan. One eye was bloodshot.

A short leather skirt barely covered her arse. She was carrying a small black bag and an Alba CD player.

Ralph started laughing.

"Is there a Mr. Joel Gosling here?" the woman said.

Joel raised his hand cautiously. "That's, uh, me..."

Frank sat next to Magnus on the sofa.

"I'm afraid you're under arrest, Mr. Gosling," she said.

"Read him his rights!" said Ralph. He finished his beer and grabbed another one.

"You're not a real police officer, are you?" Joel asked the woman.

In the corner her minder smirked and shook his head.

"Luckily for you, I'm not, my dear," she said. "But I've heard you've been a very bad boy."

On the sofa, Frank, Ralph and Magnus struggled to stop from breaking into fits of laughter.

Joel swallowed. "You're a stripper, aren't you?"

"I'll let you decide that, my dear. Now come sit down on this chair and we'll get on with your interrogation."

"Brilliant," said Ralph. He turned to Frank. "You owe me fifty quid for the stripper, okay?"

"Fifty quid? Bloody hell, Ralph."

"She was the cheapest one I could get on such short notice."

"Yeah, looks like it."

"Pay me tomorrow, mate."

Joel sat down on the chair, guided by the stripper. She smiled at him. He tried to return the smile, but it came out as an awkward grimace.

"My fiancée's gonna kill me if she finds out."

"Don't worry, my dear," the stripper said. She undid her uniform and took off her skirt. Leathery breasts and a pot belly. Sagging buttocks the same colour as a creosoted fence. The back of her thong vanished into darkness. She placed the CD player on the floor then reached into her bag and produced a bottle of squirty cream.

Joel went pale.

The stripper pressed a button on the CD player. Britney Spears began to sing 'I'm a Slave 4 U'. The stripper wiggled her arse and giggled.

"She's got cellulite," Ralph whispered as he took out his camera-phone.

CHAPTER FIVE

Two hours later the stripper was gone, and Joel was unconscious, a bottle of beer in his hand and whipped cream smeared around his mouth. Frank dozed on the sofa. Ralph was on the floor, snoring loudly, his stomach gurgling.

"Lightweights," said Magnus. He smiled and swayed. A warm numbness filled his body. He ate the last slice of pizza and licked grease from his fingers.

The house was silent apart from the creak and groan of its wooden joints and brick walls, reshaping itself in the night.

Magnus walked outside. The breeze stirred the grass. The Corsa was a squat shadow. He liked the darkness. It was peaceful and there were so few moments of peace these days. He filled his lungs with the night air.

The moon was blanketed by clouds. Abyssal darkness surrounded the house, like the voids between galaxies. No lights from towns or villages. This was how the land would have been before the rise of man.

The gaps in the cloud cover were filled with stars. Constellations aflame. Distant suns. Ancient suns.

Dying suns. Some had been dead for millennia. Beautiful.

He had read about solar flares; about what would happen if one reached out and enveloped the earth. A temperature of twenty million degrees kelvin would turn the oceans to steam and drown the world in fire. Suck the oxygen from the air. Turn every organism to ash. Cities would be destroyed by immense walls of flame and the planet would be left as a burnt piece of dead rock floating in space.

He felt small and unworthy like bacteria.

His hands shook as he took out a packet of cigarettes. He was supposed to have quit the habit. He lit one, took a long drag on it. The smoke was chemical bliss inside him; made his pulse quicken, made his bones feel like feathers.

He checked his mobile. Three missed calls from Debbie. Another text message. He read it, shaking his head.

He was sick of her. He was sick of taking care of her and the boys. She had burdened him for five years, with her illness, her complexes and her paranoia. She had drained him of his strength and his will. They hadn't had sex in over a year and the last time they had he had struggled to hide his disgust at her obese, sweaty, stinking body. Sores on the inside of her thighs where the skin had rubbed together and chafed. Hairy legs. Pubic hair spilling from her underwear like a gathering of spider legs. Skin the colour of the filling in a sausage roll. She often forgot to take her medication, causing mood swings and temper tantrums.

Magnus toked on the cigarette, looked at the stars, wished they could take him away.

Sometimes, lying in bed as she grunted and snored next to him, he fantasised about burying her in a custom-made coffin and crying crocodile tears at her graveside. He often thought of caving in her face with a hammer and laughing in relief as he did so. He thought of murder. Then he would be free.

But he couldn't kill Debbie. He was a coward. He'd never even been in a fight. And he still loved her. That was the worst part about it. He couldn't help himself. He had known about her problems when they first met. There had been an attraction on a fundamental level. She had been slim, but curvy in the right places. The sex had been fantastic; the way she would lower herself onto him, grind upon him, press her skin against his. It had been primal, manic fucking. She used to bite him, make him bleed sometimes. He had loved that.

But as the years passed, and they got married, her condition worsened. She changed into nothing more than a mound of useless meat.

But he still loved her.

He finished the cigarette, dropped it, put it out with his foot. He spat.

The clouds lifted, revealing the scarred moon in its cradle. Silver light fell over the countryside. A patchwork quilt of fields.

Thunder roared above, and Magnus jumped. He watched the moon vanish. The stars were gone and the clouds were moving and broiling like an ocean in heavy weather. Thunder boomed again. There was a great pressure upon him, trying to push him into the earth and pressing down on him.

Something was in the sky above him, directly overhead. Something huge and silent. He sensed rather than saw it.

His nose began to bleed.

Magnus fell down, sprawled on the ground. His bowels felt like a sack of hot soup.

The thunder sounded like the giant bones of skeletal gods grinding together.

Magnus curled into a ball. He began to cry. A childhood terror gripped him. The fear of monsters and being lost in the darkness.

He whimpered. The ground was cold, sucking at his warmth.

The world faded away.

* * *

Ralph awoke, ran his tongue over furred teeth. A shard of pepperoni was stuck between two molars. He gave up trying to loosen it with his tongue. He burped and it tasted of stomach fluids. He was shivering.

He sat up, hands over his face, groaning. The world tilted to one side.

Looking through the window, he saw the sky brightening. The wall clock ticked like a pulse. Just past four-thirty. The room was strewn with the wreckage of the night. The smell of stale beer. He wiped his mouth.

Someone had eaten the last of the pizza. Ralph growled. Cold air nipped at his bare arms.

Frank and Joel were asleep. He remembered the stripper through a haze of booze, and laughed.

Magnus was gone.

Ralph stood, put his hand on the sofa to stay upright. His bladder was swollen. His stomach gurgled and turned. He burped again. His heart was a heavy weight within his chest, swimming in acid.

The front door was open. Birdsong. He stumbled to the doorway.

"Magnus?"

No answer.

Thunder boomed far away. Dark clouds to the east.

Magnus was lying on the dewy grass, curled up, his arms wrapped around his chest. His clothes were damp. His glasses were askew. A crust of dried blood between his nose and top lip.

Ralph crouched and shook him by the shoulders. "Magnus, wake up. What you doing out here?"

Magnus opened his eyes, confused and groggy. The bones in his neck clicked when he turned towards Ralph.

"I had a nightmare," he said, his voice small.

Ralph lifted Magnus's left eyelid. He examined the eye for signs of something more exotic than beer and vodka. "Have you been smoking those Jamaican woodbines again?"

"I gave up weed a long time ago, Ralph."

"Let's get you inside."

"I don't think it was a nightmare." Magnus wiped dew from his face. He looked up at Ralph, his eyes regaining some focus. He blinked. Drool glistened on his mouth.

Ralph helped him to his feet.

Magnus watched the sky as they went inside.

CHAPTER SIX

Later that morning, Frank popped two aspirin into his mouth and washed them down with water. He was sitting next to Ralph on the sofa. Magnus was at the kitchen table, head bowed, drinking coffee and eating toast.

"I feel like shit," said Ralph, massaging his temples with his fingers.

"Join the club," Frank said. "I need to brush my teeth."

The toilet flushed from the other side of the cottage. Joel entered the living room, wearing a baggy t-shirt and boxer shorts. Homer Simpson slippers. His hair was stuck up in ragged tufts. He held his stomach. His face was pale. Watery, puffy eyes. His skinny legs were hairless.

Ralph grinned. "You look very sharp this morning."

Joel collapsed onto the armchair, stared at the ceiling. He groaned. "I suppose the stripper was your idea?"

Ralph chuckled. "Someone had to liven up your stag weekend."

"Yeah, cheers for that," Joel said sourly.

"My pleasure. You've still got squirty cream around your mouth."

Joel went to wipe his mouth but then realised Ralph was messing with him.

"Don't be cruel," Frank said. "Give him a break."

"Fair enough. He's been through enough."

"Please don't put any photos or video on Facebook," Joel said.

"Oh, come on," Ralph complained.

"Please, Ralph. Anya will kill me."

"No, she won't. Polish girls are very open-minded."

"I'm begging you."

"Don't guilt trip me."

"Please…"

Ralph stroked his chin. He shook his head. "Okay then. You spoil all the fun."

"Where's Magnus?" asked Joel.

Frank sucked on his inhaler, grimaced. "Out in the kitchen."

"Is he okay? Has Debbie been calling him again?"

"No," said Ralph. "It's something else."

"Like what?"

Ralph said, "I found him outside, asleep on the grass."

"What was he doing out there? Is he back on the weed?"

Ralph hesitated. "I don't think so. He said he had a nightmare...but then said it wasn't a nightmare. His nose had been bleeding."

"Is he doing coke?"

"Magnus wouldn't do that shit," Frank said.

Joel frowned. "Hope he's alright."

"I think so," Ralph said. "He's a bit shaken up, that's all."

Magnus appeared in the doorway, steam rising from a cup of coffee in his hand. A muscle twitched in his face. "I can hear you all from the kitchen."

The other men said nothing.

Magnus eyed the three of them in turn. He took a mouthful of coffee and swallowed. "I went outside to have a cigarette. You were all asleep. I was looking at the sky. Then something else was above me. I fell down and it felt like I was being crushed. I don't know what it was."

"Are you sure?" asked Ralph.

Joel looked at Magnus's nostrils for signs of white powder.

Magnus noticed him. "I haven't been doing drugs, okay?"

Joel looked at him. "Sorry, mate."

Magnus returned to the kitchen.

The room stayed silent behind him.

* * *

There was no more thunder. No rain.

The men spent the rest of the morning recovering from hangovers. Frank and Joel cooked fried breakfasts for everyone. Sausages, fried eggs, fried bread, mushrooms, baked beans and bacon. Ralph asked for black pudding and was told to go and buy it himself if he wanted some. Joel didn't finish his breakfast, so he gave the rest to Ralph, apart from the mushrooms, which Ralph gave to Magnus.

In the afternoon Ralph played Frank at darts. They drank coffee between turns. Ralph had once played for their county. He beat Frank without trying too hard and he let Frank know it.

"You've got a dart player's physique," Frank told him.

Ralph smiled and threw a double-top. "I think that's five games to nil."

Frank put down his darts.

Ralph took the five pound note from Frank's hand, folded it into his wallet.

"Well played," said Frank.

"Don't forget you still owe me for the stripper."

"I'll pay you when we get home."

"No probs."

Outside, the day grew darker. But rain still did not come.

* * *

Magnus turned off his mobile and put it his pocket. He gritted his teeth, rested his forehead against the kitchen table.

Debbie wouldn't stop calling.

Magnus went outside. The clouds were like concrete. Summer was in its death-throes, although it had been a dreary summer anyway. Autumn was almost here.

"Ah, fuck it," he said.

He took out his mobile and switched it on. He waited.

The mobile rang, vibrating in his hand. His ringtone was a Johnny Cash song.

Debbie was calling. He sighed, ran a hand over his shaven head.

He put the phone to one ear. "Hello?"

Debbie's voice, pleading and pathetic: "*Are you coming home?*"

* * *

Joel needed to stretch his legs. The lukewarm shower hadn't refreshed him. The water had seemed greasy. He had brushed his teeth twice to remove the taste of alcohol from his mouth.

The grass was damp. The hems of his jeans were wet. He walked the fields around the house. He wore a jacket to keep out the creeping cold. The breeze ruffled his hair.

He remembered parts of last night; the stripper dancing around him, her groin writhing in front of his face. She had touched his face, and her fingertips had been too warm and yellowed from nicotine. He remembered the others laughing. He didn't want to think about what would happen if Anya found out.

But he hadn't done anything wrong, had he? Why should he feel guilty when he had no control over what had happened?

Still, he felt like he had betrayed Anya, even though all he had done was lick sickly-sweet squirty cream from the stripper's bellybutton. But that was enough for him. He was wracked with anxiety and the hot panic-fever of guilt. He was jittery.

He huffed air out of his mouth and frowned.

There was nobody out here. The fields opened out before him. Low hedgerows and oak trees. A family of deer were grazing in a field. The chirp and twitter of songbirds. A crow flashed overhead, squawking like it was mocking him.

Joel glanced back at the house. He halted and looked down the footpath, the way he had been heading.

"Oh well," he muttered. "Here goes…"

He had his mobile in his hand. It shook a little. Too much adrenaline flooding his veins. Fast heart rate. His guts squirmed. He wanted to take a dump. He dialled Anya's number. Part of him hoped she would answer; another part of him prayed she wouldn't so he could put this off a bit longer.

She answered almost immediately.

"Hello, love," he said. "How're you?"

Anya coughed, cleared her throat. "Hi, Joel. How is my future husband this morning? Still drunk?" He loved her accent. Fucking loved it. Her English was excellent. Ever since he'd been a young lad he'd been captivated by women with Eastern European accents. Russian, Slovakian, Polish, it didn't matter.

"No, just a bit hung-over," he replied.

"This is a surprise. I thought you still be in bed. You have good night?"

"I have to admit something."

A pause on the other end of the line. He pictured her looking worried, waiting for him to say he had cheated on her.

"Admit?"

"There was a stripper last night."

A pause. He heard her breathing. He waited. Closed his eyes.

"I know," she said.

He opened his eyes one at a time. "What? You know?"

"I know what happened."

"I'm sorry. Please forgive me. The others were jeering me, goading me. I thought that if I wimped out of it I'd look like a fool. I didn't do anything with the stripper, I promise. She was old and skanky."

"*Skanky*, Joel?"

"Yes. It means dirty, unclean."

"Oh."

He listened to her tone of voice. His heart pounded against his ribcage. He felt woozy and panicky.

"Are you still there, Anya?"

"It is okay, Joel. You did nothing wrong."

"Really?"

She was giggling. "I knew you would have stripper. Ralph and Magnus told me before you left. They asked for my…uh, permission."

"So you really don't mind?"

"Joel, what you think me and my friends did on my hen party?"

"You had a stripper?"

"Yes. I had to lick cream from his abs. Was fun. I was drunk."

A stab of jealousy in his chest. "I did that as well."

"Lick cream from man's abs?"

"No," he said. "I had to lick squirty cream from her bellybutton."

She laughed. He laughed along with her, relieved. The anxiety faded.

"You realise how much I love you?" Joel asked her.

"Tell me."

"I'll show you when I get home tomorrow."

"I look forward to that."

"I'll bring the squirty cream."

She laughed again. Always easy to make her laugh, even with his bad jokes. He adored her for it. Other women had been mere infatuations that ended badly, as most did. It didn't matter. He only wanted her.

"I love you too, Joel. My husband."

"Not yet."

"Soon."

"I've got to go now," he said. "I think it's going to rain."

They said their goodbyes. Joel returned the mobile to his pocket.

He saw three dots in the sky, approaching from the east.

He heard the muffled stutter of helicopter rotors slicing the air.

Joel whistled.

The Chinook helicopters headed towards him. Tandem rotors. Grey-green fuselage. The distinctive RAF low-visibility roundel: two concentric circles; a red circle inside a larger blue circle. Moving fast and flying low. Their roar was deafening. He covered his ears, opened his mouth.

They passed directly over him. He ducked instinctively and watched them until they faded away into the distance, heading west.

He headed back to the house.

CHAPTER SEVEN

Monday morning. Dark clouds filled the sky. The previous evening had been spent slumped in the living room watching old Hammer films eating various unhealthy snacks.

The Corsa was idling on the driveway, Frank waiting behind the wheel while Magnus and Ralph got in the back of the car. Joel had triple-checked that the cottage's lights and electrical switches were turned off and the back door had been locked. Now he was re-checking the front door, testing the doorknob to see if it would turn and the door would open.

"It's locked," Ralph called through the open window. "You just locked it, you OCD freak."

Joel glanced back, glared, and then tried the door again. He put the keys in his jacket pocket and got into the car.

"Don't think I'll be drinking again for a while," said Magnus.

"Nor me," Joel said, slumped in his seat.

"Wimps," Ralph said.

51

Frank put the car in gear, started down the track. He guided the car around the same potholes that had annoyed him on the way to the cottage.

Frank glanced towards the western horizon. A plume of smoke was climbing the sky. Maybe a house on fire. The direction they would be heading.

Magnus had noticed it too. "It looks pretty."

* * *

Frank slowed the Corsa to a crawl. The four men stared ahead.

A red Toyota Yaris was on the grass verge, its back end sticking out onto the road. The driver's door was open. The engine was still running. The exhaust coughed petrol fumes.

Frank edged the car forward until it was parallel to the Toyota. Joel wound down the window and peered out. The open-door alarm was beeping. The headlights were on.

No driver and no passengers.

"Maybe they've gone for a piss in the bushes," said Ralph.

Joel glanced up and down the road. "Maybe it's an ambush."

"What do you mean?" asked Frank.

"Maybe they're waiting for us to get out of the car and rob us."

Ralph chuckled. "You think Dick Turpin's gonna steal our wallets?"

"Shut up," said Joel.

"Should we wait in case the driver returns?" asked Magnus. "Feels weird leaving the car parked there with its door wide open."

"It hasn't been parked," said Frank. "It's been abandoned."

Joel's voice was low. "Why?"

"Let's find out." Frank parked the Corsa by the side of the road. He got out. Ralph and Magnus followed him to the Toyota.

Joel hesitated behind them. "Are you sure this is the right thing to do?"

Frank went to the driver's side. The car was gleaming, seemingly fresh from the dealer's showroom. A long scratch ran along the side of the car, etched into the chassis. Something glistened within the scratch-mark. Some kind of fluid.

Frank looked inside. A strawberry-scented air-freshener hung from the rear-view mirror. Static hissed from the radio. The faint garble of distant voices. Frank turned off the lights and the engine.

"What if the driver comes back?" said Joel.

"What if he doesn't? Check the boot."

"Why?" asked Ralph.

"For a body."

Ralph looked at Frank.

"I'm not joking."

Ralph opened the boot. Frank joined him.

"Just a spare tyre, a foot pump and a bottle of water," Ralph said.

Joel peered over their shoulders. "Why would someone just leave their car here with its engine running?"

Ralph closed the boot. "Maybe they were injured and couldn't drive."

Joel put his hands in his pockets. "But if they were injured, why would they leave the car?"

"Should we call the police?" Magnus suggested.

"If we can't find the driver, then yes," said Frank.

Magnus was looking downwards. "I've found some drops of blood on the road, heading away from the car."

"I'm calling the police," said Joel. He took out his mobile and dialled. Put the mobile to his ear. He waited, frowning.

Frank looked at him. "What's wrong?"

"I can't get through."

"What?"

"The network's down. Try your phones."

"I've got nothing. No signal. No fucking network." Ralph tapped his phone as if doing so would solve the problem.

"Same here," said Magnus. "I was wondering why Debbie hadn't called me in a while."

Frank couldn't even get a ringtone when he dialled.

"Bollocks," said Ralph.

"What do we do?" Joel was glancing up and down the road again.

There was thunder in the distance.

"This is fucking weird," said Magnus. "I think we should head to Wishford, or even that farmhouse we passed on the way to the cottage. Tell someone about this."

"Tell them what?" said Ralph. "That we found an abandoned car? What's a bloody farmer gonna do about it?"

"We have to tell someone," said Frank. "Maybe they'll have a landline telephone we can use. And if the driver is walking the road, we'll catch up with him."

Joel nodded eagerly. "That sounds good. I don't want to stay here."

CHAPTER EIGHT

Nobody was walking the road.

"Maybe they travelled across the fields instead," said Joel.

They approached the farm, a dark house at the top of a slope of gravel and dirt. There was a mud-streaked Land Rover and a rusting transit van with flat tyres and missing windows. A tractor was parked by a barn. Crows lined the roof of the barn, pecking at one another and cawing insults.

Frank stopped the car in front of the house. He got out. The others stayed inside. He turned back to them. They looked at him, hesitant to leave the car. He shrugged.

Ralph was first to relent. Joel and Magnus followed him.

They walked to the house.

The house was in poor condition, with scarred walls with paint peeling off in small flakes. The smell of dampness and wood-rot. Cracked roof tiles. The front door was open. A leering brass face for a knocker. Frank was reluctant to touch it.

Scattered boot prints in the dirt.

There were two downstairs windows at the front of the house. The curtains were drawn.

"Think anyone's home?" Joel glanced around nervously. "Looks like the house is empty."

"Why would they leave the door open?" asked Frank.

Magnus wiped his glasses with his sleeve. "Maybe they're at the back of the house."

"Looks haunted," said Ralph with a little grin.

"That's helpful." Joel said, and then looked over his shoulder, as if someone was standing behind him.

Frank rapped his knuckles three times on the door. Three dull thuds. Too loud in the silence. He waited, listening for movement inside the house.

No response.

Frank knocked again.

Ralph stepped back and looked up at the upstairs windows. "Maybe the farmer's on the toilet squeezing one out."

"Let's just go to the village," said Joel.

Frank ignored him. He took a step towards the doorway and hesitated.

"What're you doing, Frank?" Joel asked.

"Taking a look." He slowly stepped inside. "Hello? Anyone home?"

Joel was right behind him. "Farmers have shotguns. He might think we're burglars..."

"Calm down," Frank whispered. "And lower your voice."

"This isn't right. We can't just walk into someone's house, even if the front door's left open."

"We already have."

They stopped in the middle of the hallway. Joel stood close to Frank. Magnus and Ralph paused at the doorway.

Frank looked around. The hallway had shadowed corners. Muddy wellington boots were left by the front door. Coats and jackets hung from a rack on the wall. Umbrellas and walking sticks collected in a stand. Two doorways led to a living room and a kitchen. A wooden staircase ascended into darkness. Wooden beams supported the ceiling, draped in cobwebs. Frank had a phobia of spiders ever since he'd left a glass of water by his bed overnight when he was a kid, and had woken in the morning, taken a sip of the water and realised too late that a spider had fallen into the glass and drowned. The spider's legs had brushed his lips as he went to drink.

He shivered at the memory. He could hear the scuttling of arachnids in the silent recesses of the house.

"Hello?" Frank called out. "We're sorry to enter uninvited but we've got a bit of a problem. We found an abandoned car nearby, wondered if the driver's come here..."

No answer.

Joel stood at the foot of the stairway, fidgeting with his hands. "Let's get out of here. No one's home."

"Joel's right," said Ralph. "They must be out somewhere."

"No," said Frank. "Something doesn't feel right." He walked into the living room and was swallowed by the darkness. He opened the curtains. Sudden grey light revealed a dirty and stained carpet. Peeling wallpaper. An old television with a layer of dust on it. A cold fireplace below a mantelpiece topped with clay figurines. There were photos of a middle-aged couple. Paintings of the English countryside on the walls, and old furniture that belonged in a museum. No sign of life.

Ralph flicked the light switch. "The power's out. You think that's the farmer's wife in the photo?"

"Could be his sister, but I doubt it," said Frank.

"Could be both," Ralph said.

"We're from Somerset, mate. We've got the monopoly on inbreeding."

"How dare you insult our home county," Ralph joked.

Frank tried the house phone. No dial tone.

With Ralph's help, Frank searched the rest of the house while Magnus and Joel stayed in the hallway.

The back door had been left open. It looked out on a small garden with an allotment lined with cabbages and rhubarb. A greenhouse with shelves of tomatoes growing.

A clothesline with a few drying towels on it, and a basket of damp washing on the ground.

There was a loud crashing-like sound from far away, echoing around the fields. Like a thunderclap.

"What was that?" said Ralph.

Frank tried to determine which direction it had come from. "It wasn't thunder."

"Can we please leave now?" Joel asked them as they returned inside.

Ralph and Frank exchanged a look.

"Might as well head to the village," said Frank. "We'll find a phone that works, call the police, and tell them about the abandoned car."

"Then we can go home?" Joel said.

"Yeah."

"Good. At last."

CHAPTER NINE

Two miles outside Wishford.

Ralph was telling a dirty joke about nuns and an archbishop, when a horse ran onto the road from an adjacent field, tottering on weak legs.

Frank saw the animal too late.

The Corsa clipped the horse. Frank hit the brakes, but the car was already out of control. The tyres shrieked. The horse made a terrible sound. The car swerved off the road, shuddered along the embankment, too fast, and crashed into an oak tree. Hard impact. Scream of metal. The bonnet buckled and flew open. The seat belt cut into Frank's chest and his neck twinged sharply as he was pitched forward. The airbag deployed and cushioned him.

Frank slumped on his seat.

Steam rose from the engine. The smell of petrol and burnt rubber.

The car jolted to a stop. The engine died.

Frank blinked. The inside of his head danced. Thumping heartbeat.

Joel rubbed his face with one trembling hand. Ralph and Magnus moaned from the backseat. Luckily, they were all wearing seatbelts.

Frank checked himself for injury. He moved his limbs, stretched his tendons and muscles. His chest was tight, so he used his inhaler and then took a deep breath of air.

"Is everyone alright?" he said.

Joel looked at him. Wide eyes and wet lips. He nodded at Frank but said nothing.

"You two in the back okay?"

Magnus gave a lethargic thumbs-up.

"Yeah," Ralph said. "Fucking hell. What the fuck was that?"

"A horse," Magnus said. "Did you see it? It was injured."

"It was all cut up," said Frank.

* * *

The horse, a white mare, had collapsed on the road. The men stood around her. She was still alive. Her back legs were broken.

Frank was gazing at the horse. "I'm sorry."

The others looked at him.

"It's not your fault," said Magnus.

"Look at her," said Ralph. "Poor girl."

The mare was making a pathetic mewling sound. Her eyes were bulbous with pain and fear. She buckled and her front legs kicked. The men, apart from Ralph, stepped back.

Something had torn at the horse's left flank. Several deep cuts. Bones and flesh. Flaps of ragged skin. Blood on the road. The stench of shit and offal lingered in the air.

"Something attacked it," said Magnus.

"I broke her legs," said Frank.

"It wasn't your fault, Frank," Magnus said. "Nothing you could have done about it."

"It's like a wolf or a lion mauled it," Joel said.

Ralph gave a terse shake of his head. "Not in this country, mate."

"Might have escaped from a zoo."

"Shut up," Frank said. "Both of you."

"We should put her out of her misery," said Ralph. "She's lost too much blood. She's suffering."

"You mean kill it?" asked Magnus.

Ralph looked at him, then Frank, and nodded.

Joel was silent.

"I can't do that," Magnus said, rubbing a hand over his face.

"You won't have to," said Ralph. He crouched, stroked the mare's neck. "I'll do it."

The mare whined. Splintered bone protruded from one of the wounds.

"He's right," said Frank. "You sure you can do it, Ralph?"

"I hate seeing animals suffer."

"It'll have to be quick. What can we use?"

"Is that crowbar still in the boot?"

Frank nodded. He fetched the crowbar and handed it over.

Ralph stood over the stricken animal. The others watched him. The mare was silent now. He looked into her eyes, raised the crowbar.

"You'll have to hit her hard," said Frank. "Horses have thick skulls."

"Make it quick," said Magnus.

Ralph hesitated. His eyes were moist. His mouth was a grey bloodless line. His arms shook.

"Get it over and done with," said Joel. "Quickly."

The horse made a pained sound.

The crowbar sagged in Ralph's hands. "I can't do it. I can't kill her."

"Come on, mate," said Frank. "It's better this way."

Ralph glanced at him, raised the crowbar, but he faltered again, and stepped away, shaking his head. "I'm sorry. Can't do it."

Frank took the crowbar. He couldn't look into the mare's eyes so he closed his own.

He raised the crowbar with both hands and held his breath.

The horse's breathing was very slow.

Opened his eyes.

"Sorry. I haven't got it in me."

Frank offered the crowbar to Magnus and Joel. They shook their heads, looked away. Ralph turned away. His shoulders sagged. He stared at his feet.

"There's nothing we can do," Frank said, to himself more than the others. He, Magnus and Joel returned to the car to check the damage.

Ralph stayed with the horse and watched over her until her eyes glazed over and the rise and fall of her chest faltered.

He stroked her mane, whispering softly, until she died.

* * *

They tried to move the mare to the roadside, but she was too heavy, so they were forced to leave her on the road. Ralph got blood on his hands. He wiped them on the grass.

"You okay, Ralph?" asked Frank.

"Yeah, fucking dandy."

"First the abandoned car," said Magnus. "Then the farmhouse. Now this."

"And what do we do about the Corsa?" said Joel. He sat down by the car. "Does anyone know how to fix it?"

"You must be joking," said Frank. "The radiator's shot to pieces. The bonnet's fucked. The grille is broken. We need a mechanic."

"We need several mechanics," said Ralph.

Frank patted the Corsa's roof. "We'll have to walk to Wishford. Get some help there. We still need to report the abandoned car as well."

"You want to leave your car here?" asked Joel.

"I don't see much option. Our phones aren't working. I've tried calling the RAC. Got any other ideas?"

"We could stay here until someone drives past."

"No chance. I don't really fancy spending the next few hours in the middle of nowhere waiting for another car to come along."

Joel shrugged. "We might get lucky."

"We might get arse-raped," said Ralph, unhelpfully.

"How many cars have you seen along this stretch of road since we left the farm?" said Frank. "Do you want to wait all day and night?"

Joel fumbled with his mobile. "But it's a long walk to Wishford."

Frank began to unload their bags. "If you're so keen to stay with the car, you're welcome to look after it on your own."

"No, that's okay."

"Good. Carry your own bag. Let's get going."

CHAPTER TEN

An hour later they were less than a mile from Wishford.

Church bells were ringing. Smoke was rising from the village.

Joel's mouth twitched. "Is there a wedding? Is someone's house on fire?"

"Weird," Ralph muttered, scratching his face with the end of the crowbar.

"During World War Two," Frank said, "church bells were to be rung if the Nazis invaded."

Magnus shot him a puzzled look. "Are you trying to say that the Germans have landed?"

Frank didn't answer.

Ralph was tired. He was a strong man, but he had no stamina. His fitness routine consisted of having sex with ugly women and walking to the pub, usually on the same night but in a different order. Sweat dripped from his brow. He gulped water from a bottle.

The image of the dead horse was burned into his mind. He hated himself for not putting the horse out of its misery. He looked at the crowbar and wondered if he could ever use it to kill a living thing.

He wished the bells would stop ringing.

They came across another house. Locked, silent and empty. No car in the driveway. Maybe whoever lived there was on holiday.

Ahead of them, a road-sign concreted into the grass verge: WISHFORD.

They entered the village.

"At last," Joel said. "My feet are killing me. Are there any public telephones around here?"

"What about a mechanic's workshop?" Magnus asked.

"Where's the nearest police station?" said Frank.

"Horsham, probably," said Ralph.

"Typical."

Rows of houses. Trimmed lawns. Expensive cars parked in gravel driveways. Trees and pruned hedges. Rows of flowers in bloom.

A deserted place. But things had been left behind.

A dropped handbag on a driveway, its contents spilled; a bicycle left by the side of the road, its front wheel spinning slowly; a child's red baseball cap.

They passed one house with its front door open; Ralph noticed shadowy shapes huddled just out of focus. He didn't tell the others just in case he had imagined them.

Joel said, "Something is very wrong."

Ralph grunted. "Nice one, Miss Marple."

The bells stopped ringing. Throbbing silence. Ralph's eardrums resonated in the sudden absence of sound. The anticipation of bad things. A feeling of dread. He swallowed hard.

A shriek echoed down the street and around the houses.

Magnus's eyes widened. "Jesus Christ, what was that?"

"I don't know," said Frank. "Maybe a dog? We better keep moving."

They continued to the centre of the village. Ralph and Frank entered the village shop. No staff or customers greeted them. Tins of food had been stacked neatly on shelves. No signs of catastrophe or trouble. As if everyone had winked out of existence.

Frank grabbed some bottles of water and a few chocolate bars; handed them out to the others while they checked their phones for signal. The screen on Ralph's mobile was blank. He put it back in his pocket and turned to his friends, noting how their faces were too pale, too tight around their skulls. He ate his chocolate bar in two bites.

Frank stared down the street; Joel sipped water and glanced behind them as if expecting an attack; Magnus was absently rubbing his mouth like he was trying to wipe away the crumbs of his last meal. Spit came away with his fingers. A muscle moved just below his right eye.

Ralph slapped the palm of one hand with the crowbar.

"What the fuck is going on?"

* * *

They heard the shriek again. It was louder.

"That ain't a fucking dog," said Ralph.

"I don't feel well," said Magnus. His eyes were moving quickly, glancing around. He swayed on his feet and Joel took hold of him by the shoulders. His face shined with sweat.

"You okay, mate?"

"Not really." His eyelids drooped. "Feel dizzy and hot."

Joel touched Magnus's forehead. "He's burning up."

"We keep walking," said Frank.

"Where to?" asked Joel.

"Maybe the church, if whoever was ringing the bells is still there."

"Fair enough."

Magnus exhaled through his teeth. He held onto Joel.

The four men moved on. They kept to the middle of the road. Ralph held the crowbar like he was craving violence, spoiling for a fight.

The sky was turning darker. Grey becoming charcoal. Low clouds, their undersides painted with shadow. There was a deep, short rumble far away in the sky. Frank thought about thunder and how it should sound. Not like that.

They reached the end of a T-junction. Half a dozen cars were parked along the side of the road. Frank led them onto Carpenter Street. This road would lead them out of the village, eventually.

"What's that sound?" said Ralph. He raised the crowbar.

They rounded a corner. A young woman was lying on her stomach, trying to raise herself up with her arms. She was wearing a jumper and jeans. White trainers. She made a horrible noise, as if her stomach was trying to climb up her throat. Her eyes bulged and she was crying, her shoulders hitching with each sob.

When the woman sensed them, her neck turned slowly.

"Christ on a fucking bike!" Ralph said.

"Oh shit." Joel forgot to keep hold of Magnus; he folded at the knees. Joel grabbed him again and held him up.

Frank took a step towards the woman. He held out his hands. "Are you okay?"

The woman looked at him.

"We're not going to hurt you," Frank said, keeping his voice low and steady.

"What's that on her neck?" said Ralph, pointing.

Frank saw, about two inches below the woman's left ear, a puncture mark weeping a clear fluid. The skin around the hole was red and sore.

"Looks like a wasp sting," said Frank.

"It would have to be a big fucking wasp."

"There're no such things as giant wasps," said Joel. He didn't sound convinced.

"Help me," the woman said. She held out one hand to them.

Frank couldn't take his eyes from the woman. He took a step towards her.

"What's wrong with her?" said Joel.

"Fuck knows," Ralph said.

"Help me," the woman muttered. She turned onto her back, breathing hard. Her face was vaguely child-like in the dirty light.

"Do you think she has something contagious?" Ralph asked.

The men backed away from her.

"What happened to you?" said Frank.

She didn't answer.

"Let's get out of here," Ralph said.

"We can't just leave her," said Frank.

Magnus let out a moan.

Ralph looked at Frank. "Can't we? We've got our own problems. I'm not touching her."

"So compassionate, as always."

"Ralph's right," said Joel. "What if she is contagious?"

"She needs help," said Frank.

"We all need help." Ralph let out a humourless laugh.

Frank glared at him.

Ralph shook his head. "If you want to help her, mate, be my guest."

Frank looked at the woman. The wound on her neck had become redder and swollen. Frank thought that if he touched the mark, it would feel spongy and moist. He shuddered with revulsion.

"Go on then, Frank," said Ralph. "You want to be a Good Samaritan. Stay here and help her."

"Let's go," said Joel. "We can get help for her and come back."

Magnus drifted lazily on his feet, dazed. Joel and Ralph were struggling to keep him upright and stable.

"What *happened* to you?" Frank asked the woman.

She stared at Frank. She tried to speak but her words dissolved into murmurs and sobs.

The terrible shriek echoed towards them again. It didn't sound human. More like an animal sound, but not one any of them knew.

"What the hell is making that noise?" said Joel. He was looking back the way they had walked. He was saucer-eyed. He chewed on his bottom lip.

Ralph said, "We need to get some help for Magnus first before we help this woman. We'll find some help and come back for her."

Frank didn't believe Ralph, but he nodded. "Okay."

"Good idea," said Joel. "Let's go."

Frank hesitated. He didn't want to leave the woman here. For some reason he felt responsible for her. He didn't know why. If he left the woman here, she would die. She would die alone.

"C'mon, Frank," Ralph said. "She's not our problem."

Magnus was staring at the woman. His nose was bleeding.

Joel pulled a tissue from his pocket. He wiped Magnus's nose with it, then held it there.

"You look like shit, Magnus," said Ralph.

"I'm okay," said Magnus. His voice was slurred. He took the tissue from Joel's hand and held it under his nose. "I'm fine."

Behind them, another shriek rang out. Closer. Much closer.

"Fuck this," Ralph said. He pulled Frank with him as he and Joel helped Magnus along.

Frank glanced back at the woman. Ralph was swearing under his breath.

"Please don't leave me," the woman said. Desperation in her voice. "Don't leave me here."

Frank kept walking. He looked away.

From beyond the street, another shriek rang out.

CHAPTER ELEVEN

"What's wrong with Magnus?" asked Joel. His face was all sharp angles and creases.

Frank looked back as the unseen thing shrieked again. A stab of remorse pricked his chest. They had left the woman behind, back there. *He* had left the woman behind. He could have helped her.

"Hurry up, Frank," Ralph called to him.

"Feels like someone's playing a joke on us," said Joel. "Some kids or bored villagers trying to scare some outsiders. This can't be happening, can it? It has to be some kind of prank…"

"If it is a practical joke," Ralph said, "I'm going to beat the fuck out of the little shits."

Frank hurried forwards. Something made him look up at the sky; he sensed a presence above him, hidden in the clouds. Then it was gone. He looked back at his friends.

Ralph was slapping Magnus's face lightly, trying to keep him awake. "We need to stop. He's dead weight."

"What is making that shrieking?" said Joel. "I don't want to be caught in the open when that thing shows up."

Ralph pointed to the open front door of a house across the street. "What about in there? Magnus needs somewhere to rest. We can't drag him much further."

"We don't know who's in there," Joel said.

"I don't give a fuck," said Ralph. "We can't stay out here. What do you think, Frank?"

Frank looked at the open door inviting them inside. A grey dimness lurked beyond it.

The shrieking thing called out again; a wailing, desperate sound. He tried not to imagine the mouth that made such a noise. He imagined something wet and dripping. He imagined a toothless mouth with fleshy slippery gums and tongue running over clammy white lips.

"Frank," Ralph said, clicking his fingers at him. "What do you think?"

Frank looked back down the street.

"Frank!"

He looked at Ralph. "Okay."

Ralph and Joel hauled Magnus towards the house. There was a blue Nissan on the driveway.

Frank followed then stopped at the door. Joel was calling out to see if the house was occupied. No answer. Ralph helped Magnus sit down on the hallway floor, slumped against the wall. He muttered under his breath.

Joel returned from the kitchen. He had already checked the living room. "Nobody home. Don't know about upstairs, though."

"Shut the door, Frank," said Ralph.

"I'm going back."

Ralph's eyes widened. "Oh, for fuck's sake, mate. Why?"

"It's not right to leave her."

"Please don't go," said Joel. "Stay here, Frank."

"I'm sorry. I have to do it."

"Don't be a dickhead," Ralph said. "We have to look after Magnus, not some woman we don't even know."

Frank handed his bag to Joel. "I can't leave her back there."

"Here." Ralph tossed Frank the crowbar.

He caught it.

"Get back here in one piece."

Then Frank was gone.

CHAPTER TWELVE

Frank hid behind the back of a white transit van parked by the side of the road. He gripped the crowbar and peered around the side of the van.

The woman was gone.

A sliver of panic and guilt stabbed him in the gut. Something had happened to the woman. He had had the chance to save her but neglected it. Maybe someone else had helped her. Maybe not.

Frank's body sagged and he rubbed his face with one moist, clammy palm.

Something moved on the other side of the van. The patter of feet and the scrape of something on the road. Frank froze. His temples throbbed.

Something shrieked.

The sound filled Frank's head. He clenched his teeth, fought the urge to scream, pins in his eardrums.

The shrieking thing swiped against the van. A scraping sound, like nails over metal.

Frank crouched and looked under the van.

The naked legs and bare feet of a man. Gangrenous lesions on his calves. *It is human.* The man grunted, a terrible livestock sound, like a cow drowning in a mud pit. Frank was struck by a stink like something left to rot in the sun by the side of a road.

Frank realised that if he could look under the van at the man, then the man could do exactly the same. He edged to the rear of the vehicle, towards the wheel, for cover. The man breathed loudly through a gasping mouth. The fevered breaths of a sick animal.

The man *skittered*. Wet grunted breaths grew more rapid.

The man was moving around the side of the van, towards him.

Frank got onto his hands and knees and scrambled under the vehicle. The cloying stink of oil and diesel. He stayed low to the ground, kissing the road. The cold hard tarmac bit at his hands. He tucked in his limbs. He held his breath. Sweat dripped from his face. His pulse thudded hotly between his ears and he thought the man might be able to hear his heartbeat.

The man's bare feet stopped next to him. Long toenails yellowed, curved and fungal. Calloused heels wrapped in dead, flaking skin.

I'm a fool for coming back here.

The man shrieked again, the sound of swollen and infected vocal chords.

Frank closed his eyes. He did not want to see the man's face when he stooped to drag him from his hiding place.

CHAPTER THIRTEEN

Ralph examined the blade of the kitchen knife in his hand. It was sharp and he liked it.

Judging by the framed photos on the walls, the house belonged to a young family. Mum, dad, and a little boy no more than ten years old. Ralph wondered where they were now. He had searched for the Nissan's keys, but couldn't find them.

He wondered if the family was dead.

They had laid Magnus on the sofa. He was barely conscious but his nose had stopped bleeding. Now he was a limp shape, eyelids fluttering, muttering nonsense words and moaning gently. His head was resting on a cushion. Joel laid a damp cloth over his forehead after cleaning the blood from around his nose and mouth.

Ralph found a Tupperware box full of chocolate bars in the kitchen cupboard. He gave one to Joel, one to save for Magnus when he awoke, and one for Frank when he returned. Ralph didn't save one for the woman Frank had gone to rescue. He took two for himself and ate them without pause.

"What's happening out there?" asked Joel. "Where is everybody?" He let out a nervous, juddering sigh. "I've got work tomorrow…"

Magnus groaned.

"Fuck knows," said Ralph. "Have you tried the TV?"

"The power's out. Do you think it's only happened to this village, or do you think it's happened elsewhere? Maybe the people were evacuated for some reason. What if this area is contaminated with something? Radiation or a biological agent of some kind. We could be in the middle of a quarantine zone. The government might want to hush it up, keep it all secret. There could be squads of soldiers in bio-hazard suits executing on sight anyone they think is contaminated."

Ralph's mouth turned sour. "We don't know what's happened. No point in jumping to conclusions."

"What about the woman that Frank went back to help? What happened to her?"

"Dunno."

"What was that puncture wound on her neck?"

Ralph took in a deep breath. Joel eyed him nervously, hands held together like an old maid.

"I don't know, mate."

"And what's wrong with Magnus? Is he sick? Is there something worse than that wrong with him?"

Ralph thought exactly the same. "He'll be fine. Once Frank gets back we'll decide what to do, and we'll get out of here. Calm the fuck down."

"One of us should've gone with Frank. We shouldn't have let him go on his own."

"Would you rather have gone with Frank? Or would you have wanted to stay here and look after Magnus on your own?"

"Neither."

"Frank will be okay. He'll be back soon."

"I wish I had your confidence."

"Just take it easy. We're safe in here."

"Okay."

"I'm going to see if I can find tablets or something to help Magnus."

"Okay."

CHAPTER FOURTEEN

There were great booms in the distance, like the footfalls of a behemoth raised from the earth. Distant thunder. The ground reverberated.

Frank had not moved for an hour. His limbs were stiff, like ice sculptures draped in cloth. He was too scared to leave his hiding place.

Night would fall soon. The only light was a diseased, greasy hue. He didn't want to be out here in the dark. He had heard strange noises earlier. Muted calls from far away; and voices that were no more than whispers in his ear. Footfalls down the street. The sound of running.

The shrieking man-thing was gone. He had staggered away over half an hour ago, sniffing the air and mewling like he was in pain.

Frank let out a small laugh and there was hysteria within it. He closed his mouth, scolded himself silently. With some effort he moved his limbs. He composed himself. A quick scan of the street at his level. No movement. No spindly legs waiting for him.

He crawled out from under the van, scraping his palms and the heels of his hands. He winced, ignoring the temptation to look at the grazes on his skin. He watched the street as he rose into a crouch. Waited, watched. He stood up, his back to the side of the van, flat against it. The breeze was cold and touched the nape of his neck.

The street was deserted. There were shadows but they remained still and were only threatening in the vague shape of them in the silent spaces.

The flapping whisper of wings above him. A flock of birds shot overhead. They filled the sky, thousands of dark, frail-boned bodies moving as one organism. He envied their freedom, envied their flight.

The birds faded into the distance. They were the first animals he'd seen since arriving here. No cats or dogs. Nothing.

He had to get back to the others. They would be worried about him. He started down the street.

CHAPTER FIFTEEN

Something scratched against the front door.

Ralph and Joel looked at each other. Joel's eyes were starkly white, and Ralph gestured for Joel to stay put and then stepped into the hallway. He had locked the door straight after Frank stepped outside.

More scratching. Slow and lethargic. Weak.

His fingers tightened around the knife handle. He hesitated, feeling like a little boy who was scared because a stranger was at the door. Then he stepped forward, his trainers padding softly on the carpet. Joel was behind him, eyes wide and alarmed. He was about to speak but Ralph shushed him with a raised hand. Ralph looked through the spy-hole in the door.

"What's out there?" Joel asked.

From what he could see there was nobody behind the door, unless the visitor was less than five feet tall or a child. His mind created an image of some grinning pygmy-creature waiting for him. Or maybe the visitor couldn't be seen because it had crawled here and was now lying at the doorstep, crippled and bleeding. Maybe it was Frank, and he was badly injured.

Ralph breathed out. He kept his eye to the hole. He sensed Joel's apprehension behind him, radiating like heat, a mass of trembling flesh barely held together by his clothes.

"Ralph?"

He crouched and opened the letterbox, looking left and right, listening for the sound of breathing or a shuffle of movement. He closed the letterbox and stood.

"It might be Frank," said Joel.

"It might not be."

"He might be in trouble."

Ralph chewed on his lip.

"Frank?" Joel said, raising his voice.

Something heavy crashed into the door, causing it to shudder on its hinges. Ralph fell back on to the foot of the stairway, scrambling half-way up the stairs on his back. Joel retreated down the hallway towards the kitchen.

"What the fuck?" said Ralph.

Another crash. The door shook. The bolt held. There was the sudden, sharp crack of wood splintering.

Ralph raised the knife.

Another crash reverberated throughout the house. The door was beginning to buckle.

Then it stopped.

Ralph was breathing hard. His skin was greased with cold sweat.

"I think it's gone," whispered Joel.

"I hope so."

"I think I've pissed myself a bit."

Ralph stared at the door.

The echo of violence hung in the air. Ralph could feel it throbbing against his skin.

Joel crept towards the door, hands planted against the walls at his sides, his fingernails digging into the white wallpaper.

Magnus appeared in the doorway to the living room.

Joel yelped and backed into the wall. "Magnus, you're awake."

Looking towards the door, Magnus's voice was barely audible. "They want us to let them in. We shouldn't let them in."

CHAPTER SIXTEEN

Ralph closed the curtains and then peered between them through the living room window. Darkness shrouded the street. Whatever had crashed against the front door was out there, maybe watching the house, and maybe thinking of other ways to gain entry.

They had barricaded the front and back doors with furniture; anything they could get their hands on that wasn't nailed down. Tables and chairs. The sofa and armchairs. A Welsh dresser decorated with china cups hanging on dainty little hooks.

His body was awash with adrenaline and he was jittery. His stomach felt full of crawling millipedes. He turned away from the window. With the curtains closed the room was dark, but Joel had found two candles under the sink and lit them with Magnus's cigarette lighter. The small flickering flames made shadows dance and cavort like oily wraiths. Ralph and Joel had a torch each, switched off to save the batteries. Magnus and Joel were sitting on the carpet, across from each other. Joel eyed Magnus unsurely, as if he was a stranger. Joel was holding a bread knife he had taken from the kitchen.

Magnus was without a weapon. Ralph made sure of that.

"What happened to you, Magnus?" asked Joel. He sniffed, wiped his nose. His mobile was on his lap, its screen blank and useless.

Magnus looked at him. "I don't know. I felt weird. Like something was in my head trying to push its way out of my brain. It drained all of the energy from me."

"Your nose kept bleeding as well," Joel said.

"I know. I feel much better now."

"What was wrong with you?" asked Ralph, standing against the wall.

Magnus didn't look at him. "How should I know?"

Ralph's face looked ghoulish in the candlelight. "Do you know who was banging at the door, Magnus?"

"I don't know who it was. I knew they wanted to come in and see us." Magnus scratched a patch of skin under his jaw. "Remember when I saw something in the sky on Saturday night…before I passed out?"

"Yeah," said Ralph. "I found you outside half-frozen."

"Since then I've had that strange feeling – I just thought it was an extended hangover – but when we arrived in the village it got worse. It's not too bad now; it's fading, I think. I can't explain it."

"Do you know what happened here?"

"I have no idea. I'm sorry, but I don't."

Ralph saw something in his friend's face. Magnus wasn't telling the entire truth.

"And what about Frank?" said Joel. "Should we search for him? Do we wait here for him?"

Ralph said, "It was his choice to go out there. He should've listened to me. Fucking idiot."

"We can't leave him out there," said Joel.

"You want to go out there?" Ralph's voice had risen. "Our phones don't work, so it's not as if we can give him a quick call to see if he's okay, is it?

Joel looked away.

"Maybe something got him," said Magnus.

Ralph hated the silence that followed. He thought of Frank out there in the dark and immediately despised himself for letting Frank go alone.

Magnus said, "Whoever came to the door knows we're here so maybe we should leave, find another place to hide."

"I'm not going out there," said Joel. He pressed at the keypad on his phone then discarded it.

Magnus eyed Ralph. "What do you think?"

Ralph said nothing, just walked to the window and looked out at the silent, empty street.

CHAPTER SEVENTEEN

The woman emerged from the darkness beneath a dead streetlight. The woman Frank had returned to help. She lurched forwards and stopped a few yards in front of him. Frank halted. His breath caught in his throat. He raised the crowbar and said nothing as his eyes were drawn to her.

She was naked, but Frank felt no attraction towards her. She stank of piss and madness. Sagging breasts little more than flaps of skin. She was hunched over, and her spine curved so much that it was protruding from her back, the vertebrae shifting with her movements. Her limbs were thin and her hair was falling out. The puncture wound on her neck had scabbed over.

A grin twisted her pink, fleshy lips. Her face was so slack it seemed like the skin would slough off her skull the next time she shook her head.

"What's wrong with you?" No air was left in Frank's lungs. He grasped for his inhaler but his hand couldn't find it.

She didn't answer. Her body began to buckle and dance, her limbs flailing, her fingers clawing at the air.

She let out a small moan and raised her head towards the sky, her mouth still open. A silent scream from the darkness of her throat.

The blood drained from Frank's face. His heart stuck in his gullet. He couldn't take his eyes away from her.

Bones clicked and joints popped wetly. Something changed in her face, and the skin stretched tighter over her cheekbones. She held out her hands and the fingers upon them lengthened.

She stared at Frank and let out a screech that wasn't a human sound. Her breath came in shivering fits.

Frank stepped back.

She came for him.

CHAPTER EIGHTEEN

They were sitting on the floor.

"I need a piss," said Magnus.

Ralph shrugged. He was squeezing his stress ball. "You don't need my permission."

Joel looked at them but said nothing.

"Is the toilet upstairs?"

Ralph nodded. "Knock yourself out."

Magnus looked unsure.

"Aren't scared of the dark, are you?" Ralph said. "Piss in the kitchen sink if you have to."

"That's disgusting," said Joel.

Ralph let out a tired, short laugh. "Just go upstairs, Magnus. You'll be fine. The bad things are outside, not in here."

Magnus swallowed. A draught passed through the room and touched him with icy fingers. He fought back a shiver.

Ralph handed Joel's torch to Magnus. "Have a good one."

Magnus rose, switched on the torch and went out into the hallway. He checked the barricaded front door then stood at the foot of the stairway. He pointed the torch up the stairs, staring at the shadows created by the invading light. He put his free hand on the bannister, breathed in then breathed out. His bladder felt tight and swollen. He noticed the beige carpet, darkened with grime over the years, beneath his feet and around him.

He thought of Debbie and the boys. He checked his mobile again. No signal. Only a few hours left in the battery.

"I'm sorry, Debbie," he whispered, staring at the phone.

Something creaked upstairs; the shifting and shrinking of floorboards. He shook his head. There was a dry lump in his throat. The muscles in his face were stiff and the blood quickened in his veins.

A hand on his shoulder; Magnus whirled. Ralph looked at him.

"What're you doing, Ralph? Almost scared me to death."

"Sorry." He held up his hands. "I'll wait here for you, mate."

Magnus nodded. "Cheers."

"I'm glad you're feeling better."

"Same here."

Magnus started up the stairs.

Up there, beyond the wooden hill, the darkness waited for him and seemed to thicken in anticipation.

* * *

Magnus emptied his bladder. He didn't flush the toilet; he was too worried about making any loud noises. He closed the toilet lid, sat down upon it. Looked at his trembling hands. He thought of the thing he'd seen in the sky. The thing – the presence – had touched him, he was sure of it.

He held his face in his hands. Took off his glasses, rubbed his tired eyes and squeezed them shut. When he opened them, white spots danced in his vision. He exhaled through gritted teeth. He stared at the floor until his eyes dried and his vision cleared.

The bathroom was a small, neat space. No mould in the damp, shadowed places where moisture gathered. The roll of toilet paper was nearly used up. There was a hint of bleach in the air.

Magnus walked to the sink. A child's toothbrush in a glass jar. Wisps of matted hair around the plughole. He squirted liquid soap on to his palms, rubbed his hands together. He rinsed away the lather then dried his hands on a towel.

He stared at himself in the mirror above the sink. The reflection of a dead-eyed man with narrow shoulders and a glass jaw. A ghost. Shadows under his eyes. Every wrinkle and crease in his face was starkly visible in the torchlight. The stress of being married to Debbie, of her constant demands and insecurities, was ageing him. He patted his stomach; he had a paunch. A pair of soft man-breasts developing slowly. He was skinny everywhere else. His bones felt frail and brittle, yet his limbs felt heavy, as if they were full of water.

"Getting old," he muttered.

He used to play football for the village team each week, along with Frank and Joel; Ralph was too lazy to play football so he just watched from the touchline, shouting abuse and grunting advice. They had been young men then. Before his sons were born. Before Debbie's 'condition' had fully infested her mind and made her a burden.

Good old days, he thought. Nostalgia was like a drug.

He almost laughed, but then remembered Frank was out there.

They should have been out there searching for him.

The ceiling creaked. He looked up, listened. He placed his hands on the sink.

There it was again. Pressure upon wood and plaster.

Something in the attic. But Ralph had said they checked the house for anyone alive.

They had forgotten about the attic.

A dull ache formed at the front of his skull. He spat into the sink, watched his phlegm dribble into the plughole. He was relieved to see it was bloodless.

More creaking, moving away from him. Light, quick footfalls. Something small. Magnus's eyes tracked them.

He pointed the torch at the ceiling, followed the footfalls out of the bathroom and onto the landing.

The footfalls stopped above him, next to the closed attic hatch.

The wooden cover on the hatch shifted with a quiet scrape. Magnus tensed. The torchlight trembled upon the ceiling. A thin line of darkness appeared at the hatch. The smell of dust and neglect came to him, and the undeniable sense he was being watched, scrutinised, maybe even evaluated as a threat; or even worse, something to be hunted and chased.

The dark line widened. The hatch cover moved. He saw a glint of gleaming eyes and a face that was all bone and sallow skin.

Magnus turned and stumbled down the stairs.

Ralph was waiting for him. "What's wrong?"

"Something up there. Something in the attic."

Ralph looked up the stairs. "We didn't check the attic."

"What's wrong?" Joel asked from the living room.

There was a soft thud on the landing. The creak of a door.

"We woke someone up," said Magnus.

CHAPTER NINETEEN

The woman was on Frank's heels, her ragged panting in his ears, draining the strength from his body. Part of him just wanted to fall down and let her take him.

He didn't look back.

Almost full dark. Almost night. He ran past empty gardens and dark houses. His legs throbbed and screamed. His chest grew tighter as he went. Fear and adrenaline were a chemical mixture clouding his mind. His heartbeat was a metallic drumming in his ears.

The woman screamed. He felt her foul hot breath on the back of his neck.

Frank cried out. His body was jelly.

He stumbled and tripped on a patch of uneven road, twisted and fell onto his back; the woman scrambled onto him, very eager and very hungry. He held the crowbar under her jaw and pushed to stop her from snapping her head forwards. Her mouth opened. Dull ivory teeth. He caught a whiff of hellish gingivitis. Her tongue was like a worm feeling for somewhere to burrow. She radiated a terrible, stinking

111

heat. Her body was a sack of sharp bones straddling him. His cock went hard.

The woman tried to claw at his eyes. He drew back the crowbar and hit her in the face. She fell back and Frank scrambled away from her, breathing hard, shifting awkwardly on his feet like an amateur fighter.

The woman was on her knees. Skin came away from her legs, peeled by the road surface. She hissed at him through broken teeth. Her nose was smashed and broken, blood dribbling into her mouth and down her chin. Frank hadn't meant to hit her that hard. He felt guilt and shame for hurting a woman.

"I'm sorry," he said.

She began to get to her feet.

"Please stop," Frank said. "This can end now. It doesn't have to be like this. You need medical attention."

She ignored him.

"Please stay down. Stay back." His pleading tone made no difference to her.

The woman stood. She opened her mouth, her jaws clicking. Her face was monstrous in the growing dark. She took a step towards him, a great tension building in her body. A low growl emanated from her throat.

"Don't come any closer," said Frank, retreating two steps. "I've already warned you. I don't want to hurt you. I want to help you."

She lurched towards him, arms outstretched.

It happened so quickly. Time seemed to speed up. All he could see was her leering bloodied face coming towards him.

Frank hit her again with the crowbar. She collapsed at his feet. The back of her skull hit the tarmac with a dull, porcelain crack. Blood pooled underneath her head.

The world went askew. Gravity pressed down on Frank's shoulders. A sense of surrealism washed over him.

"I had to defend myself," he said. "I had to…"

The woman wasn't moving. Her eyes remained open, staring into his face.

"I didn't mean to hurt you; it was an accident. I'm sorry. I'm so sorry."

He covered his mouth with one hand. His eyes stung with tears. He muttered and cursed under his breath, shaking his head slowly.

No matter how disturbed and insane she had been, she was a woman. A human being. And he had killed her.

"What have I done?" he whispered, staring at the woman's cooling corpse, until the sharp cold air bit at his face and he regained his senses.

Noises drifted towards him over the gentle wind. He looked around the street.

Shapes and scurrying forms were emerging from their dark holes and silent places, gibbering and hungry.

They saw Frank.

Frank ran.

CHAPTER TWENTY

Ralph halted on the penultimate step and shone the torchlight into the landing's darkness. The attic hatch was open. He breathed slowly and quietly. Magnus tensed behind him, holding a brass poker. Joel was waiting at the foot of the stairs.

Ralph stepped upon the landing. The open hatch gaped like a mouth above him. He imagined something plucking him from the landing and hauling him up into the dark.

"Look," said Magnus, his voice barely audible.

The door to the bedroom, which seemed to be the boy's judging by posters of superheroes upon it, was open just enough for someone to slip through.

"It was closed before I came downstairs."

"I see it," Ralph whispered. He looked at Magnus and nodded. Magnus returned the gesture. A muscle twitched under his left eye.

Ralph placed his hand on the door. He smiled weakly at the Spider-Man poster. Spider-Man had been his favourite superhero as a kid.

He pushed the door open; a low creak, and aimed his torch into the room. Magnus did the same. Ralph paused in the doorway. The room looked like how he had left it when he searched the house earlier. A shelf full of comics. *Shrek* wallpaper. Posters of Harry Potter, Lionel Messi, and David Beckham. Action figures scattered on a desk. A few books. A box of Lego.

Only one thing was different.

"Oh shit," said Magnus.

There was a huddled shape on the bed, underneath the *Star Wars* duvet cover.

The shape was trembling in the torchlight.

Ralph and Magnus looked at each other. Magnus's Adam's apple bobbed and moved. He chewed on his bottom lip. Ralph stepped into the room and Magnus followed.

They approached the bed. Ralph felt his heart try to climb his throat.

The shape under the duvet jerked, as if hit by a spasm. The two men froze. Ralph could see Magnus's hands shaking. Ralph motioned for Magnus to pull back the duvet so he would be ready with the knife if there was something…*nasty* underneath.

Magnus reached slowly for the duvet. He gently took hold of it between a thumb and forefinger.

Ralph raised his knife.

Magnus pulled back the covers.

A little boy was on the bed. His skin was almost transparent and his eyes were too large within his face. He wore only a white vest and underpants. He shivered in the torchlight. His dark eyes found Ralph.

Magnus stepped back, his face quivering. "Look at him. Fucking hell."

Ralph couldn't speak. He ran the torch beam over the boy's bony, white limbs. A narrow chest. Thinning, coal-black hair.

The boy opened his mouth, and a pale fluid wet his lips, spooling on the mattress. A wheezy sigh. The boy had the look of disease. Ralph had seen black-and-white photos taken of inmates rescued from Nazi death camps at the end of World War Two. This boy could have stepped out from any of those old photos.

"What's wrong with him?" said Magnus, as if Ralph would know the answer. "What happened to him?"

Ralph shook his head. "I wish I knew." He covered his nose. The boy stank of vinegar-and-eggs.

Magnus said, "I think his parents left him here. Maybe he started to…*change,* so they fled. Poor little bastard."

"Yeah."

"Do you know CPR?" Magnus asked him.

Ralph shook his head.

The boy stared at Ralph. His breathing slowed gradually until it stopped. His eyes glazed over, fixing onto Ralph until what little light had resided there was gone. Ralph considered checking the boy's pulse. He didn't.

"It's as if he went to bed just so he could die," said Ralph.

"But what did he die of?"

"Maybe the same thing that was wrong with the woman we found."

"It's fucked up," Magnus muttered.

Ralph averted his gaze to the floor. "I wish we knew his name. No one should die without a name, especially not a child."

Magnus covered the boy with the duvet and retreated quickly. "What if the boy's contagious?"

Ralph didn't answer.

They returned to the landing.

Ralph looked up at the attic hatch. "So what was he doing up there? Hiding?"

"We'll never know," said Magnus. "There's no need to know. Let's just go back downstairs."

"Someone should go up there," Ralph said.

Magnus blinked. "What? Are you mental?"

"Think about it. Do you want to go downstairs knowing there might be someone else lurking in the attic? There's that thing outside that crashed against the door, and the thing that was shrieking when we first arrived in the village. Those *things*, whatever they are, are outside. We need to make sure that we're safe *inside* the house."

Magnus sighed. "I'm not having you on my shoulders. You're too heavy. We'll need a stepladder to get up there."

"Not necessarily," said Ralph.

"What do you mean?"

"You get on my shoulders."

"Fuck off."

"We have to know if the attic's empty. We might have to stay here for the night. Otherwise one of us will have to stand guard here all night."

Magnus looked up at the hatch. "Bollocks."

"Come on then."

"How do you wanna do this?"

"Either you stand on my shoulders or I give you a lift up with my hands."

"You choose."

"I'll lift you up."

"Okay. Don't let me fall."

"Don't you trust me?"

"No. Not at all."

Ralph put down his knife, then crouched beneath the hatch and cupped his hands. "Ready?"

"No." Magnus stepped forward, put his right foot into Ralph's hands, and his other foot on Ralph's right shoulder.

Ralph took his weight and wobbled; shifted his feet to steady himself. His fingers hurt under Magnus's cheap trainers.

"Do it," Magnus said. "Hurry."

Lifting with his legs, Ralph hoisted Magnus up to the hatch; Magnus gripped the hatch edges.

Ralph shook under his friend's weight. "You're heavier than you look, you skinny bastard."

"Maybe you're weaker than you look, fat bastard."

"Funny. What do you see?"

"It's pretty dark up here."

"Use your fucking torch then."

"Shut up."

Ralph held onto Magnus's legs, keeping him steady. He righted himself. His strength held. He heard Magnus shifting around above him.

"What the hell are these doing up here?"

"What is it?"

Magnus lowered a set of keys in front of Ralph's face. "One of them must be for the car out in the driveway." Magnus pocketed them.

Ralph tried to ignore the musty smell of Magnus's feet. Then Magnus's legs began to shake.

Silence.

"I think I see something," Magnus said, finally. "There's something moving up here."

"What?"

Magnus didn't answer.

"Magnus," he said, and didn't like how his voice sounded.

"Oh fuck," Magnus whispered.

"What do you see, mate?"

"Let me down."

"What's up there?"

"Fucking let me down, now!"

Ralph lowered into a crouch. Magnus stumbled onto the landing and into the wall. His face was white and his mouth was open.

"There're two of them," Magnus said.

Ralph picked up his knife, looked up at the hatch. The sound of shuffling footsteps.

"What's up there?"

"You don't want to know," said Magnus. "We have to leave."

"What the fuck is it?"

"Just move."

Magnus stumbled down the stairs. Ralph turned back and saw a face appear in the open hatch and regard him with piscine eyes. He stared at the face until its mouth curled into a grey-lipped grin. He felt his bowels drop. He ran down the stairs, jumping the last two steps. Magnus and Joel were already removing the barricade from the front door.

"Hurry up!" Ralph said.

A soft thump upstairs.

"Hurry up!"

The attic's occupants were on the landing. Shadows moved, reaching and long-limbed.

Ralph helped remove the Welsh dresser from the front door. It crashed onto the floor.

Magnus opened the door.

Cold air rushed into the house.

Joel and Ralph looked up the stairway.

Two figures stared back at them. A man and a woman. They were all limbs and bruises. Wounds like mouths on their bodies. Wet tumours and weeping cysts on their skin. Eyes shining in the torchlight.

"The boy's parents," Magnus said. "They were nesting in a corner of the attic."

The monsters began to descend the stairs. Their movements were avian-like and twitchy, their eyes set upon the men with ravenous intensity. A hunger. A need. A desperate craving for something unspeakable. Their skin glistened wet and milky.

Ralph pushed Joel out the doorway. Magnus was trying to start the car.

"We've left our bags in the house!" Joel said.

"You want to go back in and get them?" Ralph growled. He shut the front door behind him.

From the house, the two creatures shrieked and wailed for them to stay, to come back inside.

Joel reached the car, jumped onto the backseat. He banged his head on the door frame. Ralph sat in the front passenger seat. He shut his door. Locked it.

"We have to leave this place," said Ralph.

"What about Frank?" said Joel.

"He's dead, for all we know."

"We can't leave him here. We could go back to where we left the woman."

Ralph turned his head to stare at Joel. "We haven't got time. He made his choice. Feel free to get out and start looking for him."

Joel looked away, said nothing.

Ralph turned back and wished he hadn't.

From all around them, out of the shadows and the dark gardens, pale mewling things rose from their hiding places and emerged into the street. They were people, but not people. Not anymore.

"Fuck me," said Ralph. "This is nuts."

Magnus was still trying to start the car. When he turned the key in the ignition, the engine only responded with a desperate chugging sound.

"Start, you bastard!" Magnus cried. He kept glancing up at the creatures approaching the car.

"Be careful," said Joel. "You'll flood the engine."

"Hurry up!" Ralph said, watching skittering shapes moving across the street. "Come on!"

"I'm trying," he said, and his voice broke. "I'm trying…"

"Try harder."

Magnus banged his hand against the steering wheel; the horn blared. He exhaled, twisted the key so that the dashboard went dark. He waited, his eyes flicking towards the advancing things.

"What're you doing?" said Ralph. "Start the fucking car!" He checked the rear-view mirror and saw the front door of the house open. The boy's parents stepped outside towards the car.

Joel was whimpering.

"Just wait," said Magnus.

"If you don't start the car I'll stick this knife up your arse," said Ralph.

Magnus ignored him; he turned the key and the dashboard lights turned on. "Here goes…"

The parents clawed at the rear windscreen, attempting to gain entry. White tortured faces peered in at Joel and he screamed.

Magnus turned the key towards the engine; it spluttered, almost giving Ralph a coronary, but then growled and revved as Magnus pumped the accelerator. Magnus whooped, punched the air.

From the CD player recessed in the dashboard, Johnny Cash began to sing about walking the line.

Magnus let out a delirious laugh.

"Put your foot down," said Ralph.

Magnus nodded. He looked at the swarm of villagers filling the street, released the parking brake, and gunned the engine.

With a screech of tyres the car bolted down the driveway, knocking aside a man whose face was drooping on one side and knotted with swollen blisters. His left arm was a glistening appendage of coiling sinew and spikes erupting from epidermal layers.

Magnus turned onto the road. The villagers screamed to the sky; some crouched and stared, eyes shining and gleaming. Some grinned at the car as it rushed past them. Men, women, and children. Some were holding hands; others didn't even have hands. Impossible limbs grew and retracted from twitching bodies. Bloated abdomens glistened in the headlights. Other forms reached out to the car, as if begging for help. These poor creatures staggered on emaciated legs wasted down to bone. Groans and screams echoed from around the street.

Joel was shivering on the backseat. Magnus was staring straight ahead, ignoring the monstrosities.

"Fucking hell," said Ralph. "What happened to everyone? What are they?"

Neither Joel nor Magnus answered. And when Ralph thought about it, he didn't want an answer. He dropped his knife in the footwell and held his face in his hands. The edges of his mind weakened and buckled. His body wanted to shut down and hibernate. He didn't want to be here. He wanted to be at home, safe in bed, snacking on Hula Hoops and Jaffa Cakes.

"Jesus Christ," Joel was muttering. "Jesus Christ..."

Magnus glanced at Ralph, daring to look away from the road. "Do you really think Frank is dead? Do you think those things killed him?"

"Maybe they ate him," Joel whispered.

Ralph looked down the road. There were still ragged figures emerging from the houses and stalking towards the road. There were bodies on the lawns. He looked down at the pavement and saw bones scattered upon it.

The car passed out of the village, down the long, straight road.

When they'd travelled just less than a mile, a sudden light bloomed on the road ahead. Headlights.

Magnus stopped the car. Gripped the steering wheel.

"Who is that?" asked Joel, as if the others knew.

The light approached. The sound of an engine. Heavy and chugging. A large vehicle. Some type of truck.

It stopped twenty yards from them.

Several figures stepped into the light. Human. Normal, Ralph thought, but he had been fooled already today. They moved towards the car. Ralph stiffened in his seat. He had the urge to flee.

"Soldiers," Ralph muttered, finding his voice, although it sounded pathetic.

"We're saved," said Joel.

Ralph eyed the gas mask-clad soldier moving to his side of the car. The barrel of an assault rifle centred upon him; his bowels became liquid. He stared into the soldier's black, apathetic visage.

"I hope so, mate. I really hope so."

CHAPTER TWENTY-ONE

Frank was hiding in a garden outside a darkened house. His thighs throbbed and his calves ached. He was shivering. His heart was a manic, escalating slab of muscle. He held the crowbar tight to his chest, but it gave him no comfort, and the cold grass under his feet sucked all of the warmth from his body. He didn't want those things to catch him. He didn't want to die screaming. No person should die screaming.

Far off, over on the next street maybe, something screamed like a pig caught in a steel trap. He flinched, tried not to imagine what had birthed the sound. Exhaustion pulled at his body. He waited for what seemed like slow hours of torture.

He remembered the sights he had seen on his way here, running for his life through the empty streets of this dead village: human remains scattered on a road; stomachs opened up and steaming in the cold air; a crying man kneeling on a pavement, his body juddering as if caught in a seizure, bones snapping as arms and legs were bent into unnatural angles. The man had screamed when his spine protruded through the back of his shirt like an emerging dorsal fin; a tall, gangly-limbed apparition moving from house to house, peering through the windows.

A terrible, bulbous-eyed face had stared at him from the shadows of an overturned car and beckoned him inside with a long, bone-white finger.

Frank had managed to escape his pursuers, weaving down alleyways and side-streets without regard for what might have lurked within them, but the maniacs were still hunting him, wherever they were right now. Maybe they had found another unfortunate to hunt. Maybe they had forgotten about him.

Maybe they were waiting for him to emerge from his hiding place.

He gritted his teeth as nausea bloomed in his gut. He tensed his stomach muscles, fought the urge to vomit. He could still smell the corrupted stink of his pursuers; it was everywhere. They had marked the village, this ground, as their own.

Frank listened for any slight whisper or hush of movement from nearby. He dared to move his arms to restore some circulation.

There were clicking sounds out on the street. Light footfalls. The scuff of shoes upon tarmac. A low, rattling growl from a half-man's mouth.

Frank stiffened, bunching up his body into a tight ball.

The cloud cover shifted to reveal the pallid half-moon. The glimmer of stars. The galaxy revealing itself. Silver light and metallic gleam.

The road adjacent to the garden was crawling with near-human shapes.

Could they smell him? Could they hear his heartbeat?

His eyes had adapted to the dark, and now with the added moonlight he could observe the creatures in more detail than was good for him. Some of them were naked, and this lack of inhibition showed him the black spines that had erupted from their bodies and colonised their flesh. Some were crouching and sniffing at the road, trying to pick up his scent. Men and women. No children, thankfully. Pale figures that reflected the starlight. Others skittered and moaned; one of them raised its face to the sky and wailed. The sound of claws with nothing to rip or shred.

One of the creatures was gibbering to itself; Frank thought he could discern words amongst the nonsense, but nothing that made any sense.

Then they moved away down the street.

What *were* they? Had there been a radioactive or toxic leak somewhere nearby and the people were mutated?

Frank waited until they were long gone. He stood and looked out onto the street, took a few steps towards the road then stopped, listened. Muffled thumps and booms in the distance, like the noises he had heard earlier when he'd cowered underneath the van. Sounded like fireworks. They resonated under his feet. He thought he saw a white flash in the sky to the north but he might have imagined it. He was quite sure it was coming from the west, but the houses blocked every horizon. He was in the centre of the village. He had to get back to Ralph, Magnus and Joel.

Frank slipped through the open gateway and onto the pavement. Pools of stinking fluid on the road. A smell like vinegar and eggs. Spoor or urine. Maybe something else. He thought of the pickled eggs Catherine would eat when she was drunk. They always made her breath smell, but he would gladly give her a lingering kiss now, just to be away from this place.

Something moved behind him. He pivoted, raising the crowbar.

A fox emerged from one of the gardens down the street. It saw Frank, but it wasn't worried about him; there were deadlier predators on the streets tonight.

Frank watched the fox scamper across the road and into another garden.

"Good luck, mate," Frank said, and he meant it.

He went back the way he had come, back to his mates. He crept along for a few minutes, scanning the gardens and houses brimming with ocean-floor darkness. His imagination told him of dangers in every hush of the breeze and listless shadow draped over the ground. He considered entering one of the many houses around him, but something told him there would be things inside their silent dark rooms waiting for someone like him. No, he would keep walking. He contemplated running, but realised he would make too much noise with the pounding of his shoes on the road.

Dead streetlights. Empty driveways. He saw a woman's body slumped across a car bonnet; the dark stains that had leaked from her and pooled in clotted slicks. She had been opened up and emptied out. He kept moving. He walked past something that looked like moulted skin, sloughed off by some unknown thing. He prodded it with a foot, disgusted and intrigued.

He heard a car engine from the next street. He stopped. Brakes shrieking. Tyres scraping on the road. The crash of metal against something heavier and immovable. A scream cleaved the night.

Frank ran towards the scream, resisting the temptation to run the other way. He rounded the corner and stopped. He panted, his shoulders moving with each breath he gave and took.

A car had crashed into a stone wall outside a house. People were inside the car. There was an excited screech from nearby. He swallowed to wet his throat.

There was a man in the driver's seat, slumped over the steering wheel. A woman was in the front passenger seat, crying between her screams. A girl sat in the back, stunned and reeling.

An old man pulled open the driver's door and dragged out the man. The woman screamed again, made a futile effort to stop him being pulled outside.

The old man laid out the driver and knelt over him.

"Hey," Frank shouted.

The old man turned. His body was misshapen, his bones jutting from under his clothes. He was shaking like an addict. Frank halted.

The old man's face was blank, almost moronic. Sunken eyes. He turned back to the unconscious man and bent his head towards the man's face. There was a wet scraping sound. He looked like he was kissing the man, his back arching as he bobbed his head to batten onto the younger man's face.

The woman screamed when she saw what the old man was doing.

Frank stumbled over to the old man and hit him on the back with the crowbar. The old man came free from his victim with a moist rip and turned, a wheezing rattle coming from his open mouth. He had no teeth. On his neck, flaps of skin parted bloodlessly to reveal a nest of black tendrils no longer and thicker than shoelaces. The tendrils stretched and lunged at the air, wanting to envelop Frank's face and squirm into his mouth. Frank smashed the old man's face with the crowbar; he collapsed, as did his skull. The tendrils danced erratically, even as the old man stopped moving, his face a desiccated mask. His eyes had caved in and his nose was all bent cartilage and crumbling bone.

The tendrils flopped wetly onto the old man's chest, like something washed up on a beach. Frank stepped away, repulsed.

The woman was still screaming. The girl stared at Frank, her palm pressed against the window.

Frank ran to the car, opened the back door. "Come on, get out."

"That was Mr. Stewart," she said. She had red hair, and he had a sudden image of another girl with red hair. A girl he loved.

On the other side of the car, two men had opened the woman's door and grabbed her. There was something wrong with the men's faces and their hands. They ripped the woman from her seat just as Frank pulled the girl from the car. She didn't fight him. She only looked back at the car and called for her mother.

The woman screamed. The men piled upon her. The sounds of paper being torn, but it wasn't paper. She stopped screaming.

"We can't help her," Frank told the girl as he led her away. "I'm sorry."

Frank looked down at the man, whose mouth was too wide and bloody for him to be alive. His eyes were open. He must have awoken when the tendrils invaded him. His teeth were stained red and his tongue was gone. The flesh on his cheeks had been gnawed away. His throat was a red wound.

The stink of vinegar and rotten eggs.

"That's my dad."

"I'm sorry."

"Is he dead?"

Frank didn't answer. He was looking down the road. A group of people were running towards them. He couldn't see them clearly. He didn't want to see them clearly. He looked the way the car had come and saw the church tower looming above the houses a few hundred yards away. He remembered the church bells had rung earlier. Maybe someone was there.

The girl was crying.

Frank picked her up and ran down the road. A loose-faced woman wearing a stained cotton nightdress stepped from the darkness. The girl yelped. The woman's arms trembled and jerked. She stared at the ground and vanished back into the shadows.

He kept running, getting closer to the church; the spired tower tall and dark.

The main gates appeared ahead of them.

Things that were once people screamed and cried behind them. Getting closer.

Frank could feel the girl's small body shaking against him.

They reached the gates. A row of sentinel-like trees around the graveyard's periphery, deep shadows beneath them. Frank pushed through the gates onto the stone pathway winding through the graveyard. In the pale moonlight he could make out gravestones jutting from the ground and a war memorial to the men who'd died in both World Wars. The church was darker than the sky. There was light inside, visible through the stained-glass windows. Hope flared inside him.

"We're nearly there," Frank whispered.

He stopped.

There were people in the graveyard, mewling and crying to one another amongst the graves. The church's large, arched double-doors were thirty yards away. They could make it, but what if the doors were locked?

Shapes moved like mourners trying to find the right grave at which to grieve. Frank looked towards the stone pathway and saw a figure on its hands and knees, crawling away from the church. A woman. He would have to get past her.

Frank moved. He kept some distance between them and the woman. She was making a clicking sound in her throat.

They reached the church doors. Frank twisted the ring-shaped metal handle. There was movement to his right; a teenage boy stepped from a pool of shadow into the moonlight. His shoulders were slumped and narrow. His face was a riot of wounds and writhing barbs. Frank opened the door and rushed inside the church. The door shut loudly, but he was just relieved to be inside. They found themselves in a small vestibule.

Frank made sure the main doors were shut tight. There was nothing to push against them. He wondered if *they* had the wit to open doors.

Candles had been lit. Someone was in here, or had been recently. Frank put the girl down. She looked at the stone floor.

"Stay close," he whispered. "I'll take care of you."

The girl said nothing. Barely a nod of her head.

With the girl following him, Frank walked slowly up the aisle. Absurdly, he thought of his wedding day, years ago. He looked around. Stained glass and saints. Tall stone columns scarred by age. Wooden beams and arches built by men long-dead and buried. The floor radiated a dry cold. Rows of pews. Stained and worn wood, dissected by a long, carpeted aisle leading towards the altar. The air was cold, fetid and old. Dry. Thick enough to snatch handfuls. Their footsteps echoed around the empty spaces. The candles threw shadows like slick-limbed spirits. Frank's heart jumped at every small sound and whisper of breeze. Inside, he was a riot of fear, nerves and horror.

Churches made Frank nervous. Even on his wedding day he'd been worried about setting foot inside one. All that piousness and judgement. He'd never found a reason to believe in God...or any other god. He needed evidence to believe in something. Due to his father's gentle encouragement, he stopped believing in Santa Claus and The Tooth Fairy when he was barely seven years old. Father had been a taciturn, honest man and he taught Frank to be pragmatic and sensible in life; that problems could be solved with common sense and simple solutions. His father said once that "dreamers never get anywhere. That's why so many writers and artists kill themselves".

Frank was his father's son.

The nave was empty. About halfway up the aisle, Frank stopped. The girl stopped beside him. His skin prickled. The sound of creaking wood and shifting stone. He imagined the church as a living organism born from deep within the earth; groomed, sculpted and adorned by men.

Frank sat the girl down on a pew. She was malleable and compliant. Understanding in her hooded, green eyes. He bent down to her eye level. Her face was pale and dirty.

"I'm going to take a look around," Frank said, keeping his voice low, keeping the fear out of it. "I'll see if anyone's around. Are you okay to wait here? Don't worry, I won't go too far."

She stared into his face. The corners of her mouth moved, like she wanted to talk.

"Okay. I'll be back in a minute." He offered her a tired smile. She looked down at the floor between her dangling legs. She remained there like someone's lost doll. Frank went to touch her on the shoulder but withdrew his hand at the last moment. He felt bad for leaving her.

Again, he gave her that same feeble half-smile; he wished he'd stop doing that. He felt foolish. What good would a smile do when her parents were dead?

"My name's Frank," he said, placing his hand on his chest.

She glanced slowly up at him. Blinked. Looked down again.

Frank searched the other pews. Nobody was hiding in the pulpit or the lectern. The rest of the nave was deserted. Effigies of the Virgin Mary, and St. George fighting the dragon. Cold blank stares from carved faces. He checked the chancel and around the altar. A monolithic organ melded to the wall. He stood before the linen-covered altar, intimidated by the grandeur of the holy paraphernalia: the alter crucifix; the tabernacle; the chalice used for communion; the rows of candles. He felt the weight of history and age inside this place. It was stifling and claustrophobic. There were two doors flanking the chancel.

His footsteps echoed and bounced off the stone walls, making it sound like he was being followed.

Everything was cold.

He kept looking back to make sure the girl was still where he had left her. She was still gazing at the floor.

He checked the north and south transepts flanking the chancel. In a dark corner where the east and north walls met, Frank found a fungal-like growth that stretched from the floor to about five feet high. Pulpy

141

and ripe-smelling. He didn't touch it. It was the colour of algae and stank like pond water.

Frank returned to the girl. She was lying on the pew, eyes shut. A prayer cushion under her head.

He took off his jacket and placed it over her.

Silence, apart from an occasional distant sound from outside. A scream or a cry penetrating the thick walls.

He wondered who had lit the candles and who had rang the bell earlier. Maybe whoever had done so had already moved on. Maybe they were dead. Maybe they were beyond one of the doors he had declined to investigate. It wasn't important right now. All that mattered, for now, was that they had shelter for the night.

After blocking the main door with a bookcase full of hymn books, he took out his mobile. No signal. He sat down in the pew one up from the girl. She was wearing blue jeans with patterns of flowers and a white jumper under her pink jacket. White trainers. A green butterfly hair clip amongst her red hair. She reminded him so much of his daughter, and the mere thought of it almost brought him to tears.

He would keep the girl safe. He would watch over the girl all night. He would protect her. He wouldn't let it happen again.

"I'll look after you," he whispered.

In the morning he would decide what to do next.

CHAPTER TWENTY-TWO

Frank awoke to weak light washing into the church. He checked his watch. Almost six in the morning. He yawned, rubbed his eyes. Groaned sour breath from between furred teeth. Because he had slept sitting upright his spine felt like a rod of hot metal.

The girl was gone.

He got up, straightened himself out, and looked around. Maybe she was hiding.

"Little girl," he said.

No reply. His jacket was on the floor. He picked it up and put it back on.

She wouldn't be stupid enough to go outside, would she?

He searched the inside of the church. The main doors were shut. Sudden guilt stabbed him. Panic stirred his guts. He had promised to take care of her. Then he remembered the two doors in the chancel. Frank opened the door to the right and walked into a plainly-decorated, musty room. A light covering of dust on skirting boards. A broken cobweb hung from the ceiling. The room was the sacristy, if he remembered correctly. There was an old porcelain sink, cracked and stained. Vestments hung up in a wardrobe. Communion equipment. A pile of white linen.

The girl wasn't there.

He took the door to the next room. He could smell alcohol.

There was a dead man at an antique oak desk, slumped back on his chair, his face raised to the ceiling. A half-full bottle of whiskey and some empty blister packs of painkillers. An empty glass.

Frank stepped towards the body.

A porcine-faced priest. His dog collar was yellowed and grimy. Grey whiskers sprouted from a double-chin. Bulging stomach touching the edge of the desk. His hands were dangling by his sides. His eyes were open and dull, cloudy with dust.

A bookshelf on the wall, lined with hardcovers. One was about campanology.

"Bell-ringing," Frank said. "Solves that mystery then."

Frank checked the priest's pulse. Nothing. Still fairly warm. Couldn't have been dead for long. Rigor hadn't set in yet. Maybe he had died while Frank and the girl had been sleeping.

"Fucking hell," Frank muttered. "I'm sorry."

"You shouldn't swear," a quiet voice said behind him.

Frank turned sharply. His heart leapt into his gullet.

The girl was huddled in the corner, where the walls met the floor, her arms folded over herself and her face tilted downwards. Small eyes regarded him over thin wrists. She had been crying, judging by the red around her eyes.

"I've been trying to find you," said Frank. "Are you okay?"

"Yeah."

"Are you sure? You're not hurt?"

"I'm okay."

"What are you doing in here?"

"I was exploring. I found him." She nodded at the priest. "Did he kill himself?"

"I think so."

"Why?"

"I don't know."

"Was he sad?"

"Maybe."

"How did he do it?"

Frank looked at the desktop. "He took a lot of tablets and drank a lot of whiskey. Then he went to sleep."

"Will he still go to Heaven?"

"If he believed in it, then yes."

"What does that mean?"

"He believed in Heaven, so that's where he'll go."

"Do you believe in Heaven?"

"Of course I do," he lied. "I'm sure he's in Heaven…with the angels and all that jazz."

"So why did the man kill himself?"

"I don't know."

"Because of the bad people?"

"Maybe."

"Was he scared of the bad people?"

"Probably."

"I'm scared," she said.

"You don't have to be scared," Frank said. "Everything will be okay."

"My mummy and daddy are dead, aren't they?"

He hesitated. "I'm sorry."

"I miss them."

"It's okay to miss them. It's okay to be sad."

"Do you think they're in Heaven?"

"Yes, definitely."

"Should I do what the priest did? If I do that, will I meet my mummy and daddy in Heaven?"

Frank didn't know what to say.

"You don't believe in Heaven, do you?"

"I don't know. I won't know until I die."

"Would you die just to find out?"

"No," Frank said. "I've got a wife and friends. I want to see them again."

Her eyes drilled into his. "What if they're dead?"

Frank wiped sweat from his upper lip. "We should get out of here, find somewhere safe."

"The village is full of monsters," the girl said.

"We have to get out of here."

She looked at him, unsure. "Mummy told me I'm not supposed to go anywhere with strangers."

"Your mum was very wise. But it's okay, I won't hurt you. I'll take care of you. I won't let anything hurt you."

"Your name is Frank," she said.

"That's right. I can't be a stranger if you know my name, can I? You remembered."

She raised her eyebrows. "You only told me last night."

Frank couldn't help a grin. He held out his hand. "What do you say?"

She nodded, got to her feet. She hesitated, but then approached Frank slowly. She took his hand. Her palm was warm and clammy.

Frank smiled at her. "I'll look after you."

"Okay."

"What's your name?"

She wiped her nose with the back of her hand. Her green eyes were full of sadness. "Florence."

"Nice to meet you, Florence. How old are you?"

"Eleven."

"A proper grown up then."

She ignored Frank and pointed at the priest. "Do we have to bury him? That's what you're supposed to do when someone dies, isn't it?"

"I think he's past caring. I'll get some linen from the next room and cover him up. At least that's something. Do you know what happened here, Florence? In the village."

She stared at the floor. "It started yesterday morning, I think. I was at home with my mum and dad. We heard screaming and shouting outside. I saw Mr Stewart who lived next door. There was something wrong with him. Mr Stewart was the one who killed my dad."

"I'm so sorry, Florence."

She looked up at him.

"I won't let any of the bad people hurt you."

She nodded. There were dark patches around her eyes. A frame of red hair; stray curls of it touching her chin.

"Do you live in the village?" she asked him.

"My friends are in the village, hiding in a house. Waiting for me. We're from a small village called Shepton Beauchamp. It's in Somerset."

"Your friends might be dead," Florence said.

"They might be."

"I can't go home, can I?" she said.

"I'm afraid not, Florence. It's too dangerous. We have to get out of the village."

"And go where?"

"Somewhere safe."

CHAPTER TWENTY-THREE

When they returned to the nave, Frank glanced at the black growth in the north transept. Bits of fungal matter on the floor beneath the wall, as if it had burst at some point.

There was a scuttling sound amongst the pews to their right.

"What was that?" Florence's voice was quiet and scared.

Frank caught a glimpse of something black and small peering above the pews.

"Let's go," Frank whispered. "Quietly."

"Maybe it's a cat," said Florence.

Frank gripped her hand too tight. "Keep moving. Don't stop."

It came at them like a skittering black spider, low to the floor and fast, trying to cut them off before they could reach the end of the aisle. Bristling arachnid hairs covered much of its gleaming chitin-coated abdomen. Multiple insect legs on each side of its twisted body. Too many eyes, gelatinous and dripping unknown fluids.

Frank realised, with mounting horror, that the creature had a child's face mounted upon its horrific body.

"It's a little boy," said Florence.

He picked up the girl and ran. The creature chased them, its busy legs tapping on the floor and its wheezing breath getting louder. Frank opened the main doors, glanced back. His legs quivered. The boy-creature bolted towards them. Its face was horrid and yawning. Its mouth was a quivering rip in flesh, sheathing an emerging nest of sucking worm-mouths and blind feelers.

Frank shut the doors too loud. He glanced around the graveyard. Slack, feverish faces turned towards them.

The boy-creature hit the door on the other side, scratching and scraping and searching for a way out. Frank stumbled down the pathway, avoiding the desperate lunges of bony fingers and grasping hands. A man came after them, hobbling on a bad knee. His mouth was stretched too wide and his eyes were blistered and bleeding. His hands had formed into pale hooks of bone.

Frank shut the gates, hurried onto the street. He looked both ways, chose the way he had come last night. He set Florence down and they ran together.

She was quick and he barely kept pace with her, despite his longer strides.

There were screams behind them.

"Don't stop," Frank said. "The house isn't far away."

They approached the place where Florence's parents had died. There was dried blood on the road. Her parents were gone. Florence stared at the car as they passed it. Minutes later they arrived at the house. The front door was splintered like something dense had smashed into it. Frank entered the house first. Furniture was strewn around the hallway as if his mates had barricaded the door and then had to remove it to escape the house.

The downstairs rooms were empty. Ralph, Magnus and Joel had left behind their bags. Frank left the bags on the living room floor. They climbed the stairs. The bathroom was empty, as was what seemed to be the marital bedroom. Someone had pissed in the toilet and not bothered to flush it. In a boy's bedroom, they found the boy dead under a duvet, and he was...different. Florence stared at the corpse until Frank guided her onto the landing.

There was movement up in the attic. Scrambling and scratching. He knew it wasn't his mates. He didn't want to see what might look down at them from the open hatch, so they left quickly and didn't look back.

Nothing attacked them on the street. The silence was enough to bring despair. This was a dead place. Frank never wanted to return here. He glanced at Florence and wondered how she was dealing with losing her parents, her home, and her old life.

Her old life? Her life from yesterday.

How was she still functioning? Maybe it was because she was young. Or maybe it would hit her eventually. *Really* hit her. She had plenty of nightmares to come. Plenty of therapy.

Were Ralph, Magnus and Joel still alive? What had happened to them? If they were dead, how would he break the news to their families?

A hot, creeping panic tried to overcome him.

He kept watch as they moved down the road. The sky churned with grey, promising rain. He wanted to see the sun again. He wanted to go home.

But first he had to find help.

"Unless we can find a car," he said, "we're in for a long walk."

CHAPTER TWENTY-FOUR

Joel awoke and immediately regretted it when he remembered the past few hours of his life. He'd dreamt of monsters and corpses and things with gibbering mouths. He was sitting against the wall in a corner of a long, wide room, a musty blanket covering him from his neck to his knees. Plain walls of faded beige and shallow spider-web cracks. There were windows set high in one wall, letting in dull light. A large whiteboard was attached to the far wall, and tables and chairs had been stacked in corners. Posters displayed maths sums and the alphabet. There were crayon drawings of stick people and lemon-shaped suns and rabbits with large eyes and comical bucked teeth. Posters of cartoon animals with permanent grins.

The distant *tap-tap-tap* of gunfire. His heart raced.

His legs stretched out before him on a wooden floor. His entire body ached. He felt like crying. He was confused and disorientated. The strong stink of unwashed bodies filled the air; the musk of humans packed together. He trembled under the blanket. He checked his pockets and realised he had lost his wallet. It contained a photo of Anya.

"Sleeping Beauty's woken up," said Ralph. He and Magnus were either side of him. "We thought we'd have to carry you around from now on."

"You okay, Joel?" Magnus asked, face creased with concern. He had wrapped a blanket around his body.

Joel shivered, wrapped his arms around himself. "Where are we?"

"We're safe," said Ralph. "But things are pretty fucked by the sounds of it."

Joel sat up straight, cleared his throat and looked around, avoiding eye contact with the room's other occupants. Many were asleep. There seemed to be about a hundred people here. Gathered in various groups or alone. Some families. Lines of people around the walls, some staring into space or at the floor. Some were huddled with blankets over their shoulders. More people were in an adjacent classroom through an open doorway. A few were drinking from plastic cups or bottles of water. Some gnawed slowly on protein bars, chewing moronically like cows doomed for the slaughterhouse. An old woman was trying to roll a cigarette with shaking hands. A man with a severe facial tick was drinking from a bottle of cough medicine. Young and old alike here. A palpable fear lurked amongst them. A miasma of desperation, shock and disbelief. Wide-eyed denial painted upon pale traumatised faces. Sleepers having bad dreams. One man was crying into his hands and muttering a woman's name. Another man stared at the floor, his left arm in a sling and an unlit cigarette hung from his bottom lip. He had long, black hair tied into a ponytail.

Magnus handed Joel a small bottle of water.

"What's the time?" Joel downed half of the bottle in one go.

"Nearly six," said Ralph.

"In the morning? I slept through the night?"

"Yeah."

"What happened? I remember being in the car leaving the village. And the soldiers…"

Ralph and Magnus exchanged a glance.

Ralph said, "The soldiers almost shot us. You passed out. They bundled us into the back of their truck. They brought us here. The paramedics checked you over; made sure you were okay and not infected. They said it was shock."

"I feel like shit," Joel said. He wanted to throw up.

"Join the club, mate. What a stag weekend this has turned out to be…"

Magnus grunted.

"It's unbelievable," said Joel. "This can't be happening."

"Well, my friend," said Ralph. "It certainly is happening."

"The paramedics thought I was infected? Infected with what?"

"Fuck knows," said Ralph. "One of them said something about a pandemic."

"An epidemic, not a pandemic," said Magnus.

"Same thing."

"No, it's not."

"It doesn't matter," said Ralph. "Considering what we saw in Wishford I'd say we're in the deep shit."

"Where are we?" asked Joel.

"A rescue centre," said Magnus. "A primary school in Horsham."

"Are the people from Wishford here?"

Again, Ralph and Magnus exchanged a brief look.

"No, mate," said Ralph. "They're all gone. Or most of them, anyway. The people here are from other places. There are other rescue centres, apparently. We're in one of them. The police and army have cleared and sealed off this neighbourhood."

"But from what I heard," said Magnus, "Horsham's been affected as well. This is a safe zone."

"It's happened here as well?" said Joel.

"There're armed police outside," said Ralph. "They're guarding the gates. This is serious shit, mate."

"What do you mean, they're from other places?"

"This has hit the entire country. One of the coppers said it's a national emergency."

"Have you managed to contact anyone from home?"

"No" said Magnus. "Our phones still aren't working. They reckon something atmospheric is affecting them. Debbie is going to kill me."

Joel took out his mobile and tried to call Anya, but the entire network was dead. Panic flooded his stomach. He wanted to go home, see Anya. Make sure she was safe.

"So it could have happened back home?" Joel said. His face flushed with heat. He wanted to scratch his skin until he drew blood.

Magnus shrugged. "We don't know. The police told us to stay calm until they restore order."

Ralph was shaking his head.

"In all honestly, I don't think they know much either," Magnus added.

"We're refugees," said Magnus. "Everyone here is."

Jet aircraft screamed low overhead. Joel flinched.

Ralph looked up at the ceiling. "Someone said this is an invasion."

"An invasion?" said Joel. "By who?"

"By *what*," Magnus said.

"Is it terrorists?"

"No one knows," said Ralph. "But I doubt it."

"I have to get home to Anya."

"The police won't let us leave," said Magnus. "They said it's too dangerous out there. The army is fighting in the streets. You heard the gunfire, didn't you?"

"We could take our chances," said Ralph.

"We'd die out there," Magnus said.

"What about Frank?" Joel asked. "Have you heard from him? He could be in here somewhere…"

Magnus shook his head. "We haven't seen him."

"We should never have left him," said Joel. "We abandoned him."

"We didn't abandon him," said Ralph. "He left us."

"He might still be alive." There was no conviction in Magnus' voice.

"He's dead," said Joel. "Frank's dead. I can feel it."

Neither Ralph nor Magnus replied.

"Have you seen them?" a woman asked, sitting across from them.

They turned to her. She was stroking a small dog on her lap, some sort of terrier licking at her fingers with its small tongue. She looked to be in her fifties. Sharp, keen eyes that reminded Joel of one of his old schoolteachers. Greying hair down to her shoulders. A dark blanket around her body. She was shoeless.

"Excuse me?" said Joel.

"Have you seen them?"

"Seen who?" said Magnus.

"The monsters. Whatever they are."

"We've run into a few of them," Ralph said.

"You're lucky to be alive then."

"We've had a few close calls."

"What happened to you?" Joel asked her.

"Two days ago," the woman said. "Sunday morning. I was shopping. People started to collapse and convulse. They changed right before my eyes. I had to hide in a clothes shop's changing room just so I wouldn't get torn to bits by my best friend. She went crazy, sprouted something like dark growths from her back and stomach. She tore out the throat of a teenage boy. Ate bits of him. She attacked other people. But there were more like her. Poor Francine. They became monsters."

"Fuck," said Ralph. "That's mental."

"I'm sorry about your friend," said Joel. "How did you end up here?"

She stroked the dog's head with long-nailed fingers. "I managed to escape from the shop. People were dying. So much screaming. It's all a bit foggy now. I got home and Alfie here was going crazy, barking and growling. He knew what was happening, the clever boy. I tried calling my son in London but he didn't answer his phone. I called the police but the line was busy. Eventually I was picked up by a search and rescue patrol looking for survivors. I barely made it to the truck; there were monsters on my street...some were in the gardens. Me and Alfie were bundled into the lorry. They dropped us off here on Sunday night. We've been given food and water, and more people have arrived from the surrounding areas, brought here in buses and vans. People that have been evacuated."

"So this 'event' has happened all over the country," said Magnus.

"Yes, I think so. Before the power went out I saw on the BBC News the cities had been affected as well. It's worse in the cities. We're lucky, really, when you think about it."

"I've got a cousin in London," Joel said. "He's got a family."

"I think my son is dead," the woman said matter-of-factly. "I hope he's dead rather than one of those monsters. You should hope the same for your cousin and his family."

"Demons," said Joel.

"Do you have any idea what the creatures are?" said Magnus.

"Depends what you believe," she said. "I've heard many rumours in the past two days, some believable and others not so believable. I don't think it really matters, in the end. I'm sorry – where are my manners? My name's Susan Blake. You've already met little Alfie."

"Pleased to meet you, Susan," said Joel. "I'm Joel, this is Magnus, and that's Ralph."

"We're all refugees now," she said. "We're never going home."

* * *

Joel trudged to the toilets. The corridors were full of people leaning against the walls. There were plastic bags and belongings on the floor. He stepped carefully. Nobody spoke. Eyes flicked towards him but didn't linger. Through a ground floor window he looked out at the rear of the school: a high wall surrounded the playground, which had become another gathering place for other refugees. Makeshift tents covered the playground. A child was crying out there.

The toilets smelled of disinfectant and piss. Low urinals lined the wall. A row of sinks topped by bottles of semen-like liquid soap, a forgotten toothbrush and a damp roll of paper towels. Smudges of grime on the taps. Hand-dryers attached to the walls. A sign above the sinks reminded him to wash his hands after using the toilet.

He stood there for a few seconds. He felt off-kilter, confused and scared. He entered an empty cubicle – the other three were occupied. The door didn't lock properly. There was a turd amidst a soggy smattering of white paper in the toilet bowl. He screwed up his face, covered his mouth. There wasn't much paper left in the dispenser. He tore away a few sheets and used it as a glove to touch the flush lever. The dirty water rose, crested by the turd, almost to the rim of the bowl. Joel backed away, grimacing.

The water didn't rise above the rim, and the tide receded. A cloud of sewer gas drifted to him. He coughed and waved one hand in front of his face.

He raised the toilet seat, tossed the paper into the bowl.

The man in the next cubicle was grunting; weird, ape-like sounds like he was taking a painful dump. Or something else. Joel tried to ignore him; he didn't have the nerve to tell him to shut up.

When he had finished pissing he grabbed another wad of paper and lowered the toilet lid, which he wiped clean. He discarded the paper and took out the small crucifix chain from his pocket. He sat down. The grunting sounds from the next cubicle stopped.

There was marker pen graffiti on the cubicle walls. Drawings of male and female genitalia.

One scribble read: *This is the end, boys and girls.*

Another stated: *All flesh can be used.*

He hated public toilets; the last time he'd used one, in Weymouth last year, there had been a phone number scribbled on a cubicle door, underlined with the offer of 'manly sex'.

Joel wrapped the chain around his hand so the crucifix was hanging over his knuckles. The chain was warm from resting against his thigh in his pocket. He closed his eyes. He held his hands together. Joel was embarrassed by his faith. He hid it from his friends and family. Only Anya knew. She was Catholic, although she had lapsed. He knew his mates wouldn't mock him for his belief, but he was scared to tell them anyway, especially Ralph, who was a passionate atheist and hated organised religion.

He prayed silently. He prayed that his God was listening.

Because if God still cared, what was happening outside? Was it the work of the Devil? Did that mean the things that had attacked him and his friends were demons? Were they people possessed by demons?

If they were possessed, could they be saved? And if they could be saved, was killing one actually murder?

He opened his eyes. What if he had to kill one of the afflicted to protect himself or his mates? Could he do that? Why did this disaster have to happen when he was away from Anya? Was it just God's sense of humour? His idea of a joke?

Remember, your God let Frank's daughter die. Emily. Always remember her name. God let the cancer eat her alive and destroy her body.

Joel sighed. He hoped God would provide him with an answer.

He stared at the door and waited for a sign.

The walls began to vibrate. From above him came a quick throbbing that could be felt at ground level. Joel looked to the ceiling. He felt something above the building. Something in the sky moving over them. Something massive.

A sign.

He pocketed his crucifix and rushed back to the others. He didn't wash his hands.

The windows were rattling in their frames.

Susan Blake's dog barked skywards.

Every person in the room looked towards the ceiling.

Ralph got up. "I'm going to see what's happening."

Joel and Magnus followed him.

CHAPTER TWENTY-FIVE

Early morning mist. Where the monsters were hiding.

Frank held the girl's hand as they walked the road. They left Wishford behind. Frank kept an eye on the hedgerows and skeletal trees flanking them. Distant booms echoed beyond the mist. Thunder in the darkening clouds. Frank looked up, didn't like what he saw.

Florence glanced over her shoulder. "Where are we going?"

"Horsham."

"Are we going to walk all the way there?"

"If we're unlucky, yeah."

"What does that mean?"

"It means we're walking if we can't get a lift."

"That's okay. I don't mind walking."

"I do," Frank said. "I'm old."

"You're very old."

"Cheers."

They walked on.

A Ford Escort was stopped on the road.

No keys in the ignition.

"You know how to hotwire it?" asked Frank.

Florence shook her head.

"Fair enough."

"What's this?" Florence was rooting around the backseat.

"What?"

Florence handed him a man's wallet. He opened it, checked the driver's licence filed within.

Joel's wallet.

"This belongs to a good friend of mine. He was here. Hopefully the other two were here as well."

A mournful wailing came out of the mist.

Florence stared into the mist, her mouth moving silently.

"Come on, let's keep moving," Frank said.

CHAPTER TWENTY-SIX

Joel and Magnus emerged into the grey daylight. A few others followed them.

The front of the school. A car park. There were armed police here. Submachine guns, Kevlar vests and holstered pistols. They were standing guard by the school gates, staring at the sky. A road ran adjacent to the school. A row of semi-detached houses along the street.

Joel could see squad cars, a riot van, and an ambulance in the car park. There were civilians already outside. Everyone was staring at the sky.

"Oh god," someone said.

Joel felt like his legs would collapse underneath him.

A gigantic, dark shape lurked within the grey clouds. Bigger than a mountain, drifting in the sky directly overhead.

The ground was vibrating. Joel felt his bones stiffen. The filling in one of his molars tingled. He swallowed, fought rising nausea in his stomach. He had the urge to run away and curl up into a ball until the presence passed over.

More people emerged from the school. They moved slowly, cautiously.

"It's not a craft," said Magnus. "It's not a ship. It's a living thing. A dark mass. A presence."

"It's living?" Joel asked, and he was answered with a sky-cracking wail. He covered his ears, as did everyone else. The sound of its cry reverberated through his body. A deep, sombre blast of noise and the boom of air through lungs bigger than a house.

They were all insects compared to that thing.

He had thought it a sign from God.

He was wrong. This wasn't anything to do with God. And he was in awe of the presence above him. Where was it from? Was it one of many? Were humans all over the world staring up at such colossal impossibilities and asking the same questions?

A profound terror bloomed inside him. The frayed edges of mind-snapping dread.

"That's what I saw on Saturday night," said Magnus.

Ralph and Joel looked at him.

"Before you found me passed out on the grass, Ralph, I saw a presence in the sky…like that thing."

"Is it the same one?" said Joel.

"I don't know. Could be hundreds of them."

"Hundreds," muttered Ralph. "Shit."

The presence in the clouds moved away silently towards the north, rising until it vanished higher into the sky.

Joel put his hand in his pocket and touched the crucifix. But he wasn't comforted. He had the horrid feeling that God wasn't watching.

"Nothing will ever be the same," said Magnus. "The world is changing."

CHAPTER TWENTY-SEVEN

There was a house ahead, on the right side of the road. Florence saw it before Frank did; he had been glancing over his shoulder, worried they were being followed.

"Do you think people are in the house?" asked Florence.

"Maybe. They might be able to help us."

"There won't be any monsters there?"

He shook his head. "I'll look after you."

"I hope they've got chocolate biscuits."

The house was set back twenty yards from the road. A gravel driveway without a car. Tyre tracks in the damp dirt between the stones. Maybe they had evacuated. Frank kept Florence behind him. Her little footsteps on the gravel and the quiet hush of her breath.

The house was small. Red brick walls and a squat chimney. A front door framed by a wooden latticed archway.

"Maybe there're other boys and girls in there," Florence said. "Boys smell."

Frank swallowed a grunted laugh. "Yeah, we certainly do." He looked through the window into an empty kitchen. Florence watched him. He knocked on the front door.

"I don't think they're home," Florence said.

Frank knocked again.

"Maybe they're asleep," said Florence.

"Maybe." Frank sighed. He opened the door.

"Isn't that rude? Are we allowed to go in there without asking?"

"It'll be okay. Stay close. Stay quiet."

Frank stepped into the hallway. Shadows filled the air, but they retreated from the light coming through the doorway.

"What's that smell?" asked Florence.

"Something nasty," Frank said, screwing up his face. Bad meat. He went into the kitchen. A framed photo of a man, a woman, a teenage boy and two younger girls. On the worktop was an electricity bill addressed to Mr David Pulver. The smell grew stronger. He saw a hamster cage with its door hanging open. The wiry metal was bent and warped.

The sound of movement in the next room. He could see a television and a unit of free-standing bookshelves; the living room. He made sure Florence was still behind him then moved to the next doorway.

He looked into the room and wished he hadn't. Patio doors let in the daylight.

Frank couldn't speak.

He held Florence back. He made sure of that. This wasn't to be seen by her eyes.

The air left his body. The stink of slaughter made his eyes water. The room before him drifted in-and-out of focus until it remained terribly clear to him. Too clear to ever be wiped from his memory.

"What is it?" Florence asked.

"Go back to the kitchen."

"What is it?"

He struggled to answer her. His mouth was dry. He ran his free hand over his face. The hot stink of blood and freshly-slain meat, fat and gristle.

The walls were stained with red. Splatters from arteries and veins. The remains of bodies on a carpet waterlogged with blood and shit. Scraps of hair. The stumps of arms and legs. Torsos that were no more than stripped meat and bone. Shredded clothes and wet rags. A small ribcage. Slippery organs strewn on the floor. Chewed lumps of flesh. Broken and splintered bones that had been gnawed upon. Wet things glistened.

At the foot of an armchair was a spine. A damp pelt of hair that might have been a cat once; furred skull and empty eye sockets.

"Fuck," Frank whispered.

The air was hot and stifling.

A small man was crouched over what remained of a naked body; a woman, judging by the long hair and lacerated breasts. He was sobbing. The lower half of his face was coated with blood. He was topless. Hairy shoulders and a pot belly. Boxer shorts. His knees, forearms, and hands were bloody.

Frank recognised the man from the photo in the kitchen.

David Pulver clasped his hands together. As he sobbed he muttered under his breath. Frank realised the man was praying.

The man looked up at Frank. His face was a mask of torture and misery. And hunger.

"I'm sorry," the man said. The inside of his mouth was red. His tongue seemed too long. Dirty teeth. "I couldn't help myself. I tried to stop, but I couldn't stop. I couldn't stop."

Frank tried to speak.

The man's eyes were small and pathetic and remorseful. The corners of his mouth jerked. He licked his lips.

Pulver said, "Mark got away. My son. But I killed Mary and the girls. I got them. They didn't want to die. They begged me. But I couldn't help myself. I

180

had to. I didn't have a choice. Do you understand? Do you see? I didn't have a choice."

Pulver lowered his face to the body beneath him. He kissed his wife's mouth slowly. He had peeled much of the skin from her face. Pulver turned his body slightly, and Frank saw the throbbing red pustules on the man's bare back. A pale fluid was seeping from them. Pulver spoke to the woman he had butchered.

"I'm sorry," he repeated until his voice faded into silence.

Frank raised the crowbar. Pulver looked at him.

"Please kill me," Pulver said. "Please kill me before I change completely. There's nothing left for me. There's nothing left for any of us. The world is changing. *We* are changing."

"What?"

"Kill me."

Frank remained in the doorway. A tremor started in his hands and ran up his arms.

"Please kill me."

Frank stared at the stew of scarlet slush and abattoir runoff before him. He felt his stomach muscles tighten, a wave of nausea, but there was nothing to bring up. He couldn't remember the last time he had eaten.

"Kill me," Pulver said. "I'm begging you."

The pustules on the man's back throbbed violently. Something moved under his skin. Pulver's back rippled. He moaned softly and a thin sliver of drool slipped from his wet mouth.

Frank turned back to Florence. "Stay in the kitchen. Don't come in here." He closed the door, stepped towards the man, the sodden carpet squelching under his shoes. Hot itchy air pressed at his skin.

Frank stood over the man.

"Please kill me." Pulver looked up at him.

Frank hesitated.

"Please kill me."

Frank opened his mouth. No words. He felt his mind weaken, as if the man's insanity was infectious. He felt his face drain white.

"Please kill me," said Pulver. "Or I will kill you, then the little girl you've left in the kitchen. I will go out to her and do such terrible things to her. I will rip her open and eat the best parts of her; every soft bit of her."

The pustules throbbed and swelled. The man's eyes went wide. A little smile. He opened his mouth.

Frank raised the crowbar and, before the man could thank him, brought down the wrench with all the power he could summon into his shaking hands, and kept hitting Pulver until the strength had drained from him.

* * *

They walked the road. Man and girl. The world was quiet.

Frank had thrown away the crowbar after dispatching David Pulver. He could not face wiping it clean. Skull fragments and blood had stuck to the business-end of the wrench like melted confectionary.

He remembered Pulver's mad face. Those eyes like dark stains. Taking the man's life was easier than he thought it'd be, and he felt ashamed and guilty. He had killed twice, now. But he was not a killer.

But he would kill for Florence.

He'd found an axe out the back of the Pulver house, forgotten in a corner amongst other tools and discarded things. It was still sharp. A tinge of rust. It could still cut and chop.

He carried a rucksack containing some tins of food, a few cans of fizzy drink, and two packets of ready salted crisps. A blanket for Florence, a torch and a pair of binoculars. He'd emptied the cupboards in the house while Florence sat at the kitchen table, forbidden to enter the living room. He had no qualms about looting a family's home. Not now, anyway. Things had changed.

Frank's shadow shivered. He watched the mist, expecting faces to emerge from within it. He observed Florence in his peripheral vision; her head was down, the hood of her jacket over her head. Scuffling her feet on the tarmac. She hadn't spoken since they'd left the house.

"Are you okay?"

"Yeah." She didn't look at him.

"Anything you want to talk about?"

"That man was sick, wasn't he?"

"He was sick with something. Infected. He said he was changing."

"What does 'infected' mean?"

"It means to be sick."

"Like the flu?"

"Yes."

"But it's something worse than the flu?"

"Looks that way."

"Will we get sick? Infected?"

He had considered this already, and managed to convince himself they were safe from infection, or whatever it was.

What if it was airborne?

"We'll be fine," he said, hoping she didn't notice the uneven tone of his voice.

She looked at him for the first time in a while. "But everyone else is dying or becoming monsters, aren't they?"

Frank thought of Catherine waiting for him back home. How many people were dead or turning into monsters?

"I don't know."

There was gunfire in the distance.

* * *

They moved on towards Horsham. Frank led the way. Florence stayed by his side, but she was monosyllabic. Frank knew enough about loss and mourning to understand her reaction.

Thunder in the sky. Clouds, grey upon grey. The suggestion of something else in the sky, moving in silence. They both sensed it. Frank found himself staring at the sky a few times in response to some perceived threat.

They sheltered under an oak tree during a rain shower and ate lunch as they watched the downpour. Frank realised he should be at work. He wondered if he would ever return to work. He should be home, he thought. He should be with Catherine. She must be terrified right now. Did she know what was happening? Did she think he was dead?

He wanted a drink of something strong. He wished he'd taken that bottle of vodka from the Pulver house.

The rain stopped. No sun, just grey and ashen misery colouring the countryside. At least the air felt clearer, cleaner. They walked on. They found what was left of a body by the side of the road, sprawled on the grass verge. A man, judging by the size of the remains. He had been stripped and flayed. Not much left of him except tatters of meat and bone. His eyes had been taken. A ravaged corpse.

Florence said nothing. Maybe she was used to such sights.

"Let's go," Frank told her when she lingered by the body.

"Okay," she said, looking back at the remains as she followed him.

Later they heard a deep growling coming towards them. Frank halted, took hold of Florence's hand. She looked to him. Frank scanned the road ahead.

"What is it?" asked Florence.

Scuffled footfalls on tarmac and gravel, beyond the bend in the road.

Frank put his finger to his lips, shook his head. He pulled her through a gap in the hedgerow and into a field, where they crouched behind the thicket. They stayed low. The grass was wet. Frank peered through the small partings in the hedgerow, towards the road.

They waited. Florence's breathing kept pace with his heartbeat.

The scuffling footfalls became louder.

A woman shambled into view. What had once been a woman.

She was deformed. She growled at the air, rabid, hunched over and limping. Ripped jeans showing glimpses of mottled flesh on her thighs. Shoes crusted with dirt and something tinged red. Spikes of black bone had torn through her blouse, colonising her shoulders and back.

Florence stiffened beside him. The woman sniffed the air. She wheezed from her ruined mouth; the sound of air being pushed from her lungs was like metal scraping on metal. The spikes on her upper body seemed to quiver, as if they were linked to her respiratory system by tendrils of nerve.

The woman's mouth opened. Turned to the hedgerow where they hid, but she didn't see them. She was blind; her eyes were red lesions, glistening like welts. She snarled, exposing crooked, sharp teeth. The inside of her mouth was coated with black, like tooth-rot left to spread and thrive.

She knows we're here, Frank thought. He took hold of the axe. Dread in his stomach and a flutter of panic in his chest. His heartbeat surged. His mouth was dry.

The woman seemed to look directly at him. Her body went rigid, like a hunting dog sighting prey.

Frank didn't move.

A jet flew over, the roar of its engines distracting the woman, and she raised her unholy face to the sky. The jet moved away. The woman continued down the road and disappeared from sight.

Frank exhaled. Florence did the same. They looked at each other. Frank smiled. She did not return it. They waited to make sure the woman had gone before they emerged back onto the road.

Frank wondered if he should go after the woman and put her out of her misery. But he could not stomach taking another life so soon after smashing in David Pulver's skull.

The light was fading.

CHAPTER TWENTY-EIGHT

"We have to leave," said Joel. "This place is going to implode."

"We're a long way from home," said Magnus. "We wouldn't last five minutes out on the streets. Do you want to die out there?"

Ralph looked at them in turn. "We might die in here." He glanced around the classroom. People were murmuring and chattering. Crying children. Two men were arguing. Raised voices and panicked sobs.

Ralph could feel the tension and fear in the room. The thing in the sky terrified them. He felt sorry for those who were beginning to lose control. He had adjusted to the situation, and maybe a part of him was actually *enjoying* this. He wasn't sure how this had happened so easily. Maybe there was something wrong with him; a chemical imbalance or a defect in his brain.

How could this be enjoyed? He should be fucking *terrified* like the poor bastards in here with him. Like Joel and Magnus.

He was hungry. They had only been given a few cheese crackers and a cup of water each for lunch.

Supplies were running low, the police had said. But they would be re-supplied soon, they had been promised.

Ralph knew a lie when he heard one.

A loud boom from a few streets away shook the building. Someone screamed. Ralph looked at the ceiling. The light fixtures rattled. The windows trembled.

Gunshots nearby. Getting closer. Another muffled thump not too far away.

"The infected are nearly here!" a woman said.

The room went silent. More gunfire. Ralph could hear the police moving around outside.

"It's falling apart," Joel said. "We have to leave."

"And go where?" said Ralph. "We could make a stand here."

"Make a stand?" Magnus said. "This isn't Rorke's Drift, you idiot."

Ralph shrugged. "The coppers won't let us leave."

"They might not have a choice very soon," said Joel. "They'll have other things to worry about."

"Joel's right," said Magnus.

Ralph sighed. "Fair enough. Let's go outside and see what's happening."

Magnus and Joel nodded.

Another burst of gunfire made Joel jump. Mothers comforted their children. Ralph turned to see Susan

Blake sat alone, holding her dog to her chest. Ralph's eyes met hers. She gave him a little smile, but her face was drawn and pale, and the smile didn't last.

Ralph wanted to help her, but he had to look after Joel and Magnus first.

He turned back to his friends.

"On your feet, bitches. Let's go."

Refugees filled the car park at the front of the school. The police did their best to calm them, but panic and fear were more persuasive than words.

Ralph, Magnus and Joel lurked at the back of the crowd. There was no path to the front, but Ralph could see through gaps in the scrum of bodies to the road beyond the gates.

Fires lit the sky within the town. The crackle of gunfire. A baby was wailing.

A military vehicle pulled up outside; a soldier jumped out. Automatic rifle and desert fatigues. Boots pounding over tarmac. He moved quickly. He spoke to one of the police officers. The officer's face sagged as he listened.

"That doesn't look good," Ralph said.

The soldier ran back to the jeep and got in then the jeep took off down the road. The police officer relayed whatever he'd been told to his sergeant. The sergeant listened, nodded and hefted his weapon. He went to the crowd and said something.

The crowd didn't listen.

The sergeant raised his gun and fired into the air.

The crowd quietened. A few scared voices, but the police sergeant now had their attention.

"Please listen!" The sergeant was a big man, gut straining against his shirt. Sand-coloured hair and ruddy cheeks. "I've just been informed that the infected have breached the Safe Zone. Please remain calm. The army will be along very soon to evacuate you all. Please stay calm. You are all safe here. We will protect you until the army arrives."

"We need to leave now!" said a woman at the front of the crowd.

"I'm sorry, but you can't leave on your own. We cannot guarantee your protection out there."

"Can you guarantee our protection here?" asked a man.

"Yes," the sergeant said, but Ralph saw the lie in his face. "You must remain here until the transports arrive."

"Fuck off!" said another man. This sentiment was echoed by a few others.

The other police officers looked tense and scared. Only the sergeant appeared to retain any sense of composure.

"Please remain calm," the sergeant said. "There is no need to panic."

Screams came from up the street from the direction the army jeep had come.

The crowd surged towards the car park fence, almost overwhelming the police. Ralph kept Joel and Magnus close to him. He formed his hands into fists.

The refugees screamed and cried. The clamour of stinking bodies; dried sweat, dirt and fear. Shit and panic. Ralph was jostled by the people around him. Sharp elbows dug into his flanks. A woman with too much neck fat looked at him with saucer-eyes.

"Oh shit," Joel was repeating. "Oh shit, oh shit."

The infected were coming.

CHAPTER TWENTY-NINE

Frank and Florence arrived at the outskirts of Horsham just before five. The world was turning dark. Dead street lamps loomed over them.

Jets roared low and unseen overhead. A moment of silence. A flash of light. Then a great boom as something detonated. The closest Frank had ever been to a war zone was watching news reports from Afghanistan. This was surreal. This wasn't supposed to happen here. Not in Britain. Not in England.

There were so many bodies.

Most of them had bullet wounds. Executed in the street. Faces frozen into snarls and stretched grimaces. Some of the corpses were bent into unnatural angles; bones protruded from bodies and gleamed wetly. There were children here. Some of the bodies were burnt. Charred and twisted remains of people. Grinning faces. The stink of meat left too long on a grill.

A car alarm was blaring from deep within the town.

Florence said nothing as they picked their way through the dead.

"Don't be scared," Frank told her. "We'll find some help."

A fire burned on the next street. The air tasted acrid, scraping the flesh of his throat. Florence kept her hood up and covered her mouth and nose with one hand.

Frank's eyes flicked to both sides of the street. No one came out of the houses. Front doors hung open. There was fire damage to some of the houses. Scorched walls and blackened lawns. Frank swallowed, felt the burning heat of being watched from the windows, but when he turned there was no one there. He raised the axe. He stepped on broken glass. There were suitcases and bags on the road and the pavements. Scattered belongings. Abandoned cars. Frank contemplated stealing one of the cars to travel into town, but he was worried that they would be held up by roadblocks and wrecked vehicles. And bodies, of course. Also, driving around was a good way to get noticed by the things he didn't want noticing them.

"Where's everyone gone?" said Florence. "The ones who aren't dead."

"Maybe they've been evacuated."

Turning onto the next street they found a body slumped across a car bonnet, rendered genderless by the ferocity of its death. The body had been shredded and most of it had been scattered on the road.

A burst of gunfire, and they both ducked instinctively. Frank pulled Florence closer to his side and scanned the road ahead. Smoke drifting through the air gave the impression of figures moving within a grey-white veil.

They passed a dead man in a Rolls Royce, slumped over the steering wheel. Frank didn't look at him in case he began to move.

Ahead of them was a fire engine left abandoned across the road. Its crew were nowhere to be seen. Long gone. Florence stared at the vehicle as they passed it.

Frank heard weird animal sounds, shrieks and howls, from the nearby streets.

The town was being overrun.

* * *

Moving further into Horsham. More bodies. Past the point of trying to protect Florence from the sight of them.

The concussion of thunder in the sky, like mountains colliding.

Frank had expected safety and sanctuary here. He kept trying to call Catherine. His heart palpitated when he thought of her. He squeezed the phone until his hand hurt.

They couldn't stay on the streets much longer.

Florence pulled on his jacket sleeve. Frank looked down at her. She pointed up the street. A car had been abandoned across the road. Swathes of darkness and grey light beyond.

"What is it?" he said.

She kept pointing. Large, shining eyes in her face.

Frank pocketed his phone, resisting the urge to throw it away. He flexed his hands on the axe. He approached the car. Florence followed him.

He could hear wet sucking sounds. A cold hand fingered his spine. He peered at the road behind the car.

He went to say something but the words stuck in his throat.

There were bodies laid out on the road. Broken remains of people. A girl was crouched over one of the bodies. Her face was attached to its face. The girl was making the sucking sounds. There was just enough light to make out the torn pyjamas she was wearing.

Florence saw the girl and let out a whimper. The girl couldn't have been much older than her.

The girl raised her head, detaching from the dead body. Frank pulled Florence behind the car and put his free hand over her mouth. He caught a glance over the car's bonnet. The girl looked around, her gleaming feral eyes scanning the road. Her face was covered with blood. A carrion eater scavenging on the dead. She had been a little girl with a family once; a mum and a dad and dreams of boy bands.

The girl returned to her meal. Frank and Florence went around her, treading silently. Frank watched the girl all the way until they were clear.

Further on they crept around a group of people feeding on a pile of corpses. Some of the dead were wearing army fatigues. The scavengers were too busy stripping meat from bones to notice them.

Every dark corner and shadow was a threat. Small fires burned. Shop windows had been smashed. All he could smell was blood and smoke. The deeper they went into the ruined town the more they saw deformed and mutated people roaming the streets in baying packs, shrieking and screaming and dragging flayed bodies behind them. Frank noticed others lurking in shadowed alleyways and gardens, gibbering and wailing. Some of them simply stood staring at the ground or at the sky. A lot of them stared at the sky.

Frank saw people chased down and ripped apart. Some of them begged until the very end, until their vocal chords were removed by spindly fingers and hooked claws.

Some of the mutated ones hunted alone, stalking the streets like predatory insects. Frank and Florence hid behind cars and walls. They were prey. Death would not come quick if they were caught. The monsters sensed Frank and Florence, sucked in the smell of their fear and sweat. Monsters everywhere, creeping out of their holes.

He found the dark doorway of an empty book shop and pulled Florence down with him.

Slick-skinned figures skittered upon the pavements, parts of their bodies clicking and clacking and scraping together like lengths of dry bone.

Screams and shrieks and plaintive cries of hunger.

Gunfire nearby. Florence was trembling and crying. A man was shouting. Frank looked up, expecting some grinning monster to fall upon them.

"It'll be okay," Frank whispered to Florence. "It'll be okay." He decided he would kill her with the axe and then take down as many of them as he could before he succumbed. He wouldn't let the creatures take her.

Dark shapes approached them.

Frank raised the axe.

Florence whimpered.

A man's voice.

Four soldiers, faces hidden by gas masks, found them huddled in the doorway.

"Are you infected?" one of the soldiers asked them.

Frank stared at them, his mouth open.

He shook his head.

CHAPTER THIRTY

Corporal Guppy was a short and stocky man. Even behind the muffling effect of his gas mask, his voice was deep and commanding. The other soldiers – Privates Sibbick, Gawen and Pike – sounded as though they were barely out of their teens, but they killed infected people with an absent, instinctive skill.

The infected, Frank thought. *That's what they're called. Infected.*

"Keep moving," Guppy said. He and Private Gawen jogged either side of Frank and Florence. Private Sibbick was on point, his SA80 trained on the road ahead. Private Pike guarded the rear.

Sibbick raised his hand. They stopped behind him, hidden behind the corner of a house. Frank was breathing hard.

"Is she okay?" asked Guppy, nodding at Florence.

"Yeah. But she's seen a lot," said Frank. "*Too* much."

"Are you her father?"

Frank hesitated. "Yes." He swallowed, looked away. He felt Guppy's eyes on his face.

"What do you see, Sibbick?" Guppy asked.

"A single infected ahead. He's just stood there."

"Maybe he's waiting for a bus," said Gawen.

"Can we get past him?" Guppy said.

"Should be able to," said Sibbick. "He's facing the other direction."

"Okay, let's move. Keep an eye on the bastard. If he clocks us, take his head off."

They crept past the man and stopped at the next corner. The soldiers scanned the street, searching for targets.

"Where are we heading?" said Frank. "What's happening?"

"The world's ending, that's what happening," said Gawen.

"Button it, Private," said Guppy.

"Sorry, Corp." Gawen said. He looked at Florence. "Sorry, little lady."

Guppy cleared his throat. "The town's been overrun. We lost a lot of lads back there, including our CO."

"We're more fucked than a choirboy at a priests' piss up," muttered Pike. His eyes were shockingly white.

"We're heading to the school," said Guppy. "Before we were cut off from our unit, the order came through to evacuate the town. The last transports will be leaving the school soon. We haven't got much time. The town's due to be firebombed within the hour. We've lost control."

The air was sucked from Frank's lungs. "Firebomb the town. Jesus."

"We could do with Jesus right now," said Gawen.

"I only believe in my SA80," Pike said.

"Fucking atheists," said Gawen. "Heathens."

"Piss off."

"Cut the yap, lads. We'll have every hostile in the area upon us."

"Sorry, Corp," they said together.

Private Sibbick led them along the street. Gunfire and detonations from nearby. Far off screams that caused Frank's skin to burst into gooseflesh. He held Florence by the shoulders, guided her in front of him.

"What caused this?" said Frank. "What has happened?"

Guppy grunted. "Where have you been for the last few days?"

"On a stag weekend."

"Lucky bastard," said Pike.

"It's a virus," said Guppy. "As far as we know."

"How far has it spread?"

"Everywhere."

"The whole country?"

"Maybe the whole world. We're not sure."

Something cold uncoiled in Frank's stomach.

"Have you heard about any other areas of the country?"

"We haven't heard much. It's all a mess."

"A big fucking mess," Gawen said.

Frank could only shake his head. "But where has this virus come from?"

Ahead of them, Sibbick halted. The others did the same.

Guppy looked at him. "Nobody knows. And if they do, they're not telling the likes of us."

"No one tells the grunts anything," said Gawen. "Wankers."

"Stop moaning, Gawen," said Pike. "Always fucking moaning."

"Go fuck your mother," Gawen replied.

"I'd rather fuck yours."

Private Sibbick turned, addressed Guppy. "Corp, the school is on the next street."

"Good," said Guppy. "Everyone stay on their toes. Keep sharp. Let's go, lads."

They moved.

"Don't say that about my mother again, Pike," said Gawen.

"Piss off."

"Shut up," said Guppy, "or I will personally kneecap both of you and leave you here."

"Sorry, Corp," said Pike.

"Sorry," Gawen muttered.

"That's better," Guppy said.

A shadow passed overhead.

Pike stopped. "What the…"

Something came out of the sky and plucked Gawen from the street. Frank caught only a glimpse of it. Large and dark, made of sinew and bone, and stinking of wet rot. He saw its burning white eyes as it grabbed Gawen and made off with him.

Gawen screamed from above them.

The leathery flap of wings; the glimpse of a black shape against the sky.

"Holy shit," said Pike. He was breathing hard through his mask. "It took Gawen. It took him. What the fuck was that?"

Sibbick fired off a short burst into the sky.

Florence sobbed.

Then there was silence. Guppy glanced overhead.

"Keep moving. Let's go."

CHAPTER THIRTY-ONE

The infected filled the street, flocking towards the school. Twisted, wretched faces; twitching and sagging bodies. They surged and staggered with the fervour of zealots, a mindless rhythm in their appalling jerking movements.

The refugees retreated from the fence.

Joel made a small, child-like sound. His face was slack and boneless.

"We're fucked," said Magnus. He looked around at the other terrified faces, then to Ralph.

Ralph said nothing.

People were crying and screaming. The police officers aimed their weapons towards the swarm of infected bodies.

The infected reached the fence, trying to pull it down with clawed hands and even their mouths. Some of them attempted to climb the fence with black spindly limbs. More infected clawed at the gate, thrashing and roaring through wide mouths.

The police opened fire.

Bodies were ripped open and thrown back into the swarm; others collapsed where they were standing. But those behind the fallen kept coming.

The refugees headed towards the school. Ralph, Magnus and Joel were herded with the crowd. Ralph turned back to see the battle behind them.

The infected tore open the gate and skittered over its wreckage. The fence came down with it. They poured into the car park. They closed down the yards between them and the line of police officers, and the line fell as it was breached. Some of the officers turned to run, but were caught and dragged back into grasping hands and jagged sucking mouths.

Some of the infected had been soldiers.

The police sergeant fired his handgun into the thrusting mass of infected. He took down a few staggering, grasping bodies. His gun clicked empty. A group of infected brought him down and pinned him. One of them, a young woman no older than twenty with bleached-blonde hair, forced her hand into his mouth and down his throat. The sergeant bit into her arm even as he choked. An infected man buried his face in the sergeant's groin, and his mouth came away red and dripping. The woman pulled something pink and slippery from the sergeant's mouth, threw it away and then locked her mouth to his raw lips. The sergeant's eyes bulged and he tried to scream. He vanished amidst a throng of squirming bodies.

And then there were no more police.

The infected came for the refugees.

They slashed and clawed and used their teeth. They tore at the stragglers at the back of the refugee crowd. They ripped at soft flesh. There were wet tearing sounds and screams of agony and terror. The last sounds of beating hearts. A woman's scream became a liquid gurgle as her throat was removed by an Asian man with a nest of pale tongues emerging from his dripping, gasping mouth.

The infected were jackals amongst lambs, tearing through the crowd, snarling and hissing. The air stank of hot blood and slaughter. Screaming faces. Bloated faces deformed to ruin. Rows of teeth too large for their mouths.

Ralph pushed against the bodies massing around him, crushing him. He grabbed hold of Magnus and Joel. They were buffeted and slammed by flailing arms. Magnus was hit in the face; he cried out, clutching his nose.

There was no way out of the car park except into the school; otherwise they would have to go through the infected to escape onto the street. Some desperate men and women took this option and were caught before they could reach the fallen fence. They weren't seen again.

A man fell against Ralph, and tried to shoulder him out of the way, but Ralph pushed him back. The man was grabbed by a fat infected woman and dragged to the ground. She smothered him like a blubbery sea creature. Ralph turned away, elbowed his way through the crowd with Magnus and Joel behind him. He glanced back to see infected men and women clawing through the crowd of refugees, getting closer. People were dragged away and battened upon.

Ralph pushed his way to the front of the crowd, trying to get inside the school. There was only one door. The people inside the school were trying to shut the door on those outside. A few men were attempting to keep the door open, wrench it from the hands of those inside. Punches and elbows were thrown. A man spat out his teeth.

Ralph helped keep the door open. A man from the other side of the doorway tried to scratch out his eyes. Ralph batted away the man's hand and punched him in the face.

The infected tore their way through the crowd. The panicking refugees were easy prey. Men and women were turned inside out and flayed; bones were separated from meat.

CHAPTER THIRTY-TWO

The school fell to the infected. Frank, Florence and the soldiers had watched it from the street. Frank had seen the refugees overwhelmed and consumed. A slaughter. The screams lasted for a while after the school had been overrun.

Now they moved along the street. The infected were everywhere.

"What the fuck took Gawen?" Pike said, flicking his eyes towards the sky. His voice was reedy, uneven. Scared. "What the hell was that thing?"

"He's gone," said Guppy. "Nothing we can do for him now. Focus on your job."

"Is it still after us?" Pike's movements were quick and erratic. He kept muttering under his breath.

"There're many things after us tonight, Private."

"Very true," said Frank.

"Contact!" Sibbick sighted a roaming infected coming towards them. He fired three rounds.

The infected man flopped to the pavement like a boned fish.

"Keep moving," said Guppy. "We need to get out of Horsham before the bombs hit. Other units will try to regroup outside the town."

"Sounds easy," said Pike. He gunned down a naked woman running at him.

They moved past dead soldiers. This is where the battle for Horsham had taken place. Frank sensed the soldiers stiffen. There were abandoned checkpoints to the safe zone. Broken barricades and toppled sawhorses. Spent shell casings on the road. An armoured vehicle was burning, throwing light upon the faces of the dead at their feet.

Frank slipped in a mush of blood and slick remains. He pulled Florence with him. He would not let her fall behind.

Burning cars lined the street, painting the houses with the colour of flame. Shapes flitted through the smoke. The soldiers slowed, rifles aimed into the grey haze.

"Steady, lads," Guppy muttered. "Steady as you go."

An infected man with both arms deformed into tendrils emerged from the smoke. Guppy put him down; two rounds to the chest and one to the head.

"Did you see his fucking arms?" said Pike. "Mutants. Fucking maniacs."

More infected came out of the smoke. Rasping, snapping mouths and grabbing fingers.

"Check your targets, lads," Guppy said.

Sibbick and Pike sighted the approaching infected. Fired. Short bursts. The infected went down.

Frank kept hold of Florence.

"Contact!" Pike shouted as a little girl sprinted across the street. He fired. The bullets took her in the chest and throat, and she fell. Pike walked to the girl and stood over her, shaking his head.

"Fuck's sake," said Sibbick. "I hate it when the kids get it."

"Oh shit," said Pike. "Oh shit…"

"Focus, Private," said Guppy. "Come on. She's dead."

"I don't know if she was infected. I'm not sure. I don't know. Oh fuck, I killed a normal girl. Just a little girl. A little girl…"

"Get a hold of yourself, Private," said Guppy. "Breathe."

Pike shook his head. "No, Corp. I don't think she was infected. She wasn't infected. She was normal."

Frank looked down at the dead girl. She was no older than ten years old. The bullets had opened her throat. Her chest was wet and red. No expression on her face. He couldn't tell if she was infected.

217

"Calm down, Pike," said Guppy. "Calm down, son. It's okay."

"I killed a little girl. It's all fucked. Everything's fucked." Pike started to cry under his mask.

"It's okay, mate," said Sibbick. "You didn't do anything wrong."

"Let's move," said Guppy. "We're not safe here."

"That's the point, though, isn't it?" said Pike. "Nowhere is safe."

"This isn't the time. Not now."

Pike ripped off his gas mask, and his face was wet with tears. His mouth trembled. He was just a boy, really. Blonde hair and acne.

"Put your mask back on, Pike," said Guppy. "Don't be silly, lad."

"We're all fucked," Pike said. "Nearly all of my mates are dead. We're all gonna fucking die sooner or later. Like Gawen. Like everyone else. Like the lieutenant and Sergeant Baker. Like Matheson and Williams and Boyle. We're food for the monsters. Either that or we'll become monsters. There's no point anymore. We're fucked."

Guppy lunged for the young soldier, but he was too late.

Pike stuck the rifle barrel in his mouth and pulled the trigger. The back of his head exploded. He dropped. Guppy shouted. Sibbick turned away.

Pike's legs kicked and twitched, then went still.

Guppy stood over Pike, his shoulders slumped. He looked smaller than before. He crouched and took Pike's spare ammo clips. He put his hand on the young soldier's chest. Guppy straightened Pike's arms alongside his body and whispered to him.

Sibbick came over and said goodbye to Pike.

Guppy stared at the dead soldier.

"We have to keep moving, Corp," said Sibbick.

Guppy looked at Frank. "Let's go."

Frank guided Florence away from Pike's body and the mulch of brain and skull fragments on the road. She looked back at him. Her face was the colour of moonlight. She was trembling and gaunt.

Sibbick took point. Guppy walked behind Frank and Florence.

They left Pike where he had fallen.

* * *

Frank heard far off screams. He ignored them.

"Nearly there," said Guppy. "Anything, Sibbick?"

"Nothing, Corp. Just the street."

"Good."

Frank moved his greasy fingers around the axe handle. His limbs shook with adrenaline and dread. Screams and shrieks echoed around the streets. He looked at Florence and smiled. She looked away. There were more bodies here. One of them was moving, pulling itself along the ground towards them. An old woman with her legs severed at the knees. Her abdomen was bloated and puffy. She hissed at Frank. Her eyes were the colour of disease.

Frank kept walking.

"Keep moving, Frank," said Guppy. "No point dwelling."

"It's difficult."

"I know."

"What is this virus?"

"Wrath of God, maybe."

"You religious?"

"Not exactly."

"What does that mean?"

"I believe He's strictly Old Testament. I've seen too much to believe in a loving God."

"Fair enough."

They walked on.

Corpses had been piled against a shop doorway. Frank tried not to look but couldn't help glancing at their faces. Cloudy eyes and mouths hanging open.

"Who piled them up?" asked Frank.

"We did," said Guppy. "They were infected. We were trying to keep the roads clear."

"I'm getting used to seeing dead bodies."

"I have been for years. The first corpse I saw was a little boy in Iraq in the second Gulf War. He was shot accidentally by one of the lads in my squad. A high calibre round blew out his spine. He didn't die straight away, which seems to be the way of things when children are concerned. Took me a while to get over it, but I did eventually, which in itself is quite disturbing. I've seen so many dead."

Guppy glanced at Florence, probably concerned that he'd said too much to upset her, but she was staring straight ahead, holding Frank's hand. She said nothing.

"I'm sorry about Pike," said Frank.

"He was an idiot," said Guppy. "But he was a good lad. He had a brother with Down's Syndrome; talked about him all the time. He'd heard yesterday that the rescue centre his brother was at had gone silent."

Frank opened his mouth to speak but he sensed something move above them. He looked up and it was gone.

"You saw that," said Guppy. He raised his rifle and called to Sibbick.

They halted.

Frank scanned the buildings around them. The sky was dark.

"The creature that took Gawen," said Guppy.

Movement above them. A flutter of flapping skin. The breeze touched the back of Frank's neck with cold fingers.

He sniffed the air. The stink of wet rot.

"Contact!" Sibbick said and fired overhead, tracking it with his rifle.

Frank twisted his head around the street. Movement on a roof across the street caught his eye. Something was perched by the chimney, watching them. Glowing white eyes. Its body was coloured like alabaster. Its movements were jerky and quick, like a bird. A low mewling sound came from its hidden mouth.

"I see it," said Frank, his voice a whisper.

Guppy aimed at the shape on the roof. Before he could fire, the thing bobbed its head, twisted its sinewy body, and melted into the darkness.

"It followed us," said Sibbick.

"Doesn't matter," said Guppy. "Keep moving. We're too vulnerable stood in the middle of the street. We need to get out of here before we get our nuts roasted by the RAF."

They moved together, sticking to the centre of the road.

A scrabbling on one of the roofs. Frank saw the creature's eyes again. A flash of them, then they were gone.

"Keep moving," Guppy said.

Then the creature came at them from above. It shrieked. A gust of air from veined wings. Frank saw its face, once the face of a man. Now it was a slick drooping mask. A saw-toothed rictus.

Claws sliced the air above Frank's head.

Guppy and Sibbick fired at the creature.

"Where is it?" said Sibbick, looking down the barrel of his rifle, sweeping the rooftops.

"There!" said Guppy.

The creature was clinging to a wall. Its skin was almost translucent. It scrambled upwards out of sight. The creature could be heard moving over the roofs. A tile fell from a rooftop and smashed on the pavement.

"Wait a minute," said Guppy. "I think it's distracting us…"

Frank looked at him. "What do you mean?"

There were sounds behind them. The rush of a breeze and a keening cry. Another creature leapt from the other side of the street. A single flap of its wings and it was upon them.

The creature was streamlined and hairless. Its hands opened into filthy black claws.

It reached for Florence.

Sibbick flung himself between the creature and the girl. He fired his rifle. Florence screamed.

There was a maddening squeal. A shriek of pain. A ripping sound. A wet sound.

Guppy fell back and emptied the rest of his magazine.

Frank grabbed Florence and they rolled away. When he looked back the creature was gone.

Sibbick was lying on the road. His gas mask was gone, and so was most of his face.

He screamed through a ruined mouth.

CHAPTER THIRTY-THREE

The creature's claws had been busy. Private Sibbick's face, chest and stomach were missing bits. Deep lacerations. Most of the skin had been ripped away from his jaws and cheek bones. His eyes and teeth were starkly white against the red pulp of his face.

"It's okay, lad," Guppy said, on his knees beside the soldier's trembling body. "It's okay."

Guppy tried to hold him together, but the best bits of Sibbick were falling through his hands. Sibbick's screams faded into a series of broken sobs.

The creature that attacked him was lying sprawled by the pavement, riddled with bullet wounds. It had once been a man, naked and pale with lesions and tufts of wiry hair on its glistening skin. Large membranous wings curled around its limp body. Its face was a horror of teeth and soft meat.

The other creature had retreated beyond the rooftops.

Guppy pulled his mask above his face. He looked different than Frank had imagined. A soft, doughy face. A balding scalp. His hands were bloody.

"What's it done to my face, Corp?" Sibbick asked.

"You'll be fine. We'll sort you out."

"I can feel it inside me."

"You're imagining it, Private."

"It's in my blood. The filth from its claws."

Guppy was dull-eyed. "No, we'll get you some help."

"You should step away, Corp." Sibbick's voice was slurred and slow.

The two men looked at each other. Guppy nodded, stood up and wiped his hands on his thighs.

"You know what you have to do," said Sibbick. "We've discussed this. I'd rather be dead."

Guppy reloaded his rifle.

Sibbick began to shake violently. His fingers raked at the road. A damp nonsense sound came from the flapping hole of his mouth and his eyes rolled into waxen whites.

Sibbick's skin moved under his fatigues.

Guppy stepped back. Frank guided Florence to the other side of the road. He kept checking the rooftops.

Sibbick thrashed against the tarmac, tearing the skin from his hands. Now he was screaming, and it sounded like the screams Frank heard echoing amongst the streets of Wishford and Horsham.

Florence covered her ears.

Guppy turned his rifle towards the fallen soldier.

There was a single shot, and Sibbick wasn't screaming anymore. His crumpled body looked pathetic on the road.

Guppy was an abject figure, cradling his rifle, staring at Sibbick. He looked old. His face sagged.

"They killed all of my lads," Guppy said. "They're all gone."

More gunfire from other parts of the town.

Guppy looked at Frank. He said nothing. He relieved Sibbick of his ammunition. Guppy pulled down his mask, stepped around Sibbick's corpse and started down the street.

Frank and Florence followed him.

CHAPTER THIRTY-FOUR

They passed a pub with its doors hanging open. The coppery taint of blood drifted from the darkness inside. Frank thought he could see dark shapes huddled together, busy doing something, busy doing lots of things.

They hurried past.

"This is the road out of town," said Guppy. He halted, looked down the street.

"What's wrong?"

"Hostiles. Quite a few. Won't be able to go through them on foot."

Frank looked down the road. Scattered figures loitered and shifted in the moonlight, emitting low growls and mutterings. Some of them were staring at the sky.

"Don't they ever sleep?" asked Frank.

"Haven't thought to ask them yet."

"Could we use a side street to go around them?"

"It'll take too long. Haven't got time."

"What, then?"

Guppy's gaze settled on a Ford Fiesta at the side of the street. He motioned for Frank and Florence to follow him. A man was dead in the driver's seat. Guppy checked the man over then dumped him on the road.

Keys in the ignition.

"We're driving out of here. Won't make it out otherwise. I think the rest of the road is clear of obstructions."

"Apart from the infected," said Frank.

Guppy nodded.

"Will the car start?"

"Watch the road while I give her a try."

Frank stood guard. He kept Florence close. Guppy twisted the keys; the engine spluttered and gurgled like something slowly rising from the dead just so it could die again.

Frank checked to see that the infected down the road hadn't heard the sound of the engine. Luckily, they hadn't, yet.

Florence looked up at Frank. Those small, dark eyes told him nothing. Her mouth didn't move. He nodded at her, offered a strained smile.

After four attempts, the engine started. Guppy tapped the gas pedal, listened to the engine's irregular throb and thrum.

"Get in," he said. "I'm driving."

Frank sat next to Guppy in the front. Florence sat on the backseat.

"Keep your head down," Frank told her. "Don't look out the windows."

She nodded.

Guppy handed his rifle to Frank. "Look after that while I drive. Don't shoot yourself. The safety's on, but still be careful. Okay?"

Frank nodded. He held the rifle by his legs, the barrel pointing upwards. He swallowed to wet his throat. He noticed the tax disc on the windscreen was out of date by a week. A pair of miniature boxing gloves hung from the rear-view mirror. Old parking tickets around his feet. The smell of cigarette smoke had been absorbed into the car's interior.

Guppy reversed the car into the middle of the road.

"Put on your seatbelts," he said.

Frank did so, and then checked Florence did the same.

The Fiesta started down the road, approaching the infected. They saw the car and bolted towards it, their eyes gleaming in the headlights. One of the infected men had been a police officer; his mouth contorted and peeled away to reveal jagged teeth. Whatever had made them human was gone. Many of them were all eyes and teeth.

"Maniacs," said Guppy.

Frank braced himself, stared through the windscreen. He gritted his teeth, narrowed his eyes so that the sight of bodies being smashed aside wouldn't be so clear.

Impact. The judder of limbs against the car being thrown aside. Terrible faces glimpsed for a second before they vanished. Screams of the infected. Something was caught under the wheels and crushed wetly like rotten fruit. A fleshy pop of skin and fluid. A body rolled across the bonnet and hit the windscreen, cracking the glass and falling away. Blood on the glass and hands scraping at the windows. The car jolted, its suspension grinding and clanging; Frank banged his head against the side window and his vision blurred.

The screams faded behind them. Clear road. The car was juddering and shaking. Frank hoped the car would make it out of the town.

He looked back at Florence. She still had her head bowed.

"It's okay," he said. "We're safe."

CHAPTER THIRTY-FIVE

Horsham was burning. The sound of flames was like roaring wind. A firestorm.

Guppy parked the ailing car by the roadside, looking down at the town as the fire consumed it. There were muffled pops and booms. Buildings collapsed. Wood and brick structures were fuel for the fires. Detonations flashed and echoed around the low hills and fields. Red and yellow and orange rage. Smoke and flame. Incineration that was almost awe-inspiring in its devastation.

Billows of smoke reaching for the sky. The fire seemed alive; sentient and malign in its hunger.

Frank remembered taking Catherine and Emily to see fireworks on Bonfire Night at one of the fields outside Shepton Beauchamp.

He wondered how hot the fires down there burned. He thought he could smell roasting flesh. If he closed his eyes and listened hard enough, he could hear the screams of those trapped in the fire.

No one screamed for long.

Frank imagined what it would be like to be caught in the streets when the incendiary bombs hit. Burned alive. No one would survive. Not even the monsters roaming the streets.

He sucked on his inhaler twice.

"I can't believe what I'm seeing," he said. "Never thought I'd see an English town get firebombed. Especially by its own government." He stopped talking, simply because words meant nothing at that moment when faced with the swelling inferno before them; what had once been Horsham.

"I hope that there weren't many people in the town when the bombs dropped," said Frank. "Uninfected, of course."

"There would have been a few hundred, at least," said Guppy. "Maybe the infected had already killed them…or worse. The fire would have been a mercy for them."

Frank felt sick. He glanced back to see Florence asleep on the backseat.

"It won't be enough," Guppy said. "They'll have to purge every village, every town…every city, to beat them. To destroy them." He nodded at Horsham. "This is nothing. Next time it'll be nukes."

Frank couldn't take his eyes away from the fire. "Nukes?"

"I'm just a grunt, so I might be wrong. But I wouldn't be surprised. Not with the people we have

234

in charge. They'll panic. If they've already took the decision to firebomb a town, things are really bad."

"I can't believe it," said Frank.

Guppy spat. "Scorched earth." His eyes glowed yellow from the flames. "Funny thing is, when I was a lad, I used to love staring at fires. I could watch a bonfire for hours, mesmerised."

Movement in the fields below caught Frank's attention. Refugees were fleeing across the fields. The infected wouldn't be far behind.

"We can't stay here," said Guppy. "We have to find shelter for the night." He switched on the engine.

Before they moved off down the road, Frank saw flashes of light from both the north and east.

He tried not to think what they were.

CHAPTER THIRTY-SIX

Guppy stopped the car at an isolated cottage a few miles from Horsham. The windows were dark. No sign of habitation.

He woke up Florence. She was bleary-eyed and sleepy. When Frank told her they were going to stay the night in the house she looked at him and nodded.

Frank got out his torch and shone it around the empty driveway and the garden. An overgrown lawn spotted with molehills. A set of creaking, rusted swings. Garden gnomes were grinning at him. The cottage was small. White speckled walls and vines of ivy. Old wood aged by decades. Square windows with rotting frames. A flowerbed long devoid of any flowers. The cottage was a relic. Abandoned.

The front door was closed.

Guppy twisted the handle and the door opened a little. He pushed it with the barrel of his rifle. Frank stood alongside him, shining the torch inside. Florence followed them.

Darkness cleaved by torchlight. A stairway leading upstairs. The smell of dust, mildew and old clothes.

Silence, apart from a tap dripping in the kitchen at the back of the house.

"Shut the door," said Guppy. "I'll check the rooms."

* * *

Guppy searched each room. He told Frank and Florence not to enter the bedrooms. He didn't need to say why.

They bedded down in the living room. Florence took the sofa. Frank found some old blankets for her. She returned to sleep quickly. Guppy barricaded the doors with furniture. He would keep watch. Frank offered to take it in turns until first light, but Guppy refused.

Frank settled in an armchair. He missed Catherine intensely. He thought of Ralph, Magnus, and Joel, and wondered if they had been in Horsham when the bombs fell. The possibility needled his heart and turned his guts to jelly.

He fell asleep thinking about lost friends and great mountains of writhing fire.

When he woke, the silence stunned him. He wiped spittle from his mouth. His eyes were wet. He had been crying in his sleep.

Florence was a shape in the darkness, breathing slowly and steadily.

Guppy wasn't here; might have abandoned them, but Frank was too tired to care at the moment. He rose, stepped quietly over to Florence. He stood over her and her pale face became clear like a ghost in the dark. She looked so much like Emily that she could have *been* Emily. Could have been her twin.

Frank smiled at the sleeping girl. He brushed a strand of hair away from her forehead. Her blankets had fallen to the floor, so he replaced them on her body.

He stared at her for a long while.

Guppy was standing in the doorway watching him.

"Everything okay?" The soldier's voice was flat and tired.

"Florence was having a bad dream."

"You should get back to sleep."

"I'm fine. Are you alright, Corporal?"

"It's all falling apart, Frank. Pike was right."

"Do you have a family? Somewhere to go?"

"I'm leaving in the morning," Guppy said. "Heading to Lowestoft. I'm divorced, and the ex-missus got custody of our son. I've got to see if they're okay. I'm sorry to leave you and Florence, but I've got to see them. The army can't control this plague and I'm past caring about going AWOL. It doesn't matter anymore."

"Fair enough."

"You can keep the car. Use it to get to wherever you're going."

"I'm going home," said Frank. "Heading back to Somerset. I live in a small village. My wife's there…"

"Maybe things are going better back there."

"Maybe."

"The last I heard, the army had regrouped at Salisbury. My lieutenant told me that trains are being used to transport survivors to refugee camps along the coast. "

"Which coast?"

"I don't know; he didn't say. Go back to sleep, Frank. You'll need your energy in the coming days, especially if you want to take care of your daughter. Things will only get worse."

Guppy turned away and headed to the kitchen.

Frank returned to the armchair, sat down, and closed his eyes. The silence was enough to make him weep.

Things would definitely get worse.

CHAPTER THIRTY-SEVEN

Morning. The sky brightened to a desolate silence. Tendrils of cold crept over Frank's skin and seeped into his bones. He woke slowly while they ate breakfast. Chocolate biscuits, crisps, and fizzy drinks. Guppy chewed a strip of beef jerky and looked out the kitchen window. Frank was keen to get on the road. He ignored the family photos on the walls. He wanted to go home.

Guppy packed his kit and some food he had scavenged from the cupboards. Frank found a map in a desk drawer and slipped it into his pocket. Guppy gave him a small First Aid kit he'd taken from upstairs.

They walked outside. Frank checked his watch. Almost seven. Dew on the grass.

"I'm sorry to leave," said Guppy. "But I have to think of my family first."

"Good luck. It's a long walk to Lowestoft, Corporal."

"I don't doubt that." They shook hands. The soldier nodded at Florence.

"Best of luck," Guppy said to Frank. "Look after the girl. Stay safe. Get home."

"I hope you find your family."

Guppy set off across the fields. Frank watched him fade into the distance.

Frank carried their supplies to the car. He looked at the sky. The clouds looked fungal and puffy, as if they were about to burst open with spores. But there was sunlight and birdsong, and that was good enough for him.

He hoped they were good omens for the journey ahead.

* * *

The car started on the third attempt. It was dying. The roads were quiet and clear.

Frank drove slowly. The events of the last two days stuck in his mind like poison.

Florence was in the back with the bag of supplies. She looked out the windows. Occasionally she would glance at Frank in the rear-view mirror. No words were exchanged.

She looked just like Emily.

There were distant figures in the fields. They could have been mistaken for scarecrows until they moved.

Ragged shapes. Their heads turned slowly as they tracked the car.

He tried the radio. There was only white noise. He fiddled with the tuner, listening for a voice. Nothing. He switched it off.

"Where are we going?" Florence asked.

Frank glanced at her reflection. Her face was a blank. The morning's dull light painted her in grey.

"Somerset."

"What's there?"

"My home. My wife."

"Do you think it's safe there?"

"Yeah." He didn't say it as convincingly as he'd liked.

"You're not going to hurt me, are you?"

"No. Why would you say that? I'd never hurt you."

"My mum said that bad men are everywhere."

"I'm not a bad man. I'm not going to hurt you."

"I miss my mum and dad."

"I know. I'm sorry."

"Look at the people in the field."

Frank stopped the car.

There were infected in the field; three men and a woman feeding on a dead cow. They stripped the hide from the cow's body and snaffled the animal's warm insides from the opening in its stomach. They

243

crawled over the cow, miring themselves in its corpse and its many gaping, sucking wounds.

Florence shifted over to the window, placed a hand against the glass.

One of the men raised his face from the corpse and glared at them. Blood was coated around his mouth. He moved his neck in spasmodic jerking twists. His open mouth gleamed with wet red and threads of viscera.

Frank drove on.

* * *

Two miles later the car died. Frank steered it to the side of the road. They gathered their belongings. The air became colder. Frank pulled up his jacket's collar. He couldn't see any infected nearby. He held his axe in one hand. Its weight reassured him.

Crows cawed in the next field, picking at the ground, rooting for worms.

"We'll find another car," Frank said. "Don't worry."

Florence looked at the road. She brushed a strand of hair behind her ear. Her face was glum. Her eyes were dull. She wrapped her arms around herself.

"You okay?"

She nodded. Her mouth was a thin bloodless line. She looked so young. So frail. She was glass.

He would protect her.

She followed him.

Down the road they came to a pile-up. Two cars had crashed into each other. One of the cars was in a ditch; the other was on the road, shattered and torn. Glass, plastic and metal on the road. Some blood. Frank noticed a severed hand, palm turned upwards and fingers curled like a dead spider's legs. There were mangled bodies in the cars. Florence stared at them and she was silent.

In the car still on the road a man sat behind the steering wheel, his face obliterated and dripping. His lower jaw was gone. His tongue was hanging onto his lap like an unravelled scarf. A woman was wedged in the windscreen, face down on the bonnet. In the back was a little girl with the top of her head missing. She was wearing a purple coat.

Frank stood next to Florence. "It's okay."

The woman on the bonnet moved, jerked up her head and glared at them. The violence of her ejection from the seat had split her clothes. Her face was shredded. Her mouth opened slowly and some of her teeth tumbled out like dice. She made a wheezing sound. There was no way to tell if she was infected or not. She reached for them with a bloodied hand until she could reach no further. Her fingers scraped on the bonnet.

She stopped moving. Frank knew she was dead.

Florence was crying.

He put his arm around the girl and they moved on.

* * *

"I need to pee," Florence said.

Frank looked up and down the road. "Okay. Just go in the bushes. But be careful. I'll watch the road. If you see anything, shout to me, okay?"

She didn't reply as she vanished behind a hedgerow. Frank looked up at the sky. Grey upon grey. He thought he could feel rain in the air, like a light mist. Moisture on his face.

Minutes passed. He waited. Thunder in the sky.

"Florence? Are you okay?"

No reply.

"Florence?"

No answer.

A sliver of panic in his stomach, like a parasite uncurling itself.

"Florence, is everything alright in there?"

He moved towards the gap in the hedgerow where she had gone. He halted, craned his neck to peer into the field. He called her name again, and only silence followed it. He swallowed.

"Florence!"

Frank stumbled into the field. She was gone. No sign of her. No sign of a struggle. Wouldn't she have cried for help?

He looked toward the horizon, away from the road. There was an area of woodland on the other side of the field. Groves of thin trees blanketed by grey. There was a speck of pink moving away from him, growing smaller.

Florence's jacket. Florence was running.

Frank ran.

CHAPTER THIRTY-EIGHT

The trees swallowed Florence and she was gone. Branches rattled in the wind. Frank's feet thumped on the damp earth. The rucksack was a burden but he didn't discard it. A crackle of thunder pierced the air as he melted into the inky gloom between the trees. The mixed smells of bark and mulch, sticky sap and vegetation. The faint musk of animal spoor. Rotting leaves on the ground. Twigs snapped under his shoes.

"Florence!" His voice was hoarse and crazed amongst the trees. He was breathing hard. A flash of pink ahead of him. He stumbled through the bracken and the wood's leavings. The canopy above him was thick and dark. Everything was muted, dulled, soaked in grey light. The trees stretched away from him like a fairy tale forest.

Every breath became a wheeze. His ribs pressed against his lungs. He leaned against a tree and took in deep breaths through clenched teeth, closed his eyes and willed his chest to loosen. Breathe slowly, breathe deeply. Every breath counted.

He took out his inhaler, shook it. Put it to his mouth and sucked.

He closed his eyes. The insides of his eyelids were stained with white blotches. His heart was beating so hard he felt sick.

The pressure on his lungs lessened.

Better.

He opened his eyes and pocketed his inhaler.

Something unseen was thrashing amongst the trees. It wasn't Florence. Frank froze, made himself small and kept flush to the tree. Sap stuck to his hands. He tried to hold his breath, but couldn't. He didn't move. He adjusted his grip on the axe.

Silence.

He waited.

A man stumbled past. He was bloodied and gangly. Long stringy hair. His bare arms were scratched, cut and elongated so that his gnarled white hands nearly touched the ground. Black spikes were growing from his neck, weeping a clear fluid. Around them were dark red lesions. There was a colony of blistering tumours on his stomach.

The man was dragging a small boy by the ankle. Frank couldn't tell if the boy was alive or dead. The boy was naked and there was a greasy puncture wound in his sternum.

Frank hoped the boy was dead.

The man moved away, disappearing into the woods, taking his captured prey with him.

* * *

Frank reached the edge of the woods. He was halted by a ten feet high metal chain-link fence. Beyond it was a golf course, judging by the trimmed grass winding away from him down the hill.

He couldn't climb the fence. Florence must have come this way, but where had she gone? She must have slipped through the fence somewhere.

Frank hurried alongside the fence. A few minutes later he found a small opening in the links, low to the ground. He crouched. There was a scrap of pink fluff snagged on an errant metal wire. He plucked it between two fingers.

With much effort he squeezed through the opening and pulled his rucksack after him. He stood and realised he'd cut his arm on the same bit of metal that had snared a bit of Florence's jacket. It had already stopped bleeding. He wiped it on his jeans then shrugged on the rucksack again. He walked onto the fairway, trying to determine which way Florence had gone.

The fairway stretched away from him.

He shook his head.

He had never liked golf.

CHAPTER THIRTY-NINE

Frank found a golf ball left on the fairway by the last golfer to walk the course. It was white and clean, without a single blemish. He picked it up, held it in the palm of his hand, then took out a black marker from the rucksack and drew a smiley face on the ball.

He walked the fairway.

Florence was sitting on a flat green, her head bowed. A flagstick fluttered in the breeze. Frank walked towards her slowly, careful not to alarm her. He kept his axe lowered.

She did not run from him. She wiped tears from her face as Frank approached. He noticed the small puddle of vomit on the grass. Florence looked up at him with eyes like pools of water. Frank crouched next to her. He didn't touch her.

Several short bursts of gunfire rang out in the distance.

"Hey," Frank said. "Are you okay?"

There was a faint, barely noticeable, nod of her head. The corners of her mouth shivered. There was saliva on her chin; Frank took a clean tissue from his pocket and wiped it away.

"Why did you run?"

"I was scared. I want to go home. I miss my mum and dad."

"I'm sorry, but they're gone, Florence."

"I know they're gone. I want to go back in time. I want none of this to have happened. I wish I'd never met you, Frank."

"I know."

"I want to go to my aunt and uncle's place in Bordon. I want to be with them. I don't want to be with you anymore."

His chest tightened again, but not from the asthma. "There's no guarantee it'll be safe."

"I don't care. I want to be with them. They'll keep me safe."

"I've been keeping you safe, so far."

"But you're just a stranger…"

"You've been through a lot. You're traumatised."

"I want to go to Bordon. You can't stop me."

Her face was stony, resolute and pitiful; an aggrieved child.

Frank sighed. Florence would go one of two ways in the coming days, he thought. She would either store her grief in the back of her mind and adapt, or submit to grief, terror and catatonia.

Frank felt rejected and forlorn. He tried to disguise the slumping of his shoulders as fatigue. It felt like something dull and rusty had embedded in the centre of his chest.

"It's not safe," Frank said. "You've seen the things out there."

"I don't care. I'm fast enough to outrun them. I outran you."

"You can't outrun everything."

"Then I'll hide when I have to. I don't need you to look after me."

Frank said nothing. He listened to the calling wind.

Florence sniffled. Her nose was wet.

"I'll do a deal with you," said Frank.

"What kind of deal?"

"I'm heading that way anyway. I'll take you to Bordon. I'll get you to your aunt and uncle then you can do what you like. I'll look after you on the way there. Deal?"

Florence thought about it, looked at the ground, then at Frank.

Frank offered his hand. She took it reluctantly. Her hand was hot and moist.

"No more running off," he said. "Understood? Promise not to do that again?"

She nodded.

"Here," he said, taking the golf ball from inside his jacket.

"What's that?"

"What does it look like? It's a golf ball. We're on a golf course, after all."

"Did you draw the face on it?"

"That's how I found it."

"You're lying."

"I'm not. Cross my heart."

"Hope to die?"

"Not for a long time."

"You're stupid."

"I know. But I'm old, so it's okay."

He handed the ball to her. She looked at it as if it were the steaming leavings of a mongrel dog.

"Take it," Frank said. "It's yours."

"What am I gonna do with it?"

"Probably nothing. Just keep it on you. Call it a peace offering."

She put the ball in her pocket.

"Don't lose it," Frank said.

She shook her head at him.

"We're just outside Broadbridge Heath. We'll find a car. It'll be okay."

Florence stood.

"Shall we go?" Frank asked.

She nodded.

Frank saw something dark on the grass at the edge of the green. He walked over to it, bent down to examine it.

"What is it?" said Florence.

Frank picked up the shard of dark metal. He turned it over. It had been ripped from something. He looked around. He walked to the top of the slope. Florence followed.

There was another piece of metal at the crest of the hill. He picked it up. It was bigger than the first piece and ragged. He looked down the slope.

More pieces of metal on the fairway.

They walked down the slope and found more wreckage on the way. Two hundred yards down, the fairway curved to the right, and Frank saw from where the debris had come.

A helicopter had crash-landed at the edge of the fairway, where it had come to rest against a large oak tree. Crumpled and torn. Bits missing. There was no smoke and no fire. One of the rotors had torn loose and gouged shallow furrows into the earth, where it was now stuck in the ground like the marker for a makeshift grave. Florence touched it then took her hand away as if it were hot. She prodded a warped sheet of metal with her foot.

More wreckage had been shed during its landing, scattered around the crash site. Scraps of plastic. Frank could smell oil.

They approached the downed helicopter. The fuselage was pitted with dents and scratches, and had been ripped open. Wires and cables. Cracked glass. It must have been a privately-owned helicopter. It had been painted the colours of the Union Jack.

The pilot was dead in his seat. The cockpit had been compromised and warped. He was slumped forwards. Blood stained his white shirt. His eyes were open. His neck was too limp and his head was set at an obscene angle.

Frank looked inside the fuselage. A row of seats. A middle-aged man in an expensive suit was slumped in a corner. A spiked tree-branch had impaled him through his chest and out the other side of his body so that it pierced the back of his seat. He was meat on a stick, and he was starting to smell.

Frank found a red plastic case and opened it on the grass outside. A flare gun and spare flares packed in foam. He put the case in his rucksack.

"There was someone else here, as well," said Florence. She pointed at a faint trail of blood on the grass.

"Let's follow the trail," Frank said.

CHAPTER FORTY

The woman was sitting against a tree at the edge of the golf course. A dotted ribbon of red led to her. She was holding the left side of her stomach. She saw them coming and her eyes widened in a mixture of hope, elation and fear.

"Please help me."

Frank and Florence crouched next to her. Her eyes were wet, sharp and clear with pain. Her face was pale. Red on her lips that wasn't lipstick. Bleached white teeth. The hand over her stomach wound was sticky with blood, of which she had lost a lot. She was wearing a ripped white blouse, and Frank tried not to let his eyes linger on the sight of her bra strap clinging to her pale skin. A black skirt ended well above her knees. Bare legs. There was blood in her long blonde hair and smeared over her forehead. A yellow-black bruise under her bloodshot left eye.

"Please help me."

"It's okay," said Frank. "Take it easy." He didn't know what else to say to her. He offered a thin, forced smile.

He checked the wound in her stomach. She winced when she moved away her hand. The wound was deep. He replaced her hand upon it.

"You need to get me to a hospital," she said.

"Calm down," Frank said. "We'll help you." He didn't know how, though. He had no medical training; hadn't even done a First Aid course.

"I need to get to a hospital."

Frank took out the First Aid kit from his rucksack. He placed some gauze on her wound, told her to keep pressure on it. It wasn't much, but it was better than nothing.

"What's your name?" Frank asked her.

"Caitlin."

"Hey, Caitlin, I'm Frank. This is Florence."

"Florence is a nice name."

Florence kept her distance from the woman.

"They're both dead, aren't they?" Caitlin said.

"The men in the helicopter. Yeah. What happened?"

"We escaped from London." Her eyes fluttered. "Tim and I were heading for France. He had a chateau in the countryside."

"Is Tim the man in the suit?" said Frank.

"Yes. I was his secretary. He said he would protect me, get us out of the country, to somewhere safe. He was a decent man."

"I'm sure he was," said Frank. "What happened in London?"

"The plague happened," she said. "It was all panic and slaughter. Killings in the streets. You wouldn't believe it."

"I might do," said Frank.

"After we heard the rescue camp at Wembley stadium had been overrun, we decided to get out of the city. We'd already been told that the Royal Family had been evacuated, along with what remained of the government. If it was good enough for them, it was good enough for us. Nothing to stay for. It was Hell. Think of the worst things you've ever seen and that's nowhere near what I've witnessed. The city was falling apart. There were monsters. I remember seeing people running and fighting in the streets, ripping one another to bits as we flew over them. Bodies everywhere. Packs of infected. After leaving London, our pilot had a seizure of some kind, like he had caught the plague or something, and we crashed. Woke up with a hole in my stomach. I think my right ankle's broken. I crawled here. You have to help me."

"We will," said Frank. "We'll think of something."

There was a shriek from the other side of the trees. Another voice yipped and bayed in response.

"Was that one of them?" Caitlin said.

"It's okay," said Frank. "Don't panic."

"You have to help me get out of here. Don't leave me here!"

"We won't leave you, I promise."

More shrieks and screams. Closer. Florence looked at Frank, breathing fast, her eyes wide.

"I don't want to die here," said Caitlin. "I don't want to die."

"You won't die," said Frank. He looked at Florence. "We'll carry her."

They pulled Caitlin to her feet. She screamed as her ankle took her weight.

The infected were coming through the trees.

"Come on!" said Frank. He put Caitlin's left arm around his shoulders and held her up. Florence held on to the woman, helped her along. They moved slowly. Not fast enough.

Caitlin was crying. She screamed in Frank's ear and he almost dropped her.

"I don't want to die!" she wailed.

Frank looked back. Wished he hadn't.

Too late.

The infected poured out of the trees. Five of them. Ragged men and women. Two of them had been transformed into *things* with claws instead of hands and wide mouths snapping at the air. One of them was lop-sided with glistening bulbous growths the colour of mould.

They were screaming and howling. They lusted after blood and meat.

"Keep moving!" Frank said. The fairway opened up before them. Nowhere to hide. An open range where they would be run down and gutted. A killing ground.

Caitlin slipped from Frank's grip and fell down. She cried and screamed. Frank glanced back at the infected then picked her back up. He dragged her with all his strength.

"They're coming," said Florence.

The infected screamed.

Florence was crying.

Caitlin was dead weight.

Frank would not let the infected hurt Florence. He had promised to protect her. He knew what he had to do, and he hated himself for it.

He let Caitlin go.

She fell down.

"Don't leave me!" she said, scrambling after him, her eyes pleading. "Please don't leave me!"

"I'm sorry. I'm so sorry," Frank said.

"You can't leave me! You can't fucking leave me!"

"I have to. I'm so sorry."

"You fucking bastard! You fucking cunt! You're murdering me!"

Frank grabbed Florence and pulled her along. They ran. The infected were closing in.

Florence screamed.

Frank looked back to see the infected falling upon Caitlin. They swarmed her. One of the men ripped her leg away at the knee and buried his mouth in the gristle of her calf muscle. They dismembered her upon the grass while she was alive and lapped at her precious fluids and snaffled the exquisite morsels of her abdomen.

The infected didn't come after Frank and Florence. They would be sated for a while.

Caitlin was still screaming when the infected tore out her heart.

Her screams would stay with Frank for a long time.

CHAPTER FORTY-ONE

Broadbridge Heath was desolate and silent.

They reached the centre of the village. The doors of the village hall were open and a rotting stench drifted from within. They didn't look inside. There were crashed cars. No bodies. There was a bus ahead of them, abandoned across the road.

Frank could still hear Caitlin's screams inside his head. They would fade eventually, but not for a long while, and he was okay with that. He had to keep Florence safe. Her safety was his responsibility.

Florence hadn't spoken to him since they'd escaped the golf course.

"I'm not a bad man, Florence. I had to leave Caitlin behind. I didn't have a choice."

Florence's face was shaded with dull blotches. "Would you do the same to me?"

"Do what?"

"Leave me behind for the monsters."

Frank crouched before her and held her softly by her shoulders. She didn't flinch away from him.

"I would never leave you behind, understand?" His voice was louder than he intended, and he saw it in her face. He lowered his tone, tried to smile. "I left Caitlin behind so you and I could live. So we could survive. I did it to protect you, Florence. Caitlin was a stranger; you're my friend, Florence, right?"

"I think so."

"Friends do anything for each other. I wouldn't leave a friend behind."

Doubt in her expression. "Is it my fault that she died? Because you wanted to save me?"

"No, of course not. Don't ever think that. Caitlin would have died anyway. She had lost too much blood."

"But would you leave me behind if I was really badly injured?"

"I would have stayed with you, Florence. I wouldn't leave you alone."

"Okay."

"I promised to get you to Bordon. And I'll do that."

"Okay."

He let her go, stepped back. Looked down at her.

He heard a car approaching from behind them. He turned.

Florence heard it, too. "Who's that? Do you think they'll give us a lift?"

"Let's hope so."

A white transit van appeared at the top of the road, heading towards them. Frank guided Florence to the side of the road. The van picked up speed. Frank made sure the axe was visible by his side. He kept Florence behind him. The van slowed and braked to a clumsy stop next to them. The engine idled. The two men in the van looked at Frank, then at Florence, then back to Frank. No one said anything. The driver wound down the side window.

"Hello," said the driver, a chubby balding man with glasses and a goatee beard.

"Hello," said Frank. He nodded at the men.

"Hey there," said the other man. He was wiry and scraggly, wearing gardening gloves and a beanie hat. He was rodent-like. Small eyes like marbles.

"Where you heading?" the chubby man asked.

"We're looking for the nearest rescue centre," said Frank.

"That's cool. My name's Bertram. This is Mackie." He cocked a thumb at the wiry man.

Mackie waved. "Hey."

The men stared at Frank as waiting for him to introduce himself. He said nothing.

Bertram grinned. "Where you coming from?"

"Horsham," Frank said.

"Bloody hell. You got out of there just in time. I watched it burn."

Frank nodded. "So did we."

Bertram looked at Florence. "Hey there, little lady, you look a bit pale. Are you okay? Are you sick?"

"She's fine," said Frank. "Just a bit shaken up with all that's happened."

"You her father?"

"What's it to you?"

Bertram's grin faded. "Just making conversation, my friend."

Mackie waved at Florence. His beady eyes gleamed.

"We could give you both a lift," said Bertram. "Wherever you're going…"

"We've got sweets," Mackie said.

"No, thanks," said Frank. "We're fine."

"You sure?" said Bertram. "It's dangerous out here, especially looking after a little girl. Come on, we'll give you a lift. Hop in the back. It's no trouble. No trouble at all."

"Yeah," said Mackie. "We insist. Come on, man. Look after your little girl."

"What do you think, little lady?" said Bertram. "Do you want a ride in the van? You'll be safe. I promise. We'll have some fun."

"Don't talk to her," said Frank.

"No need to be rude, my friend," Bertram said. His mouth turned up at the corners like a knife-cut in pale meat.

"Dickhead," said Mackie, shaking his head at Frank.

Bertram looked at Frank. "It's too dangerous on the road, my friend. You really want to put your little girl in danger?"

"It's no concern of yours."

"We're just trying to help." Bertram looked at Florence. "Would you like some help, little lady?"

"I said don't talk to her," Frank said. He took hold of Florence's hand and they walked away.

Bertram and Mackie were laughing behind them.

"Why are they laughing?" asked Florence.

"Ignore them," said Frank. "Now, those men are strangers."

"My mum always told me not to talk to strangers."

"That's good advice. Exactly."

"Hey, come back!" Bertram said.

"Keep walking," said Frank.

The van pulled up alongside them.

They kept walking. Frank didn't look at the van.

The van kept pace with them.

"There's no need to be belligerent, my friend," said Bertram. "We have to stick together in times like these."

"Dark times," said Mackie. "Dangerous times. People are dying."

"Come on," Bertram said. "We're trying to help you both."

Frank halted, turned to them, keeping himself between Florence and the men. "Listen, fellas...I'm very grateful for the offer, but we're fine."

"You think that axe will protect you?" said Mackie.

"It's a shame you won't accept our kind offer," said Bertram. "Do you think if I beeped the horn any infected people in this village would head this way?"

"I reckon they would," Mackie said. "Bet they're pretty hungry."

"We're not asking for any trouble," said Frank. "Please leave us alone. I'm asking nicely, lads."

Both Bertram and Mackie grinned.

Frank didn't like the way they eyed Florence. He stared at them. He could not appear to be weak.

"Come on, get in the van," said Bertram. "We'll have a road trip."

"Yeah, good idea!" Mackie said.

"I'll say it for the last time," Frank muttered. "No."

Bertram shook his head. "Well, I'm sorry if that's how you feel, my friend."

Mackie sniggered. "Yeah, we're really sorry."

The back of the van opened and a man in a black balaclava and a black jacket leaped out. Frank only noticed the baseball bat in the man's hands as it was swinging towards him, and he managed to raise his arms just as the bat connected with the side of his neck, nullifying the force of the swing. The man's assault was clumsy and mistimed, but effective. Frank went down and hit the back of his head on the pavement. He dropped his axe and the rucksack.

The man in black swore and spat at Frank. The bat fell upon Frank's ribs, stomach and legs. Frank shielded his face and tried to kick at the man.

"Florence!" he shouted.

Florence screamed. Bertram had hold of her. Mackie was giggling. Florence was thrown in the back of the van.

Frank called out to her.

A glancing blow from the bat on his forehead, and everything blurred. He groaned. He called out to Florence. She was yelling for him, begging him to help her.

The man with the bat stood over him and laughed, snatching Frank's bag from the ground.

"Come on!" said Bertram. "Leave him. The infected will hear all the noise. Let's go!"

The man kicked him in the stomach and returned to the van.

Frank watched them drive away. He was sprawled on the pavement. The sound of the van's engine receded. His eyelids were heavy. He looked at the sky. The world around him swam in fluid; shapes were distorted, dancing like squalls. The darkness behind his eyes was dotted with pinholes of light. He felt tired. The pavement was cold underneath him.

He had let down Florence. He had failed her. His daughter was dead. Emily…Florence…Emily…Florence. Both of them were gone, now. His fault both times. His fault he had lost them.

Somewhere, maybe far away or maybe nearby, the infected were screaming. The sounds of monsters gathering for a hunt.

Frank passed out.

CHAPTER FORTY-TWO

Faces formed around him, shifting out of the darkness like pale stains seeping through cloth. Loved ones and old friends. Catherine smiled at him, but there was something wrong with her face. Something wrong with her mouth and how it opened to tempt him with its slick tongue. Her breath was the stench of spoiled meat and digestive juices; bile and rot and all things torn from quivering bodies.

He saw Ralph, Magnus and Joel. They were charred skeletal corpses with white eyes and ivory grins. Their bones clicked as they shuffled their limbs to welcome him.

He saw Caitlin, the woman he'd abandoned to the infected. She was now a monster, all glistening spikes of black bone and a snapping mouth opened just for him.

He saw David Pulver stuffing bits of his children into his mouth.

He saw Corporal Guppy and his lads. They were all dead, piled atop of one another, flies droning around them and rats squirming between their decomposing bodies, chewing and gnawing on their soft meat.

Then he saw Emily, his dead daughter. But she was alive, here. She slowly assumed the shape of Florence. They were the same, both of his girls. They came to him as shivering, naked forms and they embraced him, burying their little mouths into his tender stomach. They loved him. And he loved them back.

He loved his girls.

* * *

A white room. Catherine was sitting next to him. White walls, white floor, white ceiling. Plastic chairs creaking with every movement; metal legs that scraped the floor. The smell of strong disinfectant and rubber gloves.

Catherine was crying as Frank held her. He was crying, too.

A heart monitor was beeping.

Emily was a withered body under white sheets, riddled with tubes and tumours. Her hair had fallen out. Ten years old. She was as pale as the room she would die in. Dark shadows under her eyes. She had faded into a paper-thin form of skin and bone. A rag doll with a little girl's face. The drugs kept her in oblivion. It was better this way. She would slip away and she wouldn't even know.

They whispered their daughter's name.

The beeping of the heart monitor stopped and became an uninterrupted wail.

* * *

Frank's eyes snapped open. His head throbbed with each heartbeat.

Dark shapes overhead.

The infected were upon him.

Cold hands flailed at his arms and legs.

One of the infected said his name.

That was not possible.

His name was spoken again. Louder. Clearer. A voice he recognised.

"Frank! Frank, are you okay? Talk to me, Frank!"

He opened his eyes. Three figures crouching over him. He was hallucinating, surely.

Ralph, Magnus and Joel looked down at him.

"Ghosts," Frank muttered. "Lots of ghosts…" His mouth was dry, his tongue swollen like a ripened fruit. His gums were tender and his jaw felt bruised and sore. His stomach was a broiling mess of stinking juices. He raised one hand to a lump on his forehead and winced, then threw up on Ralph's shoes. Coughed up bile, spit and the undigested dregs of that morning's breakfast.

"Charming," said the ghost of Ralph. "Ain't seen you in ages, and you chunder on my best trainers."

"Sorry," Frank slurred, forgetting what he was sorry for.

"Is he okay?" said Joel's shade. "I thought he was dead."

"Broken bones?" said Magnus. He looked into Frank's face. "Frank, are you okay? What happened to you?"

"Looks like he got in a fight," Ralph said. "And lost it."

"Let's move him," said Joel. "Get him off the street."

"The monster's nearby," said Magnus. "It followed us." His face was loose like a poorly-made mask.

Frank smiled at his dead friends. Ralph and Magnus hoisted him to his feet. The street around him was a spinning carousel. His bones felt brittle, his skin so tight over them it might split if his friends moved him too suddenly.

"Hurry up," said Joel. "It's coming."

They dragged him down the street and climbed aboard an abandoned bus. Frank's eyes bulged at the dead driver sagging over the steering wheel. The dead man's uniform was straining at his swollen body.

"I used to ride the bus to school," said Frank.

"We all did, mate," said Ralph.

He swooned, and the world became dark.

* * *

Frank came to on the seat of the bus. He could smell piss and vomit. Staleness. The peculiar musk of public transport that birthed images of sagging pensioners, grey-faced women, and chavs scowling at thin air. Then his own odour of old sweat and clammy hands.

Ralph held him down. He shook his head and put his finger to Frank's mouth. On the other side of the aisle Magnus and Joel cowered behind a seat.

Something creaked at the front of the bus. Something had joined them. Frank peered around the side of the seat in front of him and looked down the aisle.

In the aisle was a grey and naked bipedal creature with mottled skin and spindly legs. Once a man, but now something else. The sound of its breath was a wet gurgle. The top half of its skeletal body was all writhing tentacles dripping gelatinous fluids onto the floor. The creature turned its body towards them. Tentacles dotted with tiny suckers, and at the centre of the tentacles was a human face, grey and anguished, pulled tight across angles of bone. And, as Frank watched, the face opened like a fleshy flower to reveal a circular pink maw rimmed with tiny sharp teeth. An inner face. A whip-like red tongue squirmed within the maw.

Frank felt his legs go weak.

The creature turned away and appraised the dead driver. Its tentacles latched onto the man's back, dragged his bulk from the seat towards its pink maw and red tongue.

The dead man's head vanished within the clutch of tentacles. His body jerked, trembling to the sounds of grinding and sucking.

The creature plucked the man from his seat and pulled him outside to be dragged away.

The men regarded one another, and they were silent.

CHAPTER FORTY-THREE

They stayed on the bus. It was quiet outside.

"I thought you were ghosts," said Frank. "I thought you were all dead. I can't tell you how pleased I am to see you all."

There had been much back-slapping and man-hugs earlier. The camaraderie was a lift to his spirits. Frank felt some hope, for the first time in a while.

Frank checked for his inhaler in his pocket and was relieved that it hadn't fallen out. Joel's wallet was there too. He handed over the wallet. Joel nodded tersely and thanked him.

Frank thought about Florence. He tried not to think about what those men would do to her. Best not to linger on it. Madness waited on that path.

"What happened to you, lads?" Frank asked.

"What happened to *you*?" said Ralph, his face serious. Freckles of dried blood on his face. "You abandoned us; left us in that house with freaks in the attic."

"You shouldn't have left us," said Joel.

"I'm sorry," Frank said.

Magnus looked at him. "What happened?"

Frank recounted the events up to when they found him on the pavement outside. They were silent as he told them of the last two days; about finding Florence and rescuing her from Wishford.

"Fucking hell," said Magnus. "This is insane."

"That poor girl," Ralph muttered. "She survives all of that carnage just to be abducted by a few perverts in a van."

"Monsters, everywhere," Magnus said.

"A plague," said Joel. "It's almost Biblical."

"Let's not start that nonsense," said Ralph.

Magnus cleaned his glasses. "A virus."

"How is it transmitted?" asked Joel. "By bites? By blood and saliva?"

"If it's airborne we're all fucked," Magnus said.

Ralph scratched himself. "You're lucky to be alive, Frank. I wish you didn't try to save every person who needs help. We need to look after ourselves, not other people. I told you that before you left us. I wish you would listen to me."

"Yes, I know, Ralph. But you don't know what I've been through. You don't know what I've seen. I had to kill a man who was eating his dead family. I've watched people get slaughtered by monsters. Florence lost her parents to the infected, saw them die, so I had to take care of her. I tried to protect her but I failed. Don't talk down to me, Ralph. We've all made bad decisions and done things in the last day that we regret, so why don't you just back off for once?"

Ralph held eye contact with him. "I'm sorry, Frank. You've got some bollocks, I'll give you that. I didn't mean to..."

"Don't worry about it," Frank said. "Doesn't matter now."

"Kiss and make up, lads," said Magnus. He grinned.

Frank shook his head.

Ralph grunted, looked away. He was holding the flare gun Frank had found.

"Be careful with that," said Frank.

Ralph tapped the flare gun against his forehead and winked.

Frank appraised his friends. Studied the small details that told of what had happened to them. They looked like he felt, and he felt like sun-fried shit in a shoebox. They were exhausted and stressed. Hunted and haunted. Pale faces and red-rimmed eyes. He wondered what terrible things they had seen. Ralph appeared to be coping better than Joel and Magnus, although there were dark bruises under his eyes, and his thickening beard made his face seem heavy and spade-like. There was a plain white plastic bag on his lap. The bag bulged.

"What's in the bag?" asked Frank.

Ralph put the bag on the floor. "Not much. Things we've scavenged on the way here. A torch, a bottle of water, a packet of painkillers, a packet of biscuits…"

"Better than nothing, I suppose."

"Yeah," Ralph said.

Joel was rubbing the left side of his jaw, a nervous tic that Frank recognised. There was something in his other hand, which was clenched into a fist. He was taking great pains to keep it hidden.

Magnus was trembling and blinking his eyes. He ran his hands over his shaven head. He looked ready to drop. His jacket was torn and there were stains on his trousers. Frank tried not to guess what they were.

In the distance, something roared.

Night was coming.

Ralph shut the doors.

Time to hide when the darkness arrived.

* * *

"We managed to get out of Wishford," said Ralph. He was looking at Frank, his face caught in shadow as the light faded. He told Frank about the attack on the rescue centre.

"We were lucky," said Magnus.

"How did you escape?" Frank was sitting on a seat, sipping from a water bottle.

"We hid in the kitchen, in a big cupboard where they stored food. We barricaded the door. The infected didn't find us. We waited, listening to the screams. Then everything went silent. Eventually we crept out. There were only a few infected remaining at the school; they must have left in search of more victims. We managed to sneak outside and down the street. We were lucky to get out of the town alive. People were fleeing the town. We were running across the fields outside of Horsham when the bombs hit. Still can't believe they firebombed a town."

"Things are bad, if that's the government's solution to the plague," said Joel.

"But to firebomb a town on British soil? This isn't the fucking Blitz," said Magnus.

"There wasn't a choice," said Frank. "The town was overrun. The infected were everywhere. I saw them. We all did."

Magnus cleared his throat. "And that enormous thing in the sky," he said. "We all saw it."

"What do you think it was?"

"It was alive. It wasn't a ship or a craft. It was organic."

"We don't know that," said Ralph. "It could have been anything."

Joel said, "Yeah, Ralph's right."

"It was like a god," muttered Magnus.

"It can't be a god," said Joel. He went to say something else, but stopped himself. He shook his head. He looked sick.

"It doesn't matter," said Ralph. "We have to worry about the things down here with us."

A few moments of silence. Almost full dark outside. They were four huddled darkening forms amongst the stinking seats.

"It's the entire country, isn't it?" said Joel. "It's everywhere."

"Seems that way, from what we've heard," said Ralph.

"You think it's global?" Magnus's voice was hoarse.

No one answered at first. Then Ralph spoke.

"That doesn't concern us at the moment, lads. We have to get home before we start worrying about the rest of the world. They don't care about us. Fuck them, for now. This is England."

"He's xenophobic and borderline racist," said Joel. "But he's right."

"Suck my balls," Ralph said. "But thanks for agreeing with me."

"I'm sorry about Florence," Joel said to Frank. "Even when everything's falling apart, people are still bastards."

"People are always bastards," Ralph said. "Maybe even more so when things are bad."

Magnus was nodding.

"Wish we could catch the men that took her," said Ralph. "Fuck knows what they'll do to her. I'd cut off their bollocks if I got my hands on them."

"She's gone," said Frank. His acceptance shamed him. He had lost Florence just like he had lost his daughter. He should be searching for her. But it was dark, the men would be far away by now, and Frank was terrified of the things lurking in the dark.

CHAPTER FORTY-FOUR

oel awoke to the sound of helicopters flying over the village. He rubbed his eyes, yawned into his hand. A gradual increase in light as dawn broke outside. There was too much grey in the world and it depressed him.

The country is dying, he thought absently.

He checked to make sure his small crucifix was in his pocket. He couldn't see the helicopters but the air trembled with their presence. They flew close to the rooftops, and by the time he rose from his seat they were gone.

Joel looked at the other men. By the movement of their faces, they were dreaming. Magnus muttered something under his breath. Ralph's mouth hung open towards the roof, catching dust.

Joel looked at Frank and smiled. He was relieved that Frank was alive. They were all together again. Joel was adamant the four of them would never fragment again on the way home. He felt something like love for his mates.

After checking his mobile phone, which was almost dead, Joel ate a biscuit and looked out at the street to the side of the bus. He thought of Anya and if they would be alive by the time of the wedding.

Would there even *be* a wedding?

Not if everyone was dead and the country was burning.

He stretched the muscles in his face. He cleared his throat, wetted his mouth with short sips of lukewarm water from the only bottle in the plastic bag. He liked the quiet, before the others awoke. The village outside was a dead place and there was plenty of quiet. Only the birds in the trees lining the street broke the morning's silence.

Joel sat down and wondered what sights he would see today. He took the photo of himself and Anya from his wallet. He smiled at it. He missed her deep in his stomach. He put the photo back in the wallet and pocketed it.

Then the infected came.

Joel ducked down in the aisle. He froze. His heartbeat filled his head. He breathed slowly through his mouth, peering through the window on the right side of the bus.

The infected came prowling through the street, amongst the abandoned cars. He did a quick count. Fourteen, in all. Deformed faces and jutting, twitching limbs held close to their bodies. Glazed eyes secreting dark fluids. They revolted him. How could God have allowed such things to exist? Were they His creations? Were they really demons? Was the pestilence blighting England actually a demonic plague?

Did that mean the Devil was roaming the land? And if that was true, what was God going to do about it?

Joel noticed one of them, a young boy, was limping at the back of the pack and making an awful, slow mewling that made Joel's heart sink. The boy crouched over a scrap of bloody clothing on the road and picked it up, holding it to his face and taking deep breaths from it. Joel watched him, amazed and horrified.

Was the boy a demon? Was that pathetic creature something unholy and damned?

Some of the pack scratched and scraped their fingernails on the side of the bus. Joel's teeth fillings tingled. He shivered and cold tendrils coiled around his bones.

Joel stepped down the aisle, watching the infected move down the road. He stopped near the front of the bus, waiting for the pack to leave.

The infected moved clear of the bus.

Joel slumped on a seat.

Behind him, the others were waking up.

* * *

Ralph found a Ford Fiesta with its keys in the footwell and no bodies inside. There was a small, still-working torch in the glove compartment, which they added to the one already in the plastic bag. The car had a quarter-tank of petrol. Ralph volunteered to drive. Joel sat in the front with him. Magnus and Frank were in the back.

Frank seemed to be recovering from his beating yesterday. He was bruised and winced whenever he moved too quickly. Every few minutes, Ralph glanced in the mirror at Frank, but Frank never met his eyes. Frank talked about the girl he'd travelled with. He talked about her too much.

They left Broadbridge Heath just before eight. No sign of the infected Joel had seen earlier. No sign of anyone.

"What's the plan?" asked Magnus.

"We're going home," Ralph said.

"Sounds too easy."

"It won't be. We've been lucky so far. Our luck won't last."

"Nothing like thinking positively," said Joel.

They travelled through other villages and hamlets. Lone infected lurked outside houses and by roadsides. They stared at the car as it passed.

Crashed vehicles by the road. Frank noticed a Dyno-Rod van on its side. The driver, a heavyset man with long hair, lay next to it, gutted and spilled open. A few hundred yards down the road, a tractor had crashed through a fence and into a tree. Smoke drifted from its engine.

Ralph stopped the car by an abandoned grocer's van. The men stared at the pool of oranges that had spilled from the open back doors. Two women, their faces streaked with soot, were filling plastic bags with fruit. They mouthed insults and threats at the men while discreetly displaying the knives tucked into their tracksuit bottoms.

The road dissected fields; groups of people were travelling across them. Frank remembered that they were called refugees, now. Some groups walked the roads. Ralph beeped the horn at them when they blocked the way. Men glared and swore at him. An old woman put one palm against the window and begged them to take her with them.

"Please help me. Please help me." A reedy, pathetic voice. Her nose was bloody.

"We're not stopping," said Ralph. He stared straight ahead. "We're not stopping for anybody."

"Where are they going?" said Magnus.

"Anywhere that's safe."

"They're heading west," said Frank. "Like us."

Two men were fighting by the side of the road, swapping punches while a young woman encouraged them, waving her hands and shouting. She looked feverish. The other refugees ignored them, not even sparing them a glance.

Heading towards the village of Slinfold, the numbers of refugees lessened until the road was empty again.

The petrol tank ran empty and the car shuddered to a halt. No other cars around from which they could siphon petrol.

"Bollocks," said Ralph. "Looks like we're walking."

"I don't feel too good," said Joel, holding his stomach.

They left the car behind.

CHAPTER FORTY-FIVE

They walked. Frank's legs were throbbing. He ached from the beating he'd taken yesterday. He kept thinking of Florence. Guilt and shame made his stomach boil. He popped two painkillers with a sip of water. He felt used up. They weren't even halfway home.

Two miles outside the village Joel vomited onto the grass verge, doubling over and retching until he cried and his eyes were red-ringed and sore. He spat by his feet.

"Are you okay, mate?" said Magnus.

"Feel like shit."

"Did you get bitten or scratched by one of the infected?" Ralph asked.

Joel wiped his mouth. "You're trying to ask me if I've got the plague? What is wrong with you?"

Ralph was unmoved. "I'm just asking. Don't take it personally."

"Don't take it personally? You think I'm going to turn into one of those monsters?"

"I didn't say that. I just wanted to make sure."

"Piss off."

"Were you bitten or scratched, though, Joel?" asked Magnus.

Joel shook his head, glared at Magnus. "No, I wasn't. I'm fine."

"Okay," said Ralph. "Do you still feel sick?"

"No."

"Good. Let's keep moving. We need to get to Slinford before it gets dark."

"We've got hours yet," said Magnus.

"I know, but we're walking. Think about it, genius. I don't want to be caught in the open when night falls."

"I suppose you're right."

Frank looked around the fields. He imagined the infected coming out of the dark to kill him and his mates. He shivered and looked at the cold grey sky.

* * *

One mile later they rounded a bend in the road and stopped. They stared down the road, none of them saying a word. There was thunder in the distance. Frank felt it inside his head. When the sky roared, his skull trembled. He rubbed his eyes.

"What the fuck?" said Magnus. His voice was a tired whine.

"Kids," said Joel.

The children were standing in the centre of a crossroads twenty yards away, their faces turned towards the sky.

Frank expected to see some great shadow looming above the children. Grey clouds that were almost black, but there was no shadow and no discernible threat.

He could almost reach up and push his hand into the clouds. But would he still have had his hand when he pulled it out?

The children didn't move. Necks craned towards the sky. Eyes open, mouths shut tight like they were keeping a secret only they should know. Six boys and three girls. None of them were over ten years old. Dirty clothes and blood on their skin. Red around their mouths. Most of them were barefoot. One of the boys wore only a pair of pants and socks soiled with dirt.

Ralph said, "They're infected."

"Are you sure?" asked Joel.

"Look at them."

"Why haven't they attacked us yet, then?"

"Something else has their attention."

Magnus ran a hand over his face. "Oh for Christ's sake."

Frank took a few steps forward. He had a horrible feeling that Florence was among them. He looked for her unmistakeable mane of red hair. She wasn't there. He looked at their hands. The children were twiddling their fingers by their sides. The closer he got to them the more the air thickened. Almost electric, like the silent moments before a thunderstorm.

The others stopped behind him.

"Be careful, lads," said Ralph.

"What're they doing?" Joel said. "What are they looking at?"

"The things in the sky," said Magnus. "Like what we saw back in Horsham. The thing that drifted over the school."

"You can't be sure of that. How do you know?"

"What else could it be?" said Ralph. "Look at them."

Joel looked. His face seemed to droop. He swallowed, took a deep breath and looked ready to be sick again.

"I remember," said Joel, "when we were little and we used to go on walks across the fields. When we used to stop and sit down to eat our packed lunches, I would lie on the grass and look up at the sky when there were no clouds and there was just blue. It used to make me feel weird. Dizzy, almost. And small. I used to think the world would suddenly turn upside down and I would drop into that blue sky and keep on falling."

"I remember you freaking out once," said Ralph. "Crying because you were worried you'd fall into space. I took the piss out of you for weeks afterwards."

"Yeah," said Joel, with a scowl. "I was only eight years old. Thanks for being so understanding, mate."

Magnus shifted his feet. "Will they attack us if we get too close?"

"Let's just go through them," said Ralph.

"What?" Magnus said. "Are you mental?"

Ralph shrugged, looked puzzled. "Why not? They'll either ignore us or they won't."

"What if they *don't* ignore us?"

Ralph tapped the flare gun against his leg. "Then we'll sort it out."

"Ralph is right, unfortunately" said Frank. "What choice do we have, lads?"

"Are you prepared to kill a child?" said Joel. "Even if it's infected? Could any of you live with that?"

"Could you?" said Ralph. "You might have to before we get home."

"Not if I can help it."

Ralph shook his head. "If you want to stay alive, you will."

"Stop arguing," said Magnus. "This isn't the time."

Joel and Ralph glared at each other. Joel looked away.

"Do you hear that?" said Magnus.

"Hear what?" Joel said.

"Vehicles. Engines."

On one of the roads approaching the crossroads, several trucks were heading their way.

"Looks like a convoy," said Ralph.

A jeep headed the convoy. Armoured cars with mounted machine guns.

"Hide," said Ralph.

Frank turned to him. "Why hide from the army? They can help us."

Ralph grabbed Frank, pushed him to the roadside. Magnus and Joel followed. They hid in a soggy ditch overgrown with grass and stinging nettles, and stinking of stagnant water.

"I've got a bad feeling," said Ralph. "Keep your heads down."

"This is insane," said Frank.

Ralph glared at him. "Just wait."

Frank peered over the top of the ditch, wincing as a nettle stung his hand. The army convoy stopped near the children. His heart went a little faster. A squad of soldiers jumped down from one of the trucks.

The children didn't react. They stared at the sky.

"Maybe the soldiers will put them in one of the trucks," said Magnus. He chewed on the inside of his mouth. "Maybe they'll take the kids to some sort of sanctuary."

No one answered. Frank watched the soldiers gather in a line behind the children. One of the soldiers was shouting, but Frank couldn't tell what he was saying.

The children were content to look at the sky, lost in the clouds.

"Don't look," said Ralph.

But Frank looked. So did the others.

Frank's eyes felt hot and stinging. He didn't want to watch but couldn't stop himself.

The soldiers raised their rifles and took aim.

The children stared at the sky.

The soldiers opened fire.

The children fell.

And they would never look at the sky again.

CHAPTER FORTY-SIX

Joel said, "I need to stop."

"Come on, mate," said Ralph. "We're almost at the village. It's getting dark."

"Darker than it should be," said Magnus.

Joel darted to the side of the road, bent over and vomited onto the grass. Magnus went to him and patted between his shoulder blades.

"Take it easy, Joel. Take it easy."

Ralph shook his head and snorted.

After Joel finished vomiting he stepped back on to the road. He ignored Ralph. There were globs of spit and mucus in his facial hair. He wiped them away, coughing and spitting.

"You okay, Joel?" said Frank.

"They killed those children," he said.

"The children were infected," said Ralph. "The soldiers didn't have a choice."

"Why did you make us hide?"

Frank remembered walking past the pile of children's bodies that the soldiers had made. He had felt voyeuristic and disrespectful looking at the small corpses.

"How do you think the soldiers would've reacted to us witnessing them kill a bunch of kids? Do you think they would have let us go on our merry fucking way? They would've shot us."

"Shot us?" said Joel. "Our own army wouldn't shoot us. We're not infected. They're on our side. They're supposed to help us."

"Take your head out of your arse for a minute, Joel. They wouldn't have let us get away. They wouldn't let that sort of thing get out. They would've shot us and dumped our bodies with the children. No one would ever have found out."

"Don't insult me," said Joel. "Fuck off."

Ralph stepped towards him.

Frank and Magnus moved between them and Frank put his hands on Ralph's shoulders. "Calm down, mate. Count to ten or something. There's no need for this."

Ralph glared at Frank, cracking his knuckles. Then his face cleared, his body loosened, and he nodded, suddenly ashamed.

"Sorry," Ralph muttered.

"It's okay." Frank turned. "You okay, Joel?"

Joel nodded. He didn't look at Ralph.

They walked onwards.

* * *

Slinfold was silent. The men entered the village while dusk fell.

They walked up the high street of dark houses and shadowed windows. No infected came at them. No distant shrieks or screams. No birdsong. No sounds of animals. There was a red Range Rover on its side and dried blood around it. A pair of polished shoes had been left by the edge of the pavement, as if someone would return soon to collect them. There was a strange smell in the air, faint, but noticeable once you knew it was there. A chemical taint. Something Frank associated with public swimming pools and cupboards full of cleaning agents.

Dead birds littered the ground. Blackbirds, sparrows and crows. Black, beady eyes. Yellow beaks and grey beaks. Dark feathers fluttering in the breeze.

Magnus's mouth fell open when he saw the carpet of avian bodies.

"Another ghost town," said Ralph, switching on his torch and lighting up the shop doorways he passed.

"Where is everyone?" asked Frank.

"No idea."

"There they are." Joel nodded towards the end of the street.

Bodies piled on top of one another. A large mound of corpses.

Frank spat.

They walked to the bodies. No one spoke. The top of the pile was higher than the tallest of them; Joel was over six feet tall but the pile of remains towered over him. The men were swallowed by its shadow. Frank looked down at the bodies dried out like the husks of dead crabs. Many of them had died as if reaching out for a loved one as they lay on the ground. Doughy slack faces. Bent and entwined limbs. Glazed, bulging eyes and mouths frozen in their last screams. Some of them had died raking their fingers on the road. Fluids had leaked from mouths, eyes, ears, and dried into dark stains like colonies of mould.

Frank watched a beetle crawl over a woman's face and into her mouth.

To think that Florence was among the dead here almost floored him. He didn't know if he could come back from seeing her within the tapestry of stiff limbs and waxen faces. Not again. Not after losing Emily.

There were even dead dogs and cats within the pile. Pets with collars and name tags. Frank shivered with revulsion and sadness. A pool of darkness formed in his stomach and he wanted to cry at all of the pointless death before him.

"These people weren't infected when they died," said Ralph.

"I can't see any bullet wounds," Magnus said. "None of them were shot. How long have they been dead?"

"Couldn't have been long," said Frank.

"Chemical weapons," said Ralph. "Gas, maybe. Some kind of nerve agent. Who knows what the army and the government have got tucked away waiting to be used? More shit than we'll ever know about."

"It gets worse and worse," said Magnus.

"What kind of gas?" said Frank. His great-granddad had fought at the Somme and Passchendaele during the First World War, but had died before Frank was born. Joseph Hooper never said much about his time in the trenches, Frank's father once told him, but he could imagine the hell of France and Belgium back then. Gas attacks. Mud and slaughter. Men choking, clawing at their throats as they died.

Frank wiped his sweat-soaked face. His throat had dried and closed up. He felt a great urge to touch the corpses; to reach out and touch their hands, run his fingers down a dead man's cold palm.

He suppressed a burst of laughter.

He thought he could hear someone crying far away, a sound echoing down the empty streets, but it wasn't real. He looked at his hands and they were shaking.

"So the army killed these people then piled them here?" asked Magnus.

"Looks like it," Frank said.

"Maybe it wasn't the army that did this," said Joel.

"Who else would have done this?" said Frank.

"The things in the sky, maybe," said Magnus, and the other men looked at him.

"How bad are things going to get?" said Joel, his face pale, sagging and forlorn. "Those kids and these people. All this death."

"Are we in danger?" Magnus asked.

"From what?" Ralph stared at the bodies.

"Whatever killed these people."

"We should leave," said Joel. He was holding one hand over his mouth and nose.

"If we've been contaminated," said Ralph, "it's too late now."

"Are you sure?" Joel's voice was muffled under his hand.

"If there was still a danger, we'd already be dead."

"I admire your confidence," said Magnus.

Ralph regarded the sky. "We should find somewhere to spend the night. Just because there're no infected here at the moment doesn't mean any won't pass through."

"Agreed," said Frank, turning away from the pile of bodies. His body still ached, and every time he moved was a moment of dull pain.

"We can't stay in this village," Joel said.

Ralph looked at him. "Why not?"

"Because we can't."

"We haven't got a choice."

"It doesn't seem right."

"Why? You afraid of offending those poor bastards?" Ralph gestured to the bodies.

Joel looked away.

"We'll find a house at the other end of the village," said Frank. "It'll be okay, Joel."

Joel ignored him.

"I hope there aren't more bodies," said Magnus. "I'm sick of seeing bodies."

Ralph picked something from his teeth then flicked it away. "Doesn't matter. Bodies are just bodies. It's all just meat."

CHAPTER FORTY-SEVEN

The men found an empty house and made it their own for the night. Ralph secured the doors and closed the curtains.

They made sure to check the attic.

Joel removed the family photos from the walls and formed them into a pile in the corner. No one questioned his motives. They knew why, and they were grateful.

They gathered around Frank's map in the living room. Ralph had lit a candle he'd found in a drawer, confident that the curtains would hide the light from outside. They ate a sparse meal of cold hot dogs and baked beans from tins liberated from the kitchen cupboard. Ralph found a bottle of cheap whiskey; it tasted like badger piss but warmed Frank's insides. The warmth gave him hope, numbed the edges, and made it easier to think about Florence.

Joel hardly touched his food. Ralph ate the rest of his share. Joel was silent. He was lying on the floor, sipping from a bottle of water, gazing at the ceiling.

"All we seem to do is hide in other people's houses," said Magnus. "Dead people's houses."

Ralph swigged a shot of whiskey. The candlelight made his face flicker with shadow. "Would you rather be out on the streets tonight?"

"I'd rather go for a ride on your mother," Magnus said.

No one laughed.

Ralph nodded. He tipped his almost-empty glass towards Magnus in acknowledgement. "Well played."

Magnus looked guilty. "I shouldn't be making jokes. Not after the things we've seen."

"I know what you mean," said Frank.

"It doesn't matter," Ralph said. "Things are fucked anyway. Cracking a few jokes won't make things any worse."

Magnus looked at the floor.

Ralph exhaled, a wistful look on his face. He met Frank's eye. "I thought we'd lost you, mate. I thought you were dead."

"Yeah," said Magnus, his eyes a little glazed. He rubbed his jaw.

Frank winced as his spine clicked. "I'm sorry for leaving, lads. I won't go out there on my own again."

"Good to hear," said Ralph. "Can't have you leaving me with Magnus and Joel. It's a nasty job trying to keep them from kissing and cuddling every five minutes."

The three men laughed. Joel remained unmoving.

Their laughter cut out. The men looked at the floor, as if ashamed of themselves. To Frank, it felt strange and even offensive, to laugh after what he'd seen today. He took a large swig of his drink. His throat burned. The alcohol hit his bloodstream and his head went a little fuzzy. He welcomed the buzz.

Frank was studying the map. He'd folded it into a small rectangle that showed Southern England. He placed his finger on a spot on the map.

"We're here," Frank said. "Slinfold. You see?"

Magnus and Ralph nodded.

Frank ran his finger westwards along the map. "And these are Loxwood, Ansteadbrook, Haslemore, Bordon. Various towns and villages."

"I wonder what we'll find in them," said Magnus. He didn't look optimistic as he put down his empty glass.

Frank said, "I was supposed to take Florence to her aunt and uncle in Bordon. I promised her."

"It wasn't your fault she was taken," said Ralph.

"I still feel like shit."

"We all do, mate; it's the end of the fucking world."

"She's gone," said Magnus. "There's nothing we can do about that now."

Frank downed the rest of his glass then looked at Ralph. "Refill, please."

"Good idea," Magnus said.

Ralph nodded. He replenished their glasses and his own.

They drank, grimaced at the taste of the whiskey, and then studied the map.

Frank said, "We'll skirt the northern edge of the South Downs National Park, avoiding Farnham, Basingstoke and Winchester. The next big population centre will be Salisbury."

Ralph sucked on his teeth. "The army might have razed Salisbury to the ground."

Magnus looked shocked. "Would the government do that?"

"I don't think they will," said Frank. "Guppy told me that the army is regrouping in Salisbury."

"Why in Salisbury?" asked Ralph.

"Because all the main roads go through there. He also said they were transporting refugees by train out of the city. Salisbury's important to the government and the army. They won't want to lose it to the infected."

"It's probably a fucking battleground by now."

"Let's worry about that when we get there," said Frank. "We might not even get that far."

Ralph grunted. "I'm impressed; you sound as pessimistic as me."

"I've had a bad few days," Frank said without humour. "We all have." He was struggling to hold it all together, and it wouldn't take much for him to fall apart. But that was true for all of them, he supposed.

He glanced at Joel and wondered what his friend was thinking.

"We could go around Salisbury," said Ralph. "Avoid it completely."

"That's a possibility, but it would take much longer. I want to get home as soon as possible. And maybe we can catch a ride on a train, if we're lucky."

Ralph and Magnus nodded.

Frank folded the map and put it away. "We'll try to find a car in the morning."

"Maybe something that has enough petrol to take us further than twenty miles this time," Magnus said.

Frank grabbed the whiskey bottle and topped us his glass. He noticed Ralph looking at him.

Ralph was studying him silently. There was no aggression or confrontation in Ralph's face. More like a barely-disguised expression of pity. And concern.

"What's wrong?" asked Frank.

Ralph's face softened. He looked away. "Nothing, mate. Don't hog the whiskey."

CHAPTER FORTY-EIGHT

Just before midnight Frank was in the kitchen, staring out at the darkness. The clouds had receded; the moon was revealed, stark and clear and pale. Starlit desolation. Planets and stars and all the things in-between. Pulsars and nebulas and moons. Burning constellations. Infinity.

He was looking into forever, and it stretched before him and declared he was as insignificant as one of the dead insects on the windowsill. He rubbed his face and when his hand came away damp he realised he was crying.

Past the back garden and the fields beyond, there were flashes of white light on the horizon.

He listened.

Distant booms and detonations.

"War," he whispered.

* * *

The four men watched from the back garden. They passed the whiskey bottle back and forth until it was dry.

315

The distant horizon was lit up by tracer rounds and muzzle flashes; the crack and pop of gunfire.

"I watched a documentary last week," said Ralph. "It was about World War Two. Old footage of battles and night time skirmishes. It was like this."

"Last week seems like years ago," said Frank.

"I remember watching the invasion of Iraq," said Joel. "The night-vision shots of Baghdad being bombed…" His voice trailed off.

Silence fell upon them. Nothing else to say.

Magnus asked, "Do you think we're winning?"

* * *

Frank awoke a few hours later on the living room floor. The others were asleep. He'd dreamt about monsters that wanted to eat him.

There was an approaching sound. He pulled aside the curtain over the living room window and looked onto the street. Darkness. Nothing out there but the other silent houses.

Headlights were coming up the road.

A convoy of civilian vehicles passed through the street. Frank counted them as they went past. Fifteen, in all. Cars, trucks and minibuses full of people. Refugees. Survivors.

He didn't go outside to stop them; he didn't want to leave his hiding place.

The convoy passed out of sight.

"Where are you all going?" he whispered.

He went back to sleep.

* * *

They left the house at first light. A cold breeze pushed them onward below clouds the colour of concrete and oil smoke.

The crackle of gunfire to the south.

Frank found a battered and ugly Volvo. It took four attempts to start the engine, and when it did it spluttered into a gargled cough of fumes and oil-stink.

Fighter jets sliced the sky overhead.

The men left Slinford and its dead behind. Magnus drove.

Joel seemed to have recovered slightly. He had eaten the remaining four biscuits from the plastic bag. He still looked pale, but that could have been the morning light casting his skin in shades of ivory and chalk.

There were wrecks on the roads. Shattered glass and crumpled metal. Collisions and accidents from days ago, when the outbreak had first hit. Magnus slowed the car to manoeuvre around them, careful not to puncture the tyres on the broken glass that littered the road.

They passed a car transport truck that had ploughed through a wooden fence and into a field, shedding much of its load of brand-new cars, which were now scattered around like a child's neglected toys. The transport truck was on its side. It would stay there for a long time, maybe years.

They passed a few groups of refugees on the road, but with Ralph's insistence they ignored their pleas for help. Frank looked back at the people struggling with injuries and children, and felt a stab of guilt. These people, lame and shuffling along the road, would be easy prey for the infected.

There was a silence in the car that Frank didn't like. He kept thinking of Florence. The shame and guilt he felt for losing her was strong and potent in his blood.

Then he saw something that quickened his heart and turned his mouth dry and dusty.

"Slow down," he said.

"It's just another wreck," said Ralph.

"No, it's not. Pull over. Now!"

Magnus protested, but stopped the car.

"The white van," said Frank. "That's the van they took Florence in."

"Are you sure?" said Ralph.

"Yes."

Frank was out of the car and approaching the crashed van. He stood away from it, clutching his axe in one hand. Rush of blood in his head. He swayed. He ignored the dull pain throbbing in his muscles.

The van was on its side against a sloped grass embankment. At the top of the slope were trees, their branches creaking, curled and gnarled.

The driver's door was open.

"Florence," he whispered. He opened the back doors of the van, stepped back. His eyes were wide and stinging. Insects swarmed within his ribcage, skittering over bone.

"Frank!" Ralph said.

Frank slumped. The back of the van was empty. Dirty blankets piled to one side. Empty tins of baked beans. A stink of sweat and grease. No sign of Florence.

Ralph stood behind Frank. "What the fuck are you doing, mate?"

"She was here."

"Who? The girl?"

"Her name is Florence."

Frank barged past Ralph. There was some blood on the road. A scrap of clothing. Tyre marks burned into the tarmac.

"Looks like they hit something," said Joel.

In the grime and dirt on the side of the van was a small handprint. Small fingers splayed apart. A girl's hand. Frank traced a finger around it. He went to the cab. Empty. The windscreen was cracked. There were splotches of blood on the driver's seat.

The others were standing at the front of the van, inspecting the bumper.

"They definitely hit something," said Joel.

"Blood on the bumper and number-plate," said Ralph. "Almost looks black." He touched the bonnet. "Engine's still warm."

"Where did they go?" said Magnus.

Joel looked at the blood on the road. "What did they hit? An animal?"

"One of the infected?"

"There," said Ralph. He pointed down the road.

They turned. A dark shape was lying on the embankment, ten yards away.

Ralph raised the flare gun, walked towards the prone shape. The others followed. Frank swallowed and it was like slivers of metal scraping his throat.

"Roadkill. Lovely." Ralph spat.

The woman was a broken jumble of twisted limbs. The van had thrown her this far. Skin hung in tatters from her bare legs. Her right foot was turned wrong way. When the men gathered around her, she moved, gulping a breath of air and fixing what remained of her face upon them in turn.

She hissed; the sound of sickness and hunger. Her chest rose and fell spasmodically. She reached her left hand towards them, as if imploring them for help.

From somewhere nearby rose the shrieks and wails of the infected. The woman listened to them. Her body was shaking. She screamed in reply and the men stepped away.

"Fuck this," said Ralph. "Let's go."

"What about her?" said Magnus.

Ralph looked like he'd tasted something nasty. "Forget her."

"Where did they go?" said Frank, glancing around. "Florence!"

"Shut up," said Ralph.

"Florence!"

"Shut up!" Ralph grabbed him.

"Where is she? Where did they take her?"

"She's gone."

"Ralph's right," said Magnus.

There was something small and white in the grass, half-hidden amongst dandelions and daisies. Frank recognised it. He broke from Ralph's hold and picked it up.

"What is it?" asked Magnus.

Frank turned it around in his hand. The golf ball he'd given to Florence. He imagined her holding it, terrified and alone, in the back of the van.

The smiley face grinned.

"I gave this to her. To cheer her up."

The others looked at him.

Frank stared down the road. "I think she's still alive. They couldn't have gone far."

"Fair enough," said Ralph. He took the axe from Frank's hand and walked over to the infected woman. She was making a low mewling sound, like a dying cat.

He ended her suffering.

"I'm driving," said Frank.

CHAPTER FORTY-NINE

Two miles along the road, Frank stopped the car.

A man and a woman had pinned Mackie, and were peeling him like a soft fruit.

"He's one of the men who took Florence," said Frank.

The infected had torn away Mackie's clothes, which lay strewn around them, ripped and bloody. Their mouths snapped at the man's body, picking away bits of him.

Mackie was still alive.

Frank grinned, and he didn't care.

The infected glared at the car, distracted from the meat of Mackie's tender parts. Wet mouths and mad eyes. They held Mackie tenderly. His mouth was moving. Frank couldn't hear him.

Mackie reached towards the car with a flayed, dripping-red arm.

The infected gathered him up like a pile of wet rags and dragged him off the road, where they would pull him apart in the deep shadows.

The last thing Frank saw of Mackie was his red hand trailing behind him.

* * *

Frank stopped the car on a hill looking down at the surrounding fields and roads. Ahead of them was the village of Loxwood. Ralph swept the area with the binoculars. The village looked empty.

Smoke stained every horizon. War upon the land.

"I see something," said Ralph.

"What is it?" Frank asked.

"Not sure."

Frank snatched the binoculars. Ralph pointed to where he'd been looking. Frank saw a flash of movement among the fields. A brief sighting of something pink and small at the edge of the village.

His body tightened. Adrenaline kicked in, dosing his blood.

Three figures were walking across a field towards the village. Two men and a young girl. Bertram, Florence, and the bastard with the balaclava. Both men were injured and hobbling. Bertram was holding a machete. Balaclava corralled Florence along with his baseball bat. Her head was bowed, avoiding eye contact with the men.

Rage was like bleach in Frank's veins. "It's them. It's Florence. We have to get down there before they reach the village and find a car."

Ralph took the binoculars then looked through them. "What is that down there?"

"What's wrong?" said Magnus.

When Ralph took away the binoculars from his eyes, his face was severe and concerned. Frank grabbed the binoculars.

Something was following Florence and the men, keeping its distance and hiding from them as it moved closer. A pale tumultuous form flitting between trees and patches of grassland like it was carried on the wind. It moved quickly. Very quickly.

"Oh fuck, what *is* that?" said Joel.

Frank ran to the car.

* * *

They reached the village minutes later. Frank stopped the car and they got out. A baseball bat, speckled with blood, had rolled to a stop by the kerb.

There was a soft gurgling sound from down the street.

"We were too late," said Frank.

They walked around the corner.

325

"Oh my God," said Joel. He put a hand to his face and touched his mouth.

The creature was a travesty of sagging, corpse-white skin and wheezing breath. It held the fundamental shape of a human being, but its flesh and muscle was twisted and wrinkled. Tumours bulged under its skin, expanding and retracting as it breathed through a clenching ruby-lipped mouth. It was hunched over, withered vestigial arms dangling from its body, as it steadily absorbed the man in the balaclava.

The man's arms moved in spasms. His eyes opened. His mouth opened but nothing came out. No words, just incoherent fear and terror.

"Fuck," said Magnus.

As they watched, the monster puffed out and expanded like a creeping growth, losing its human shape to a blubbery mass of mottled flesh that enveloped the man slowly, as if the creature were savouring the absorption of its prey. It was like a giant unshelled mollusc. Dozens of small yellow eyes opened on the creature's body. Prickly tendrils grew from its flanks; some of them sensed Frank and the others, and their slick tips tasted the air like awful tongues.

The man vanished beneath the monster. His muffled cries could be heard from underneath the creature's pulsing flesh.

The creature seemed to swell and enlarge even more until it was the size of a large car. The man screamed once as the creature's mass made several violent shudders, and there was a sucking, scouring sound. Slopping wetness, like a pig slurping from a bucket.

Ralph aimed the flare gun at the pulsing thing. His arm was steady. He didn't fire. He lowered the gun and shook his head. No need in wasting a flare.

He watched in awe, with something like admiration.

The creature made a moaning, pleasurable sound. Ralph realised he was fascinated by the creature...and the other creatures newly-born to the land. He liked to watch nature documentaries, and was fascinated by nature's cruelty; lions hunting gazelles and zebras; crocodiles lunging out of rivers to drag wildebeest into the water; eagles snatching monkeys from tree branches and carrying them off to their nests for their young. The dance between predator and prey.

"Amazing," he said.

The creature looked at Ralph with its many yellow eyes. Then it looked at the flare gun in his hand. It feared neither.

He respected them, the infected; the monsters, the abominations. They held no pretensions. They didn't hide anything. No delusions about what they were, unlike people. They were honest and they were truthful. Honest in their intentions to ingest or infect you. They were what they were, and nothing else. No lies, dishonesty, betrayal, hatred or ignorance.

No prejudice.

No evil.

No humanity.

The creature's protean mass began to diminish, deflating itself until it returned to its original size. The pulsing stopped, its eyes closed and its tendrils lowered to become slack and idle upon its tumorous mass.

It had fed well, and now it would sleep.

There was a cry of pain from beyond the creature.

"Florence," said Frank.

They left the creature to its gluttonous slumber and staggered down the street.

* * *

They found Florence standing over Bertram's corpse slumped against a wall. Bertram's face was raw and wet, mutilated by a sharp edge. His right eye had been cut away. His throat had been slashed. His chest was a network of red wounds.

Florence turned to the men. She was holding Bertram's machete. The blade dripped red into a pool by her feet. Blood on her face and her arms. She was shaking, but seemed unhurt.

Frank's eyes met with hers. They were shadowed with dull patches and appeared too large for her small face.

"He tried to take me away," said Florence. "He tried to touch me, so I took his knife and I…"

"It's okay. Everything's alright." Frank knelt beside her, looked into her face. He forced a smile, relief and horror flooding through him. "Are you okay? Did they hurt you?"

She shook her head. She radiated heat.

"Did they do anything to you? Anything bad?"

She knew what he meant. Again, she shook her head.

Frank took the machete from her and dropped it on the ground. Behind him, the others were staring at Florence, their mouths open. They said nothing.

"You came back for me," she said.

"I would never leave you."

Florence began to cry, and she wrapped her arms around Frank's neck and hugged him, staining him with Bertram's blood.

He didn't care. He couldn't stop smiling.

CHAPTER FIFTY

They kept to the back roads. Rain gathered in the heavy skies. The wind had picked up. Ralph stared out the window at a lone figure in the fields they passed. It was a naked man, his hands clasped over his chest like he was uttering a plea upon the sodden earth. The man's stomach was distended and rippling; suddenly, it split into a vertical slavering mouth lined with human teeth.

The man fell to his knees.

Ralph looked away.

The girl was sitting between Ralph and Frank on the backseat. She was resting her head on Frank's chest; he had his arm around her. He had cleaned her face of Bertram's blood.

Ralph had never been good with kids; they were just more annoying versions of adults. He could tolerate them, but barely.

Florence had clung to Frank ever since they'd left Loxwood. She had eyed Ralph, Magnus and Joel with suspicion, but Frank had convinced her that they were the good guys, not bad men like those who had taken her. Frank had told her that they were going to look after her and keep her safe from the monsters.

Ralph remembered the girl standing over the man she had killed. He wasn't shocked anymore. He admired her. It required strength of will to take a life.

Frank caught Ralph's eye and nodded. Ralph could tell that Frank cared deeply for the girl. They shared something. A bond. The girl's resemblance to Frank's daughter Emily was uncanny. Frank hadn't mentioned that detail before, and because Florence and Emily were so similar, Ralph was concerned about how his friend was reacting to her presence. He had seen the change in Frank even before they had found Florence in Loxwood.

Emily had died two years ago. They had all mourned her. A child's funeral was possibly the most heart-breaking thing in the world. Ralph had watched Frank and Catherine grieve and suffer, and eventually heal, but not fully, never fully. But they had recovered.

Ralph looked at Frank.

Frank was smiling.

* * *

Roads strewn with wrecks and human remains. A milk tanker was resting on its side across the width of one road. Milk had leaked to create a congealed white mud around the stricken vehicle. They had to reverse and take a side road that was no more than a muddy lane littered with broken tree branches and potholes.

A house was burning and there were people standing around it, staring at the flames.

The sky turned black for a few hours and when it rained it was like something unworldly. Something that could have been magnificent in a different time.

They passed lone travellers hitchhiking. People packed into cars, just like they were. Riders on motorbikes and bicycles.

They passed Haslemere, Hindhead, and Liphook. Dead places.

Magnus wanted to forget what he witnessed there. A dark mass birthed inside him and festered. It stayed there like an itch he couldn't scratch. He wanted to forget a lot of things. He wanted to go home.

When he saw a dead child face down by the road, he felt like crying. He kept his hands gripped onto the steering wheel so he couldn't see how badly they were shaking.

Great flocks of the infected stained the land, hunting the refugees. Monsters and men. Dead livestock littered the fields. Bodies of men, women and children by the roadside.

They passed a crashed Boeing airliner in a field of rapeseed. A torn fuselage among the garish yellow. Scattered wreckage. Rows of seats with their occupants still seated in them. Handbags and shoes. Spilled suitcases. Discarded clothes fluttering on fences and hanging on tree branches. Sheets of paper and Styrofoam cups drifted in the wind. More bodies pulverised and shredded; some had come to rest hundreds of yards from the airliner. A severed human head was on the road. The infected picked through the remains, scavenging carrion.

"My God," said Joel.

Magnus was speechless.

"Don't look," Frank told Florence.

She asked, "Are we nearly in Bordon?"

"Yes. Almost there."

CHAPTER FIFTY-ONE

Magnus stopped the car at the outskirts of Bordon. A red moped once used for pizza delivery was lying by the kerb.

Frank turned to Florence. "Where do your auntie and uncle live? Do you know where their house is?"

The girl put her hand to her mouth, concentrated on the floor. "It's near the church, I think. It's a dead-end where they live."

"A dead-end?" asked Frank.

"A cul-de-sac," said Ralph.

Florence looked at Ralph, her face creasing. "Cul-de-sac," she said slowly.

Frank said, "Do you know what road they live on? What it's called?"

She shook her head. "Their house has a wall at the bottom of their front garden. On the gate is a sign that says 'Beware of the dog'...but they haven't got a dog."

Ralph scratched his mouth. "Well, that narrows it down."

"We'll find them, Florence," Frank said.

Ralph looked at Frank and shook his head.

"I hope they're okay," said Florence. "You don't think they're dead, do you?"

"I'm sure they're fine."

Ralph was sure that Florence's aunt and uncle were either dead or infected.

Frank smiled at Florence. "It'll all be okay. Just you wait and see."

* * *

The car entered the cul-de-sac. A crescent of eight houses in a row. Cars parked on driveways; other driveways were empty. There were dried patches of dark fluid on the pavement. A woman's high-heeled shoe on the road. Houses with dark windows. Closed front doors.

Magnus pulled up outside the house.

"Is that it?" Frank asked Florence. "Is that the house?"

A 'BEWARE OF THE DOG' sign was on the gate. There was a wooden bird-bath, leaning to one side, crusted with seeds and droppings.

Florence nodded.

The house was silent and still. The curtains were closed. It looked abandoned. But appearances can be deceiving, thought Ralph.

"Let's go then," said Frank. "Florence, you stay here with Magnus and Joel, okay?"

"But I want to see my aunt and uncle…"

"You will, but I need to check it first."

"Is it safe for us to wait here?" Magnus asked.

Frank said, "If you get any trouble, beep the horn."

Magnus nodded but didn't look convinced. He glanced back at Ralph, his face drooping and weary. Ralph met his eyes, winked.

"Ready to go?" said Frank.

Ralph nodded.

"Good luck," said Joel. He handed a torch each to Frank and Ralph, who then exited the car. Ralph was holding the flare gun; Frank hefted his axe, scanning the area around them.

The world was silent. Ralph liked the silence.

"After you," said Ralph.

Frank opened the gate. The two men walked up the stone path to the house.

"What if they're still home," Ralph asked. "And they don't want visitors?"

"What?"

Ralph gestured towards the house. "What if Florence's uncle and aunt are armed to the teeth in there…?"

"They could be infected," said Frank.

"That's what I meant by 'to the teeth'."

"Idiot."

"So we'll just knock on the door and ask to come in?"

"We'll see what happens."

The lawn was snooker table green. Gnomes watched them with dead eyes and wicked smiles, having a whale of a time. White beards and pointy hats. One of the gnomes was standing by the small pond, holding a fishing rod. Goldfish sucked tiny bugs from the water's surface.

"Why are we here?" asked Ralph.

"What do you mean?"

"You know what I mean."

"I promised Florence I'd take her here so she'd stay with me. I have to show Florence that I'm here to look after her. It's the only way she'll trust me."

"You want her to stay with us, don't you?"

Frank avoided Ralph's gaze. "She's safer with us. We can look after her."

"She's not ours to look after. She's not our responsibility."

"Yes, she is. Her parents are dead. I saved her back in Wishford. We can't just leave her. She won't survive without us."

"Without you, you mean."

"What?"

"I've seen how you look at her."

"Shut up, Ralph."

"She's not Emily. She's not your daughter."

"I know that."

"Do you? I'm not sure you do. I think your judgement is clouded by her resemblance to Emily."

"Stop saying her name."

"Emily's gone. Florence can't replace her."

"Shut up," said Frank. "Please shut up."

"I'm looking after you, mate. I don't know if Joel and Magnus have noticed it, as well, but I'm sure they'd say the same as me."

"You don't know anything."

"I know more than you think. Florence can't replace Emily. Florence isn't your daughter. You can't be her surrogate father."

Ralph looked through one of the windows and cupped his face. He could only see shadows and suggestions of dim shapes. Nothing moved. His breath bled from his mouth and fogged the glass.

"I have to protect her," Frank said. "It's meant to be. What choice do we have?"

Ralph stared at him. Frank met his stare and didn't flinch.

"If her aunt and uncle are alive, do you promise to let Florence go with them?"

Frank closed his eyes. Opened them. "I promise."

"Good."

"But part of me hopes we don't find them."

"Fair enough. I figured that. But if we do, you let her go. I'll make you, if I have to. Our only aim should be getting home, not babysitting some orphaned little girl."

"What else should I have done? Abandoned her? Left her to die?"

"She's not our problem. You were never obliged to rescue her. We have to look after our own. You've risked your life to keep her safe. You could have left Catherine a widow just because of your fucking morals."

"I don't want to argue, Ralph. Florence is just a little girl."

"You should have left her to die. Survival of the fittest. Darwinism."

Frank gripped his axe tighter.

Ralph stared back at him. But then turned away from him and looked at the front door. "Do you want to knock?"

Frank twisted the door knob, pushed the door open. He looked at Ralph. "Ladies first."

Ralph stepped through the doorway.

* * *

Ralph held the flare gun and the torch, expecting something to leap at him from one of the rooms. The hallway was tidy, nothing out of place. Coats hanging on a rack. A pair of woman's tennis shoes placed together. Paintings on the wall. Looked like some sort of modern art, all weird shapes and bright colours, a nonsense greater than the sum of its parts. There was a small table in the hallway, topped with ceramic ornamental fairies, coins and an opened packet of chewing gum.

A stairway beckoned him upstairs. Ralph turned away. Frank was checking the living room. Ralph followed him. Frank opened the curtains, letting in daylight. A beige carpet. Cream-coloured walls and a three-piece-suite. No bodies. A faint smell of air freshener. Ralph saw a stack of science fiction novels on a table in the corner; Isaac Asimov, Ray Bradbury, Arthur C. Clarke, and that bloke who wrote the book *Blade Runner* was based upon. A painting of Niagara Falls above the fireplace. More photos of a man and a woman. Looked to be in their thirties. They were hugging in each photo. And smiling. Lots of smiling. Ralph already disliked them.

"Look here," said Frank.

Ralph looked. There was a photo of Florence and two adults. Her parents. Frank stared at the photo until Ralph took it from him and replaced it on the mantelpiece.

"Come on. Let's check the rest of the house."

Ralph pulled back the curtains in the kitchen. There was a smell of yeast and sweat.

A man's clothes had been discarded on the floor. A blue t-shirt and khaki trousers. Black socks and boxer shorts.

"What do you think of that?" said Ralph.

Frank crouched, prodded the t-shirt with his axe. "Weird."

"That sums up the last few days."

"They're not torn," said Frank.

"But it looks like they've been taken off in a hurry."

"True."

"Do you smell that?"

"As soon as I walked in here. It's like yeast."

"That's what I thought."

"What is it?"

"Nothing good."

There was a door leading away from the kitchen into dreamy shades of ash and darkness.

"You want to go through that door, don't you?" said Ralph.

Frank stood and looked at him.

"You know, mate, you could just tell Florence that we couldn't find her aunt and uncle, then she's all yours to look after."

A flicker passed over Frank's face. Maybe he was considering it. He shook his head. "It would be easy, wouldn't it? But it wouldn't be right. We have to do this properly."

"You and your conscience."

"What do you think's through that door?"

"Another room," said Ralph. "Maybe a cellar."

They switched on their torches.

* * *

A set of steps led down beneath the house. Frank went down first.

Their torchlights revealed a damp cellar dripping moisture from its walls. A dirty stone floor stained with mould. Cardboard boxes and junk piled in shadowed corners. Ralph's face brushed against a cobweb, and he swatted it away with his hand. He ignored the thought of a spider skittering across his body to lay eggs in a sweaty fold of his skin.

A woman was sitting cross-legged with her back against the wall directly opposite them as they stepped onto the cellar floor. Her face was revealed in the torchlight. She raised her head, her eyes glazed and large inside the moon-like frailty of her face. Her blonde hair was lank and greasy, hanging to her shoulders. Naked, save for her underwear, she grinned at the men as they halted before her.

Florence's aunt. Ralph recognised her from the photos.

She let out a short, high-pitched giggle. Wiped her mouth with the back of a pale, veiny hand.

The smell of yeast filled the air down here. It had become the air. The moist, pickling smell of fermentation.

Ralph said nothing. Frank said nothing. They directed their torch beams around the cellar.

Symbols and shapes had been carved into the wall above the woman's head. Strange eldritch sigils. Crescents and nonsense shapes; curlicues and narrow dagger-like triangles. Shapes without meaning, at least to Ralph. All of these symbols were contained within a carved sphere filling most of the wall.

And on the wall to the woman's left, there was something else. They trained their torches upon it, taking a step backwards as they realised what they were looking at.

"Fucking hell," said Ralph.

Frank's mouth fell open. He was blinking quickly, as if doing so would erase the thing on the wall from existence.

"Very soon," said the woman. A whisper.

It was like a fungus, a sack of pulsing fluids and blubber, reaching from the floor to the ceiling. Fibrous and wet, the same colour as a spider's nest, glistening in the light. Big enough to fit a man and attached to the wall by some sort of resin. Patches of it were transparent. Something moved inside it.

"It's a chrysalis." Ralph stepped forwards.

"Careful," said Frank.

Ralph shone his torch into the glistening sack, and it showed him what was curled up within the briny juice of its amniotic fluid. A shape. On the floor next to the wall there was a pile of dead rats, mice and birds.

The woman was humming a happy tune.

Wetly encased in the sack's sallow skin was a head, a torso, and legs. The curved line of a jaw and a dreamy smile. Arms folded into its body, legs raised to its chest. Foetal. In the silence Ralph thought he could hear a heartbeat that wasn't his own, muffled by the protective liquid enveloping it.

"Open your eyes," he whispered to the thing.

The sack's pulsing grew faster, reacting to his proximity.

Ralph held out the torch until it was almost touching the sack; it gurgled like an upset stomach. The creature within flinched.

Ralph wondered if it was dreaming. And what it dreamed of. What was it seeing behind its eyes?

"All flesh is useful," said the woman. "Did you know that?"

Ralph turned to her. "What does that mean?"

"You'll all be welcomed into the flesh. None of you shall go to waste. Every one of you. All the men, all the women…all the little children. All flesh is useful."

Ralph stepped back alongside Frank.

"What're you doing here?" Frank asked the woman.

She looked at him. A secretive grin. "He's going to be a beautiful butterfly. I'm waiting for him to wake up. He'll wake up soon. Maybe today."

"Who is in there?" said Frank.

"Her husband," said Ralph. "Florence's uncle."

The woman's grin faltered. "Florence? I remember that name. A little girl. Part of my blood."

"She's your niece," said Frank.

"That's right," said the woman. "I remember now. Is she here?"

"She's outside," said Frank.

"Maybe you should bring her down here. She can be a beautiful butterfly as well."

"That's not going to happen."

"Maybe not now, but eventually…"

"Never."

She giggled.

"What's happening to your husband?" said Ralph.

Her eyes searched him up and down. The grin never left her face. "He's becoming something else. He's changing. Something better than before. Something stronger."

"He's turning into a monster," said Frank.

The woman's grin consumed her face until she was all teeth and eyes. "I'm waiting for him to emerge. He'll make me like him."

Frank looked at Ralph. "We're done here."

"We could kill them."

"We don't need to. They're not a threat to us. Let them be together. They deserve that, at least."

As they left the cellar, the woman said, "Say hello to Florence for me."

CHAPTER FIFTY-TWO

After leaving Bordon they skirted the northern edge of the South Downs National Park, passing through Alton, Alresford and Kings Worthy.

Frank had told Florence that her aunt and uncle were dead. The girl accepted this without question. She was already traumatised by her parents' death and killing Bertram, so the death of her aunt and uncle didn't make much difference to her. She went to sleep with her head on Frank's chest. It was best for her to sleep.

Poor girl, Magnus thought. *How many other children are orphans now?* At least Florence wasn't alone. Magnus was glad he wasn't alone. At least they were all together.

They bypassed Winchester. The city was burning. A fire so intense it burned an afterimage in Magnus's vision.

That night they stopped the car at a rest area just outside a small village called West Tytherley. The petrol gauge was getting low, but there would be enough to reach Salisbury.

In the morning they would enter the city. Getting closer to home.

The sky darkened into night. No stars. Magnus sensed the presences in the sky and was terrified one of them would find him again.

They were all hungry and thirsty. They slept in the car that night, and they locked the doors. They made sure to lock the doors.

* * *

Joel awoke in darkness, gasping and breathing hard. A second of confusion as to where he was. He rubbed his eyes, and then pulled his jacket up to his chin. The cold air embraced him. He felt like crying. He felt weak. He pulled out his crucifix, enclosed his right hand around it and closed his eyes.

Are you listening? Are you out there? Have you abandoned us?

Abandoned. Such a terrible word.

He opened his eyes, pocketed the crucifix. He inhaled a deep breath.

The others were sleeping. Ralph was snoring.

The stars were visible through a parting in the clouds. He stared at them for a long time. He fell into a trance-like state, his mind untroubled for a while, until the clouds closed and the stars went away again.

He thought of Anya. In the light of his dying mobile phone he opened his wallet and took out the photo of them together, taken on a holiday in Norway. The freezing North. Cold enough to burrow into your skin and snap your bones. Mountains, waterfalls and ice. A land so beautiful it moved you to tears and stirred something wonderful in your soul.

He fell asleep with the photo in his hand.

* * *

Was it a dream or a memory? Or the memory of a dream?

Magnus was in the upstairs hallway of his house, outside Debbie's bedroom. He usually slept in the spare room because she took up so much space, wheezing through her blubbery mouth and wriggling in her sleep.

He was holding a tray of food. A bowl of tomato soup, Debbie's favourite. Four slices of buttered bread. A cup of sugary tea.

He could hear the boys playing downstairs. The thud and crash of the two brothers wrestling drifted up to him. Banging footsteps across the living room and out into the kitchen. One of the boys was crying. Adam, probably; he was smaller and weaker than Grant.

Glass smashed. Grant shouted. Adam was still crying.

Magnus shook his head. A vague depression settled upon him. The house smelled of dust, neglect, and Chinese takeaways rotting in a bin. A dirty carpet beneath his feet.

He looked down at the tomato soup and considered spitting into it, and then considered ejaculating into it. Cream of tomato. He wanted to throw the tray against the wall and scream. He wanted to leave. He wanted to be free again. The bond to his family was like a fraying rope gradually unravelling.

"Magnus, are you out there? I'm hungry."

His body sagged, the air rushing out of him like he was a punctured balloon. He dug his fingers into the plastic tray, fought the urge to walk downstairs and out of the house.

Never come back.

"Yes, dear. I'm coming."

Balancing the tray on one arm, he opened the door. The smell that greeted him made his eyes water. The curtains were drawn against the sunny morning. The only light in here was the lamp on the nightstand. Its glow was yellow and dirty. Old wallpaper was peeling off at the corners.

Debbie was on the bed, an obese mass beneath a stained duvet. A pallid moronic face, and bovine eyes, dull and glazed. Crumbs in one corner of her mouth. Knotted, greasy hair.

"Here you go, dear," Magnus said.

Her eyes tracked him from the door to the bedside.

"I've got your favourite, dear."

Debbie sniffed the air, glared at the tray. "I don't like tomato soup."

"But it's your favourite."

"Used to be. I like chicken soup now."

Magnus made a rigid smile and wanted to tear off her face.

"Take it away. I don't want it. I want chicken soup."

Magnus said nothing. He was imagining making her eat his shit.

Her face bloomed pink. Her eyes shined. "I'm in the mood, Magnus."

"Are you sure, dear?"

"Yes."

"Okay." He put down the tray.

"Undress," she said.

He took off his clothes and then climbed into bed as she pushed aside the duvet. She parted herself to him and she was clammy, moist and stinking. A shellfish opening its gummy cleft. A smell of hot dogs in brine and pickled vegetables. Her large hands

352

guided him into her. He wasn't fully hard. She moaned and writhed, buckling underneath him. She was cold inside.

He took hold of her upper arms and thrust his hips forwards. She raised her hands to her sagging breasts and pinched her nipples. She yelped like a newborn crawling from a broken egg. Magnus pushed again. She pulled him towards her, to kiss her mouth, and her breath was like rot.

Their mouths joined. She moaned and cried beneath him.

Her body began to envelop him. She covered him in pale blubbery flesh until Magnus was a part of her.

He screamed once before he was absorbed.

CHAPTER FIFTY-THREE

Ralph lit a cigarette and watched grey light seep into the sky. He'd stolen the cigarette and the lighter from Magnus. He took a drag, sucked the smoke into his lungs and was grateful for it. He'd given up smoking last year, but now seemed as good a time as any to restart his habit.

He breathed out, listening to the birdsong. Maybe they'd be home by the end of the day. It was possible, although he was inclined not to hope; it wasn't in his nature.

The others were up, too; hands buried in pockets against the chill of the early morning air, their plumes of breath like smoke. They were tired, grey and sullen.

The fields were wreathed in mist. Earlier, when he'd been pissing onto a grass bank, Ralph had seen a family of deer moving silently amongst the white shrouds; ethereal shapes. Nature reminding him that it was still here. He had watched the deer until they vanished into the mist, and he wished them well with a bittersweet smile.

Ralph dropped his cigarette and put it out with one foot.

The sound of engines.

Magnus and Frank were looking down the road. Joel stayed near Florence, biting his nails. Ralph walked to the car.

"What is it?" said Joel.

Ralph loaded the flare gun and pocketed the spare cartridges. "Sounds like company."

Magnus and Frank retreated to the side of the road.

A convoy of military trucks and other vehicles – jeeps and armoured cars – rounded the corner. Ralph remembered the soldiers slaughtering the infected children. He felt cold, suddenly.

"We're saved," said Joel. "We're saved, aren't we?"

The lead truck halted; the rest of the convoy did the same. A soldier jumped down from the cab of the first vehicle and approached them.

There were refugees in the backs of the trucks.

The soldier was talking to Frank and Magnus. Ralph watched. After they had finished talking, Magnus jogged back to the car.

"What's happening?" asked Joel.

Magnus smiled. "They're taking us to Salisbury. They're going to help us get home."

CHAPTER FIFTY-FOUR

Salisbury was a battleground. Smoke and fire. Smashed buildings. Roads clustered with wrecked cars and detritus. Piles of bodies at the roadsides. Streets of abandonment; of those things left behind. There were suitcases and plastic bags, some of which had spilled their contents, left by the roadside. Sporadic gunfire echoed around the city.

The convoy blasted through ruined streets, scraping viscera from the road with their wheels. Fighter jets screamed overhead. The concussion of artillery shells from outside the city made the ground tremble. The refugees in the trucks huddled together, seated on the metal benches or crammed on the floor. When Ralph and the others had climbed aboard the truck, some of the refugees greeted the sight of four grown men and a little girl with suspicion. Not surprising, really. He would have done the same.

Ralph peered through the side of the truck and saw the cathedral's spire, undamaged and resolute, reaching towards the sky. He wondered how long it would remain standing.

Everything fell eventually.

Magnus and Joel were seated either side of him while Frank was sitting on the floor with Florence. She looked at Ralph and he returned her gaze. He didn't smile at her. He turned away as the truck juddered over rubble and potholes. Ralph had heard other people talking. According to the rumours, passed about like germs in the back of the truck, the army was occupying Salisbury. The infected had claimed parts of the city, but the army had pushed them back from most areas. One man, wrapped in a dirty blanket, had said the infected had amassed near the cathedral, where they had made nests and larders to store their dead victims.

Ralph didn't know what to believe.

The convoy halted. The refugees looked at one another. Furtive glances and confusion. Murmurs and whispers amongst the crowded bodies.

They disembarked from the trucks and were corralled along the street. Frank kept Florence close to him, holding her hand. The refugees were herded down the road. Armed soldiers lined the street, watching the crowd. Side roads were blocked by armoured cars and Humvees. Helicopters buzzed the skies.

Gunfire crackled a few streets away.

"Keep moving!" a soldier was shouting. "Don't stop! Keep moving!"

"Where are we going?" asked Florence.

"Just stay close," said Frank. "Everybody stay close."

The crowd streamed into the train station car park. Cars had been shifted so there was space for people to gather. Other masses of people joined until the separate crowds became a huge swarm of refugees. A surging, confused mass of humanity. A herd of terrified animals watching for the predators.

Another soldier was standing on the roof of a tank, speaking through a loudspeaker: "Please stay calm. Move in an orderly fashion. Do not panic. Keep moving."

They moved past a machine gun nest manned by nervous-looking grunts. Ralph met eyes with one of them, a young man of no more than twenty who averted his gaze quickly.

The flow of the crowd slowed until it stopped outside the station entrance.

"Please keep calm," the soldier with the loudspeaker said. "Do not panic."

Rain began to fall.

* * *

The refugees possessing weapons, makeshift or otherwise, were forced to give them up to the army.

Frank handed over his axe without complaint. Ralph stowed the flare gun down his jeans, hoping some grubby squaddie wouldn't look down there. Baseball bats, cricket bats and knives were handed over under protest. Red Cross workers and Salvation Army volunteers distributed blankets and bottles of water. Both items ran out before even a quarter of the refugees received any.

Trains arrived at and departed the station; some travelled straight through, already laden with refugees staring out from clouded windows.

After waiting for what seemed like hours, stuck in the rain, they were finally herded into the train station and onto one of the platforms. They were all drenched and miserable. Ralph was craving a hot shower, a pint of beer, and a plate of toasted cheese sandwiches. Maybe a chicken curry with rice, naan bread, prawn crackers, and poppadums. His mouth watered. His stomach complained. His nose was running. He shivered.

"We're going home," said Joel. "At last. We're going home."

The crowd filled the platform above the tracks. People jostled for room. Small arguments broke out but were quickly subdued by the soldiers. Ralph and the others managed to get to the front of the platform, overlooking the tracks. They were careful not to get pushed off. The rain was coming down fast and hard. Ralph looked towards the horizon and it was all black clouds.

They waited. Pale and expectant faces. Shivering bodies clad in coats or jackets. Hoods pulled up to shelter heads. Huddled families waiting to be saved. Murmurs and whispers. Babies crying. An old lady kept asking anyone who would listen if the train would be arriving before it got dark. No one gave her an answer. She gave up after the eighth time of asking. Then she asked if the rain would stop soon.

More jets roared overhead, lost in the clouds. Some of the children covered their ears. A loud crash from across the city; a mushroom cloud of smoke rose above the buildings and dispersed in the breeze. Someone screamed. Someone told the screamer to shut up.

The battle for Salisbury was raging.

"Are we going on the train?" said Florence.

"Yes," Frank told her.

"Where are we going?"

"We're going to Somerset. "Have you ever been to Somerset, Florence?"

She shook her head. "I don't think so. My dad always said the people who lived there were inbred. What does that mean?"

Ralph couldn't help but laugh.

Frank hesitated. "It means they're nice people."

"Inbred," she said slowly, trying out the word in her mouth.

"We have to get out of here," said Joel. The colour of his face was like curdled milk.

"We will," said Frank. "Be patient."

Joel coughed, scratched a rash developing on the side of his neck. "Me and Anya came to Salisbury last year for a day out shopping. I bought her some nice earrings. We got the train back. We waited on this platform. The train was late, if I remember correctly."

"Sounds about right," said Frank. "I've never liked trains."

"I need a cigarette," said Magnus. "Ralph stole my last one."

An Apache helicopter flew over them then stopped and hovered over one of the streets to the north. It released its missiles at the ground. Unknown targets. An explosion. Flames bloomed and then died. The Apache banked to its left and wheeled away out of sight.

"Boom," said Ralph.

"Fucking hell," Magnus said. "It's almost unreal, isn't it?"

Ralph spat onto the tracks. "Yeah."

"I hear a train coming," said Joel.

A rush of expectation and excitement swept through the crowd. Raised voices. Someone laughed in relief.

"This next train isn't stopping," said a soldier cradling his rifle. "You'll be on the next one."

There were complaints. Dissenting voices. Insults. The soldier ignored them all.

"Where will our train take us?" said Joel. "Will it stop to let us off in Somerset? The train might go straight through Somerset. Do you think they'll let us get off at Yeovil Junction or maybe Crewkerne station?"

No one answered him. No one had a clue.

A train appeared from around the bend in the track, the ugly noise of its engine growing louder.

People were screaming on the platform. Ralph saw the train driver and realised why. The man looked terrified.

Frank turned Florence away from the train as it went past them. Joel held one hand over his mouth. The train, all five carriages of it, was filled with the infected and their victims. Blood painted the windows. Snarling faces smashing against the glass. Red handprints. Windows filled with writhing flesh. The infected screaming to be let out, driven into a frenzy by the proximity of fresh victims.

Rain was pelting the carriages. A great silence descended on the platform as the train went past.

"Infected must have gotten aboard one of the carriages," said an old man next to Ralph. "Slaughter. A fucking slaughter."

"Does that mean we can't go home?" said Joel. He looked ready to burst into tears.

"I don't know," said Frank.

A ripple of sheer panic spread through the crowd. A woman was crying, saying "Oh god, oh god," over and over until she buried her face in her hands.

Voices spoke up from the crammed bodies on the platform. High-pitched with fear as the possibility of being stranded at the station became very real.

"Are there any more trains?"

"We can't stay here!"

"Please help us!"

"All those people are dead!"

The same soldier from earlier addressed the crowd: "There'll be another train along in a minute. Please remain calm."

"Can we still use the track if that train is on it?" said a middle-aged woman carrying a toddler.

The soldier held out his hands. "Yes. It's been diverted onto another track and it'll be dealt with. There's no need to panic."

"Thank fuck for that," said Magnus.

"What if our train has infected on it?" said Joel.

"It's either that or stay here," said Ralph.

Joel looked at him, said nothing.

The sound of a train approached the platform.

"Get ready," said Frank.

CHAPTER FIFTY-FIVE

The rain lessened and became a drizzle against the windows. The train groaned and picked up speed as it headed out of Salisbury with its four carriages packed full of human cargo.

Parts of Salisbury were burning. The sky above the city was bloated by the smoke rising from the fires. The refugees had been crammed onto the train; the aisles were filled, swamped by people holding onto seats to keep their balance. A silence descended aboard the train, allied with relief, misery and a little hope. The smell of dirty bodies, wet hair and waterlogged clothes; the mutter of prayers spoken behind entwined hands. The sense of relief was palpable, but it was tempered by fear and anxiety. Whispers of quiet elation, guarded like secrets. The odour of stagnancy was so thick it had a pulse.

Ralph watched a young boy sitting on his father's lap, picking his nose and examining the stringy mucus on the tip of his finger. The man called him Sam. Ralph wondered what sights the boy had seen in the last few days; the horrors that had hunted him. Sam glanced at Ralph, blessed with the total absence of adult manners and ego, and wiped his finger on his father's jacket without his father realising. Ralph forced a thin smile. Boys would be boys, even as the country was falling into ruin.

Ralph pulled his fingers through his scraggly beard, staring at the floor. So many people around him, suffocating him. He closed his eyes, counted to ten, and then opened them. Deep breaths. His fingers felt tingly and his heart was punching against his ribcage. Too many people. He had been fine earlier when he was on his feet and his mind was occupied; but now, crammed into this metal coffin, his discomfort with large amounts of people and their close proximity was unsettling him, raising his hackles and turning his mouth dry.

Magnus was sitting next to him. Behind them were Joel and Frank, with Florence sitting on Frank's lap. The aisle was filled with standing people. A man's groin was four inches from Ralph's face, and he kept completely still so there was less chance of his nose or mouth accidentally brushing against something dangling and soft.

"You alright, mate?" said Magnus.

"Fucking rosy."

"Did you count to ten?"

"First thing I did."

"Did it help?"

"I'll let you know."

"I forgot to let you have the window-seat, mate. Sorry. Do you want to swap?"

Ralph shook his head. "No, I'm okay. Cheers, anyway."

Magnus patted him on the arm.

Ralph breathed in deeply and took out his stress-ball from one of his pockets. He squeezed it hard. He opened his palm, and the ball was a misshapen lump; it slowly reformed. He squeezed it again until his knuckles had lost their colour.

"We're going home," Magnus said. He sank back into his seat. "Never thought I'd be so glad to get on a bloody train."

"I hate trains," Ralph said. "Did I already mention that?"

"Yeah, but we're going home. It seems a bit surreal now, don't you think?"

Ralph said, "The last few days have been surreal."

"I thought we were going to die out there. We were lucky."

"We're not home yet. Not by a long way."

"Always the optimist."

"Always best to expect the worst, mate."

"And then anything else is a bonus?"

"Spot on."

"That's one way of looking at things."

"It's the only way, my friend."

"You've always been a ray of sunshine."

"I try my best."

Magnus laughed and cleaned his glasses. "Some of the things I've seen…" His voice trailed off. He was shaking his head. "Part of me still finds it hard to believe they're real. I had never seen a dead body before, Ralph."

Ralph looked at him, let him continue.

"I've been constantly terrified for the last few days. Terrified beyond anything I could've imagined. It exhausts you, digs into your sanity."

"You've done well."

"Really?"

"You're still alive, aren't you?"

Magnus looked puzzled.

"Try to get some sleep, mate," said Ralph. "A nap will do you good."

"I am pretty tired." Magnus looked out the window as the train rushed past fields, houses and roads. "Wake me if anything happens, Ralph."

"Will do."

Magnus closed his eyes.

* * *

"I'm never going home again, am I?" said Florence. Exhaustion strained her voice. Her lips were cracked. "I'll never see my house again. I'll never go home. I'll never go back to my bedroom and sleep in my bed."

Frank tried to smile for her. He didn't want to give her false hope. She would never return to Wishford and her old life. That life was dead.

"Maybe one day we'll go back there. When this has been sorted out."

"My parents will never come back."

"I'm so sorry, Florence."

"You say that a lot."

"She's right," said Joel. "You do. Stop saying sorry. It's not your fault."

"What will happen to me now?" Florence asked. "When the train stops…"

"You can stay with me and my wife. Her name is Catherine. She would love to meet you. I reckon you'd both be great friends. We'll look after you."

She eyed him. "Do you and your wife want to be my parents now?"

Her question took him by surprise.

"No one could ever replace your parents, Florence. That wouldn't be right. We're just trying to look after you."

She looked at the floor. "I'm hungry and thirsty."

"So am I," said Frank. "We'll get something when we get off the train."

"Promise?"

"I promise."

"Okay."

Frank wanted to be her father. He couldn't deny it to himself. He looked at Florence, and his chest felt full of air; but it was a good feeling.

He rested his eyes and shut out the world for a little while. He felt Florence's weight on his lap, comforting him. It gave him hope to think that such a delicate creature had survived so far when so many others were dead.

He kept his eyes shut and he could almost pretend that Emily was sitting on his lap.

CHAPTER FIFTY-SIX

Magnus awoke as the world shuddered around him. The squeal of brakes, like an animal pulped beneath the train. A hard jolt and the shock of recoil. Stillness and inertia. Voices and panic. The cry of a child being hushed by its mother.

He'd been dreaming of Debbie and the boys again. He was tired.

The train had stopped. The carriage creaked. He blinked his eyes clean, wiped them with the back of one hand. He yawned. His back and his legs ached fiercely.

The rain had eased off; only a few droplets on the windows. The other refugees were looking down the train. Disquiet and apprehension. A few whispered words. There was a vague smell of opened pores leaking sweat.

"What's happened?" Magnus asked Ralph. "Why have we stopped?"

Ralph spared him a puzzled glance and shrugged.

Magnus pressed his head to the window, tried to see towards the front of the train. Nothing. There were fields on both sides of the train, and beyond them were deep ranks of trees that led into darkness. He stared into the trees for a while. Shadows moved, stopped, and moved again. He got the feeling of something stirring within the inky darkness. His skin broke out in gooseflesh.

He looked away.

"What's going on?" Joel asked from behind. Frank was reassuring Florence.

Anxiety and pent-up anger began to take hold on the collective emotions of the refugees; a single pulse composed of their combined heartbeats, growing faster with every second that the reason for the train's stop was not revealed.

Magnus could hear voices from the next carriage. Arguments were breaking out.

Ralph was looking down the aisle, trying to see past the standing bodies.

"What's going on?" said Magnus.

"Maybe we'll be told in a minute."

The speakers in the carriage buzzed with static, and a tinny voice spoke: "*Uh, please stay calm. Do not panic. There is an obstruction on the track. Do not panic. In a moment the driver will be passing through the carriages to the other end of the train so we can reverse...*"

Cold sweat broke out on Magnus's back and ran down his spine.

The carriage rocked gently on its wheels. At the back of the carriage, a woman screamed. She was pointing out the window, towards the trees flanking the train. Someone asked her what was wrong. She shrank away from the window, her face stretched and pale.

"There's something out there!" she cried. "Something in the trees!"

Magnus looked at the trees. He moved towards the window until his nose was touching the glass. The shadows were moving again. Gaining shape. Coalescing.

Coming towards the train.

He retreated from the window.

A man burst from the trees, sprinting towards the train. He was topless. His jeans had been torn into rags. His upper body had developed dark lesions. His left arm was withered into a hooked appendage. Magnus couldn't hear him, but he could tell that from the shape of the man's mouth and the crazed intent in his eyes, he was screaming.

"Infected!" someone said.

Another man bolted from the trees, running for the train. Then, another. Four, five, six. All of them were horribly deformed.

"They're on the other side as well!" a woman cried.

Heads turned. Magnus managed to peer between the scrum of bodies blocking the aisle, and saw men and women tearing down the field towards the train.

"Oh shit," Magnus said.

The infected emerged from both sides.

Panic broke out on the carriage. The infected kept coming. The fields on either side of the train were filled with them.

Magnus looked past the infected people. He was so scared that his heart almost stopped.

Something large was coming through the trees.

CHAPTER FIFTY-SEVEN

The thing began as an amorphous shadow skulking within the tree line, and then it emerged. Frank's hands tightened around Florence; an instinctive act of protection. The other refugees saw it, too. The carriage was full of screaming and crying. A lone voice begged its god for help that wasn't coming.

The train driver, a plump and sweaty man, was trying to make his way up the aisle, towards the other end of the train. He was struggling to wriggle through the bodies crowding the carriage. He was too big. He shouted and swore at them to let him through. They ignored him, staring at the thing coming at them from out of the trees.

The creature loomed almost thirty feet tall; a spindly, dangling abomination. Frank couldn't take his eyes away from it.

Joel was shaking his head. His eyes were wide and shivering with tears. He rubbed the rash on the side of his neck. He looked at Frank, opened his mouth to speak, but words failed him.

The creature broke through the trees, pushing branches from its path. Frank couldn't see it clearly, but its tall, bloated body appeared to be pulsing. There were tendrils attached to its main mass. Then it opened its mouth, and despite the carriage interior's muffling effect, its screech was high-pitched and anguished. The carriage trembled.

The infected people reached the train and began to pound, scratch and claw upon it. The refugees looked down at them, safe for now, until they found a way inside.

The tall thing skittered across the field on rows of insect legs. It moaned dully as it moved.

"What the fuck is that?" said Ralph.

Frank saw its body in detail for the first time, and he wished it to be the last. The creature halted by the train, looming over it, casting a shadow that darkened the inside of the carriage. Its tendrils were tipped with stingers or sharpened claws. There were human faces partly-submerged within its mass, and the flailing naked arms of those people were hanging from its flesh, their fingers grasping at the air. Faces and body parts were dripping a pale fluid onto the ground. The beast was a growth of half-absorbed bodies and screaming faces. They were still alive. They were part of the creature, assimilated into its body. A monster composed of human bodies and infected flesh.

Those human eyes, so many of them, appraised the contents of the train. One of the eyes, bloodshot and staring, seemed to find Frank and focus on him. It was using the eyes of its human victims to navigate. Its body was veiny and pulsing, throbbing dully and slowly like a pig's heart. It didn't possess a face, but there was a mouth, and it opened just a little into a vulva-like aperture showing pink gums and a glistening passage leading to somewhere he didn't want to visit.

The beast had no teeth. It didn't need teeth.

One of the tendrils scraped against the window, its claw scoring a line in the glass. It left behind a smear of sticky fluid.

"What is it?" asked Joel.

The tendrils shot forward and grabbed the carriage, shaking it. People collided and fell into the aisles.

Magnus said, "I can hear the people inside it. They're talking to me. Can't you hear them?"

"What are they saying?" Frank asked.

"They want to absorb us. Eat us."

"That's good to know," said Ralph.

The beast shuddered and the faces within its body opened their mouths and screamed. It was the sound of a hundred people suffering, trapped in a feverish half-existence of agony and hunger.

"Those poor people," said Joel. "Dear God."

The ceiling of the carriage trembled; there was a ripping, screeching sound and several of the tendrils plunged through the roof, into the carriage. Part of the ceiling directly over the middle of the carriage was ripped away. The beast caught the scent of the people inside the train. The refugees retreated from the ragged hole, scrambling away, panicking and squabbling and screaming.

The tendrils descended. A woman screamed and a tendril whipped towards her and wrapped around her neck. Two men tried to grab her, but the tendril dragged her from where she cowered and took her away. The woman screamed until she was silenced by something wet and sucking. Frank thought of those pink gums and that vaginal mouth and he shivered. Bile rose in his throat. He put himself between Florence and the hole in the ceiling. She was crying.

The two men who'd attempted to save her were also grabbed by other tendrils and taken. Their screams were brief.

More of the roof was ripped away. A screech of metal. A rush of cold air. The hole grew bigger. The sudden stink of the beast, like raw meat.

More tendrils crept through the hole, twitching and jerking at every human heartbeat.

The beast screamed.

Joel screamed.

Others screamed with him.

The beast wanted them all.

The tendrils claimed other refugees, including the driver, and plucked them from the carriage. Neither the tendrils nor the people returned. The beast put its wet mouth to the hole in the roof. There was a gurgling, gagging noise. The fleshy, contracting maw widened until it covered the hole completely.

A clear fluid dripped from the mouth. The gagging sound grew louder. Something pale and wriggling appeared inside the mouth and then dropped into the aisle with a moist slap. The refugees stared at it as they retreated, screaming and shouting

"It's like it's just been born," said Frank.

"Newborn," Ralph said.

The pale thing – the newborn – was a collection of white pincer-limbs, a segmented abdomen and a glistening thorax of mottled flesh. About the size of a large dog. Its skin was wet and coated with creamy mucus dripping from its body. It unfolded itself from the carriage floor and opened its mouth, which was something that shouldn't have existed beyond the pitch-black fathoms of the seas. Sharp mandibles and clicking jaws. It stood on multiple legs, wobbling like a baby giraffe, and cried out in a high pitched shrill that turned Frank's insides to quivering jelly.

The newborn's eyes were like white grapes upon fleshy stalks. A shadow of a dark pupil within each eye. The newborn turned towards a man to its right who was cowering in his seat. The man looked back at it, his eyes wide.

The creature let out another shrill cry.

The man screamed.

The newborn pounced on him, stabbing him with its pincers, making itself part of the man's torso. The man spluttered blood from his mouth. The creature needled him, puncturing his internal organs and slicing him from groin to neck, ravaging his body. His insides fell out like a sloppy surprise.

Screams filled the carriage. The newborn separated itself from the dead man and dropped to the floor, skittering underneath the seats.

Frank looked back at the hole in the roof; into the beast's mouth as it gurgled and gagged.

Ralph was trying to undo his jeans.

"What the fuck are you doing?" Frank asked.

Ralph ignored him, reached into his jeans and produced his flare gun.

Ralph checked the gun was loaded then crept down the aisle until he was beneath the large, wet mouth. His eyes went wide. He aimed the flare gun towards the mouth. His movements were calm and deliberate.

He pulled the trigger. A flash of red light and smoke.

The beast screamed. There was pain within the sound. The flare was fizzling inside the beast. A smell of burning.

Then the carriage was shaking.

"Shit!" cried Joel.

The windows imploded. Flying glass flew and found soft flesh, faces and eyes. Screams of agony. Frank slipped, fell down in the aisle. Ralph collapsed on top of him.

There was a terrible wrenching sound. The world quaked around them. A deep roar. A feeling of moving into the air. Weightlessness that seemed to last for hours. The carriage left the ground. Then a crash. Impact. A pain in Frank's legs. His breath was stolen.

Metal and glass everywhere. Broken, screaming bodies.

By the time Frank came to his senses, he realised the carriage was upside down and he was lying on the ceiling.

Ralph was lying next to him, eyes open and unseeing.

Ralph wasn't moving.

CHAPTER FIFTY-EIGHT

There was screaming, crying and moaning. An unseen woman begged for help. The inside of the carriage was all grey light and bright splashes of blood. Broken windows and warped metal. Bodies lying at contorted angles. The world was askew. The hot smell of opened bodies.

The seats were hanging above Frank. Bags and belongings littered the ceiling.

Frank grabbed hold of Ralph's arm, shaking him. "Ralph! Ralph!"

Ralph blinked. He groaned. He sat up and spat a tooth onto his chest.

"Are you okay?" Frank said.

"Yeah. I *think*."

"You shouldn't have done that. You pissed it off."

Ralph offered a broken grin.

Florence crawled towards them.

"You okay?" Frank asked her.

She nodded, dazed but unhurt.

"Where're Magnus and Joel?" asked Ralph.

"Over here." Magnus was crouching over Joel, who was rubbing his head and moaning. Magnus's forehead was cut, weeping a lazy trickle of blood. He wiped it away before it reached his eyes.

"Are you okay?" said Frank. "Is Joel okay?"

"Yeah, I'm fine," said Magnus.

"Same here," said Joel.

"Where's that little bastard creature?" said Ralph.

"Hopefully it's dead," said Magnus.

The large beast was still outside; Frank could hear its insect legs skittering upon the ground. There were screams from the direction of the track. He looked back towards the track. Their carriage had been thrown over twenty yards. The beast had upturned the rest of the train and was picking through the remains. One of its tendrils plucked a crying man from a torn carriage and sucked him into its gaping mouth. Hundreds of people were running in every direction, most of them taken down by the infected. Others were fighting back, protecting their families. A group of men and women had formed a circle around some children. They were quickly overwhelmed by the infected and then the children were screaming. Groups of refugees were fleeing down the track, away from the train. He saw a young boy pinned to the ground by an infected woman; her arms were glistening pincers that impaled him through the chest. Then she bent down and began to strip the meat from his face with her ragged hole of a mouth.

Shadows gathered outside the upturned carriage. Footfalls and mewling sounds and strangled wails. Infected people appeared at the shattered windows, reaching inside and dragging outside anybody at the edges of the carriage. One man was pulled outside by a sinewy, hollowed-eyed woman. She went to work with her teeth and hands. The man screamed until she removed his throat with her snapping mouth.

Other refugees climbed out of the train and ran.

"Stay away from the windows," Ralph said.

"It won't matter," said Magnus. "They'll get us."

"We're surrounded," Joel muttered. "We're trapped."

Frank kept Florence close to him.

Ralph was searching around him. "Where's the flare gun?"

"It's gone," said Frank.

"We're fucked," Magnus said.

"Shut up," said Ralph. "Pull yourself together."

Frank looked through the jagged window frame. He pointed towards the trees the infected had poured from earlier.

"Our only chance is to get to those trees."

"What?" said Magnus. "The trees the infected came from?"

"Yeah."

"Fucking hell."

"I'm scared," said Florence.

"I know," said Frank. "We'll be okay. You have to be brave."

"If we're going to leave," said Ralph. "Then we should probably go now, before more infected arrive."

Frank looked at Ralph and the others. "Ready?"

"No worries," said Ralph.

Frank turned to the girl. "Are you ready?"

"Yes."

"Be brave."

"Okay."

They prepared themselves to leave the carriage. Magnus inhaled deeply then exhaled through his mouth. Ralph stared outside. Joel breathed through his nose. Frank held Florence's hand.

Then Magnus was screaming.

Frank turned. The newborn was on Magnus's back, one of its sharp limbs spearing his shoulder. The creature shrieked; its body was twisted and bleeding and most of its legs were broken. Its mouth opened, jaws connected by glistening strands of fluid, and it pulled its head back, ready to bite the back of Magnus's neck.

Magnus fell onto his stomach, the creature part of him.

Ralph rushed over and kicked at the newborn. The leg embedded within Magnus snapped. Magnus screamed. The newborn fell away, screeching. Ralph dragged Magnus away from the broken creature as it began crawling towards him on twisted legs.

It was a ruined, leaking thing, and it almost seemed pathetic.

The newborn shrieked.

Ralph stamped on the creature's back until it collapsed, pale liquid bleeding from its wounds. He pushed away its mangled form with his foot.

Magnus was crying, his face creased and sweating. "Get it out of me!"

Ralph picked up a jacket and, covering his right hand with it, used it as a protective sheath as he grabbed the snapped leg hanging from Magnus's shoulder.

"Ready, mate?"

Magnus nodded. "Do it."

Ralph pulled. Magnus screamed. The limb grinded against bone and scraped flesh then slipped free from his body, dripping his blood, and other fluids not his own. Ralph threw it and the jacket away.

Magnus's eyes fluttered and his mouth moved in a silent groan.

Ralph and Joel held him steady as he passed out.

Frank peered out from the carriage; panic and confusion greeted him. Screams filled the air. Cries for mercy. Utter chaos. He felt sick. The infected were feeding on the people they'd dragged outside. They were oblivious to everything else so total was their hunger. They stripped and flayed bodies. Ripped limbs from their sockets. Removed tongues from mouths and clutched them like trophies. A squirming woman, trying desperately to escape from their clutches, was torn into five different parts.

An infected man loped past with a dripping scalp clutched in his hand.

"Let's go," Frank said.

They crouched as they stepped outside and formed a tight huddle. Ralph and Joel grimaced as they hefted Magnus's dead weight. Frank scanned the immediate area. Packs of infected feasted on the downed refugees. Frank moved and the others behind him followed. His heart wanted to burst from his chest. He held Florence's hand, gripped it tight as he carried her. She was breathing into his ear, quick and scared. They moved amongst the slaughter and the panic, dodging other refugees and stepping over dead bodies.

The beast screamed behind them.

Frank stared across the field to the trees. He would get Florence to safety. They would make it to the trees. He would not fail.

He would not let them fail.

CHAPTER FIFTY-NINE

Some of the surviving refugees regrouped in the woods and walked westwards. They moved in a ragged, stumbling mass. Frank guessed there were approximately thirty people here. He wondered how many others had escaped. Not many, probably.

The light was fading. The beast was screaming far behind them. The survivors staggered deeper into the woods. Frank glanced over his shoulder, checking the infected weren't pursuing them. None of them had any weapons. If the infected emerged from the darkness and attacked, there would be no stopping them.

Many of the refugees were sobbing, heads bowed. How many had lost family back there? Wives and husbands? Children? He looked at Florence and thought he could never have left her behind.

Magnus was hanging limply from Ralph and Joel's arms. His shoulder had stopped bleeding.

"He's starting to get heavy," said Joel.

Ralph grimaced. "We need to find somewhere to stay the night."

"Agreed," said Frank. He looked at the other refugees. "But we might have competition for any shelter we find."

"We should go our own way," said Ralph. "The infected will be attracted to any large crowds. Better off on our own."

"What about safety in numbers?" asked Joel.

"Like herd animals?" Ralph shot him a mocking glare.

"Sort of."

"Herd animals get hunted."

"Ralph's got a point," said Frank. "Magnus needs to rest for the night. He won't be going much further."

They broke away from the group. None of the other refugees said anything or tried to convince them to stay.

An hour later they found an old barn in one of the fields outside the woods. They were alone, for now. Magnus had come to. He was groggy and quiet; face drained of colour. No sign of serious injury. They would have to watch for concussion.

The barn was a large construction. Timber battered by the elements. Old wood, stained dark. An arched roof. Big double-doors, closed but unlocked.

"There might be something nasty inside," said Joel.

Frank took Magnus's cigarette lighter. He opened the doors. The creak of rusted hinges. He stopped and waited. The others hung back behind him.

He flicked on the lighter and stuck his head inside the barn. Darkness stared back at him then retreated a little, begrudgingly, when he stepped inside with the flickering flame.

A hard dirt floor. Strands of dried straw around his feet. A smell of desiccation and mice droppings. A ladder led to another floor above him.

"Is it okay?" Joel asked from outside.

"I think so." Frank climbed the ladder, keeping hold of the lighter between two fingers and hoping any sudden breeze drifting through the worn walls wouldn't snuff it out. He didn't want to be alone in the dark.

The next floor was empty and silent.

Frank looked down the ladder, where the others had gathered on the ground floor. "It's not a Premier Inn, but it'll do."

* * *

Night fell as the sound of distant gunfire drifted around the countryside, a reminder of the war being fought. They rested on the first floor of the barn, huddled together to keep warm, hoping there would be no visitors tonight.

They slept.

Magnus awoke during the night. He was cold. There were sounds coming from outside.

Ralph was sitting in the corner, watching him. Magnus said nothing and crept slowly to the window. The glass was cloudy with smudged dirt and encrusted with mould.

The night was cleaved by moonlight.

The infected were outside. His body went rigid. The wound in his shoulder throbbed with its own heartbeat. Heat rose from his skin despite the cold.

Waves of men and women were passing through the field. The infected hissed and gibbered and mewled. Nightmare sounds.

His shoulder felt like it was burning. He clenched his teeth and bit down on his tongue, drawing blood. He tasted himself. He closed his eyes and saw flashes of memory: sunny days and sandy beaches; smiling children; a pair of dogs running around a garden as a football was kicked between a father and son; a bride and groom on their wedding day; a girl losing her virginity to her overzealous boyfriend; a school Nativity play; a woman giving birth in a delivery room.

These were not his memories.

There were voices inside his head. A mad cacophony of screaming, wailing and begging. Tortured voices. A deep, deep coldness at the heart of them. He caught fragments of names, places, and other memories. He heard babies crying. Felt the tears of proud parents and grieving widows. The sadness of lost pets and shattered dreams.

The infected remembered who they were.

But beyond that was a hunger, a need, a craving. The feel of flesh beneath his fingers. The smell of steam rising from warm bodies in the cold air.

Magnus opened his eyes. He was crying. He stood by the window and watched them until the last ones had drifted past and the field was empty. He wondered where they were going and if they had known he was watching them. He would be joining them soon, if his theory was correct. The others knew it as well; that's why Ralph was keeping watch over him.

The plague was in his blood.

He went back to where he'd been sleeping.

Ralph was still watching him.

CHAPTER SIXTY

They found a car as they entered the village of Milborne Port the next day; a Honda Civic of no use to the dead man lying next to it with his throat torn out.

Ralph removed the parcel shelf from the car and made Magnus sit in the boot, away from everyone else. Quarantine, Ralph called it, and said that if the plague was airborne it would lessen the chance of Magnus infecting the others. Magnus didn't argue. No one argued. He sat in the boot without complaint.

Frank volunteered to drive. They left the village. They passed through Sherborne; apart from scavenging birds, it was deserted. The dual carriageway to Yeovil was littered with crashed cars. Frank guided the Civic slowly around them, watching the road. An infected woman with a snapping mouth for a face bolted out from one pile-up and launched herself at their car. Her right arm was a flowering mass of urchin-like spikes. Frank steered away from her, resisting the temptation to run her down.

They reached Yeovil not long after.

A car was burning. Two bodies next to it, limbs splayed, faces torn to red ruin, insides scooped out, half-eaten and left to dry on the tarmac. There was blood smeared on the walls of houses. Bodies in gardens, lying in the grass and on flowerbeds. A dead woman on a set of swings. Lone infected looked out from the windows, screaming silently. A man was sitting in a car, staring at his lap. He was covered in blood and he was grinning. As Frank drove past, the man looked up quickly and laughed. His eyes were gone.

Some of the roads were blocked, so they had to reverse and find other roads leading to housing estates and side-streets. Kebab shops and Chinese takeaways. Blocks of flats loomed above the streets. There were people still alive in the town. Some of them watched from their windows, waving for help, uninfected and clean and doomed.

The hospital was on fire. Great towers of smoke climbed into the sky. Part of it had already collapsed.

The infected owned the streets. They saw lone survivors taken down by baying packs of monsters.

Something with tentacles and too many legs was wrapped around a pile of bodies.

Magnus was shivering in the boot of the car.

Joel looked at him. "We won't abandon you, mate."

Magnus replied, "I don't want to go back home and spread the plague. What if I infect my family? What if I kill them? What if I kill all of you?"

"We'll sort something out."

"You might as well stop and leave me by the roadside."

"We're not going to leave you, Magnus," said Frank. "We'll be with you until the end, mate. I promise. *We* all promise, don't we?"

"Yeah," said Joel.

"Yeah," said Ralph, his voice a whisper.

There were tears in Magnus's eyes. "I don't want to die. I don't want to be a monster."

CHAPTER SIXTY-ONE

Joel was the one who said it.

"What if we get home and they're all dead?"

Frank looked at him in the rear-view mirror. "We don't know what we're going to find." He thought of crows picking at Catherine's torn remains on their front lawn.

"He's got a point," said Ralph. "Everywhere else has been fucked,"

"Everywhere we've *been*," Frank said. "There could easily be places that are still surviving."

"You believe that?"

Frank ignored the question, answered it with one of his own. "I thought Ralph was the only doommonger amongst us?"

"Things change," Joel said.

* * *

Deserted roads, and fields that had been harvested long ago.

Home.

They entered the village from the south. A signpost at a crossroads next to a tall oak tree. Birdsong. Familiar roads, lanes, and fields. Things remembered. Despite the sense of dread infused within each of them, they felt welcomed. The feeling of returning to where they belonged.

Smoke was rising from the other end of the village. Frank remembered Wishford and how that village was overrun by the infected.

No one emerged from the houses to greet them. No welcoming party. Many of the doors on many of the houses had been ripped from their hinges. Smashed windows. Dried patches of blood. The signs of ruin they had grown accustomed to.

Silent houses of people they knew.

As the car coasted past Silver Street and onto Middle Street, the engine died and rattled to a stop. As if it was meant to be. Magnus was the last out onto the road, breathing slowly and holding his wounded shoulder.

Florence glanced up and down the street. "It's like my village. Where's your house, Frank?"

"At the other end of the village, along with Joel's house and Magnus's house."

"The poor end of the village," Ralph joked, and no one laughed.

Frank looked down the street. The church spire jabbed towards the sky. He saw movement near the front of a garden. The others saw it too, and turned towards it.

A dog emerged from between two cars, padding onto the road, sniffing the ground. A black Labrador.

"That's Al Copper's dog, Stumpy," said Ralph. "Look at its tail."

Ralph was right. Al Cooper was one of the drunkards that frequented the pub almost every night. He and his dog were inseparable. The Labrador's tail had been bitten off by a badger a few years ago.

"So, where's Al?" asked Joel.

"He might be around here somewhere," said Ralph. "But he might not be the same Al that we know."

Stumpy saw them watching him and raised his head. His ears pricked up and he sniffed the air for their scent. Magnus stepped forward.

The dog growled, his ears flattening against his head. His legs stiffened. He stared at Magnus.

Magnus stared back at the dog.

Stumpy turned away whimpering, and ran away down the street.

"I hope he survives," said Ralph, watching the dog disappear. "He's a good dog."

They came to the village hall on Church Street. The doors were hanging open and there was a dead body at the top of the steps leading up to the hall, unrecognisable due to the severe mutilation inflicted upon it.

More bodies inside the hall, left where they had fallen, but not left untouched by the ravaging hands of the infected. The floor was slippery in places, sticky in others. Arterial spray on the walls, insane patterns of red. The men looked for their loved ones but couldn't identify them. If they were here it would never be known.

Frank stepped back from the smell. His eyes were stinging. He breathed through his mouth.

Joel was crying and sniffling, wiping his face. "I want to wake up. Please let me wake up."

Frank put one hand on Joel's arm. He looked at Magnus, who had retreated from the doorway to stare into the sky.

Magnus said, "They're up there in the clouds. Above the clouds. They're up there waiting. I can hear them. They're speaking to me. Speaking to all of us but only some of us can hear them."

His skin was radiating heat, slick with fever. He closed his eyes, took in a breath heavy with exhaustion and sickness. His body was trembling. He had lost weight. The corners of his mouth flinched.

He spat on the ground; yellow sputum flecked with red.

"Magnus?" said Frank. "Are you okay?"

Magnus opened his eyes. He swallowed. His skin pulsed. He wore a defeated smile. Tears in his eyes.

"Not long now."

CHAPTER SIXTY-TWO

We've all come home, Ralph thought.

They arrived at his house first. He made the others stay on the street; he wanted to go into his house alone. Frank nodded in understanding and let him go.

He halted at the garden gate, composing himself, gathering his thoughts. His heartbeat was fast and strong. Adrenaline made his arms and hands tingle. He breathed through his nose, filling his lungs with clean air. For the moment, the entire world consisted of just him and the house.

The garden was just as it had been when he'd left. Mum liked to plant and to tend the flowerbeds, but Dad was in charge of the lawn and he was proud of it.

Ralph didn't want to move. He wanted to stay by the gate and hold onto the thought that his parents were alive and uninfected; that they would be inside the house waiting for him. He would walk through the door and they'd be sitting down in the living room, watching one of the old Peter Sellers films they enjoyed so much. Dad would be in his armchair with a cup of tea and a small plate of chocolate digestives.

Mum would be sitting on the sofa, sipping Bovril and petting their cat, Gus. They would be in there and they would welcome him home, and Mum would make him a cup of coffee and a bacon sandwich with brown sauce. Even Gus would welcome him home with an uninterested glance and a swish of his tail.

Past Mum's hideously beige curtains, he could see part of the kitchen and the living room. He looked for movement, but there was none. The red front door didn't open for him. No welcome for the returning son.

This house was ingrained in his memory. This house where he lived; where he grew up. This house where his childhood memories were made and treasured.

Ralph opened the gate and then walked up the garden path. He stopped at the front door, laid one hand upon it. He turned the handle and the door opened inwards. A breath of old air met him.

He stepped into the house. An oppressive silence, like a break between screams. He moved slowly into the living room. Two empty armchairs and two empty mugs. The television was dead. Old photos in silver frames. A four-day-old newspaper on the floor. Shelves of autobiographies and history books. His father's slippers next to the fireplace.

French windows looked out onto the back garden. He remembered playing football with Dad out there when he was a boy. There was nobody out there now. He wondered where the cat was. He checked every downstairs room but couldn't find his parents.

He trod lightly on the carpeted stairway. He reached the landing and paused outside his parents' bedroom. A basket of dirty laundry and a cheap painting on the wall. The door was closed. He didn't want to enter. He listened for any sound and was disappointed with silence. He steeled himself for a terrible sight. He opened the door. The smell of rot greeted him.

I hope you're both dead...

His father was face down on the bed. He'd been partially eaten and his spine was exposed, dull white nubs of bone showing through yellow fat and the red flesh of his back. The back of his neck had been gnawed away. His father's killer had ripped through his clothes to get into him. Bare feet and callouses. Grimy soles. The wonky big toe on his right foot. Long toenails; Mum had always moaned at Dad to cut them more often.

Both bedside lamps and the pillows were dotted with dried blood.

His father couldn't be dead. A part of Ralph refused to believe it. He didn't want to turn his father over and see his father's face. He didn't want to see the last expression his father wore as he died.

Ralph stared at the corpse until a sound from the bathroom stirred him.

He found his mother lying in the bath. She was covered in blood. Her eyes were dark pools and she hissed at Ralph through a red slash of a mouth.

Ralph's heart felt like a bag of stones. He held his ground, feet shifting on the linoleum floor.

"Mum," he whispered. "Mum, it's me. Ralph."

She was naked. Her fingers were elongated and tipped with onyx claws. Her right arm was hanging over the side of the bath, dripping blood onto the floor. His skin was pale and mottled with grey. He felt embarrassed at the sight of her sagging breasts and wrinkled stomach.

Shit, piss and blood filled the toilet.

His mother reached for him with her right hand.

Ralph shrank away from her.

His mother let out a plaintive mewl. She was one of *them* now. And in a second of pure white-hot agony, he realised his mother was gone forever.

He walked to his bedroom and reached under his bed, groping amongst the porn magazines and old James Herbert and Shaun Hutson paperbacks. He pulled out the baseball bat and gripped it in both hands. The base of the handle was wrapped in duct tape for better grip. His initials were carved into the wood. He returned to the bathroom, every bit of him screaming to run away, but he wouldn't. He had a job to do.

His mother waited for him. She reached out to him again, and there was something like recognition in her dark eyes as Ralph stood over her. Her mouth opened; her tongue emerged like a gleaming serpent from a cave, picking scales of dry blood from her chin.

"I'm sorry, Mum," he said. "Thank you for everything. I love you, Mum."

His mother's face was pathetic and full of woe. Maybe she whimpered. Maybe she said his name.

He brought the bat down on her head. His mother's skull gave no resistance and her body jerked as her nerve endings flared for one last time. A soft moan left her mouth. A sigh of relief.

Ralph finished her without hesitation, forcing all his strength into the final blow. He stared at her body. This broken, diseased thing that had once been his mother. He pulled on a pair of gloves, carried her to the bedroom and laid her down next to Dad.

Ralph covered them with a blanket and said goodbye.

After grabbing some bandages, gauze and painkillers for Magnus, he raided the alcohol cupboard for the last bottle of vodka, then pulled a photo of his parents from its frame and put it in his pocket. He guzzled a few mouthfuls of vodka, savouring the burn in his chest. He punched himself until his face was sore and tender, and he enjoyed the pain because pain was life and life was pain, and one could not be without the other.

CHAPTER SIXTY-THREE

They walked past places remembered from days gone by. They checked the church and found it empty. They found a man lying by a woman's grave, his throat cut by his own hand. There was a photo by his body. Frank didn't look at it for too long.

The pub, The Duke of York, was deserted. There were smashed glasses and bottles on the floor, upturned tables and chairs. Blood on the floor and on the bar, but no bodies. Frank stared at a human ear left on the bar, like an offering for them. He covered it with a towel used to clean up drink spillage.

They arrived at the street where Joel and Anya shared a semi-detached house. Fallen leaves flittered upon the road. A plastic bag coasted past. The breeze was cold and intrusive, reaching inside Frank's collar and stroking the back of his neck.

Smoke dirtied the air, made it thick and acrid.

Joel's house was burning, along with the house next to it. Joel ran down the street and fell to his knees before the raging fire. When the others caught up with him, he was crying and biting down on his left wrist. Frank crouched next to Joel, grimacing at the heat pressing against his skin. The fire's voice was deep and growling. Flames leapt from the shattered windows. The roof had collapsed; the chimney had toppled and broken on the road. There would be nothing left, save for ash and carbon, once the fire died. The fire heated the air until Frank could feel the back of his throat begin to dry and itch.

"How did it start?" asked Joel. "Why did this happen?"

The house next door was almost fully consumed by the fire. The walls had fallen and the garden was aflame.

Things popped and smashed inside Joel's house as the flames claimed them. If anyone was in there they were dead. Smoke streamed upwards, a trail of volcanic grey.

"Joel," Frank said.

Joel took his wrist from his mouth; imprints from his teeth marked his skin. His eyes were full of shock and incredulity. His mouth moved silently. A fleck of ash landed on his cheek.

"She's dead," Joel said.

"You don't know that."

"Then where is she?"

"I don't know. But I know that she's not dead."

"She's gone."

"She might be hiding somewhere else. Somewhere safe. She might be with Catherine at my house."

Joel's tears were drying from the terrible heat. Fire in his eyes. "That was our house. We were supposed to live here, together."

"She's alive," Frank said.

"Do you really believe that? How can you believe that?"

"I know because you and Anya are going to get married. We'll find her, and we'll find Catherine, and we'll find Magnus's family and we'll all be safe."

Joel's mouth worked but no words came out. His face looked like stone. His eyes were red-rimmed and bloodshot. He was at the point of exhaustion. He watched the flakes of ash dance and form shapes in the air.

The fire raged.

Joel wiped his mouth. "I'm ready to lie down. I'm not strong enough. Never was. If Anya is still alive, she's got a better chance of surviving without me. She's better off without me. I'm better off dead."

Frank slapped him across the face.

Joel gawped at him.

"Don't you ever say that again. You will stay alive and you will survive, Joel. You will survive and keep Anya safe and you will keep her alive. Do you understand me, Joel? Do you fucking understand me?"

"You really think we're going to survive, Frank? Even after all we've seen? How do you know?"

"Because I'm your best man and Ralph and Magnus are your ushers. It's our job to look after you. You're still the groom. Nothing has changed from the weekend. We will stick together. We will survive. *You* will survive, Joel. Do you believe me?"

Joel coughed weakly. "I believe you."

Frank nodded, pulled Joel to his feet. "Good. Good job, mate."

CHAPTER SIXTY-FOUR

Joel barely raised his head to see where he was walking. Ralph stared into the distance, gulping vodka like it was water.

Magnus wheezed and moaned, holding his shoulder, every breath a sucking croak, wet and throaty and thirsty. Death was like a black dog on his heels. They had bandaged and tended his wound, but a nagging voice told Frank they would have to deal with Magnus eventually. Maybe before night fell. Maybe before Frank managed to summon the will to do it himself. The thought of it hollowed him out, made him feel sick and lost. Despondent. Maybe Ralph would do it; he had the bat.

Frank looked at Florence. The girl was brave and strong and he admired her for it.

He envied her for it.

Frank stopped, looked at the road sign.

"Home," he whispered.

* * *

Frank stepped inside his house. It was like coming home from work. But no one came to greet him and there was no smell of cooking food from the kitchen.

He knew Catherine was gone.

He stood in the hallway, amongst the gathered mementoes and artefacts of their life together, and breathed in slowly. Where had Catherine gone? Had she been taken? His heart kicked fast in the hollow of his chest as he searched the house. The shadows cast by the grey light gave him the feeling he wasn't alone. He thought he could hear Catherine singing and wondered if it was her ghost returning to where she shared her life with him.

The singing faded away. He sat on the edge of their bed, one hand laid upon the mattress, hoping there would be some residual warmth from her body. He said her name. A whisper. It was good to have her name on his lips; his mouth was a perfect fit for her name. His body felt heavy with adrenaline and disappointment, and his lungs were tight and strained from inhaling smoke. His skin was tender from the heat of the fire. He gained comfort from the familiar surroundings. At least there was still comfort left in the world. He looked through Catherine's wardrobe, touching her clothes, holding them to his face and thinking about her.

"Where are you?" he asked.

He looked at the photos in the house. Then he emptied the almost-bare cupboards of the few tins of food remaining. He and Catherine were supposed to have gone grocery shopping today. The food in the fridge-freezer was already going bad; an opened pack of ham was growing stuff upon it.

Frank locked the door when he left the house. The possibility of never returning burrowed a gaping hole inside him.

The others were waiting by the road. Joel's face was full of foolish hope.

Frank shook his head.

* * *

Magnus's pace quickened and he wheezed out a moist breath. "Debbie. My boys. I'm almost home."

Frank glanced at Ralph, who was watching Magnus. Ralph took a swig of vodka.

They followed Magnus down the street. Parked cars lined one side of the road. There were a few trees whose forms were perfectly still, as if painted there by an artist's hand. The breeze had died.

Magnus stopped on the road and faced his house. Tears on his face. He was slightly hunched, his spine becoming rigid and bent. Trembling limbs. Fever and heat. Glistening skin. His eyes were growing larger, becoming piscine.

They gathered beside him. Frank put one hand on his arm, and Magnus jumped, as if woken from a daydream. His smile was heartbreaking and defeated. But he was home. The muscles moved under his face. His shoulders seemed thinner and his neck scrawnier. Veins pressed against the skin like they were trying to escape the prison of his body.

Magnus was steadily collapsing, so slowly that it was impossible to see, so discreet was the plague's workings within him. He was becoming something else; something that would make the man known as Magnus Heap as simple memory. He would be dust.

Magnus closed his eyes, and they could be seen dancing behind his eyelids, as if he were dreaming.

Then he opened his eyes. "They're inside the house. They're at home. They're waiting for me."

"How do you know they're in there?" asked Joel.

Magnus started towards his house. Frank placed one hand on Magnus's uninjured shoulder, made him turn around.

"Are you going in there alone?"

He nodded. "I have to."

"Let me come in with you."

Magnus thought about it.

"For old times' sake, mate?" said Frank.

Magnus nodded again. He looked at his friends in turn, offered them all a smile that was like a grimace painted onto a corpse.

He turned away and stared at his house.

Frank told Ralph and Joel to stay with Florence. He fell in behind Magnus.

The darkness within the windows watched them. It was oily and dense, full of unseen eyes.

* * *

The garden was a small jungle. Grass left to grow too long. Weeds were blossoming. There was a deckchair on the lawn, tilting to one side, its metal legs rusting and bent. A deflated football with some of its skin missing. Magnus bent down to pick up something from the grass: a green plastic toy soldier. Magnus put it in his pocket.

They continued to the front door. Magnus produced his keys from one pocket, fiddled with them in his hands. The clink of metal; his hands were shaking. He went to stick the key in the door but missed the keyhole. Frank offered to take the keys, but Magnus shook his head.

"No. I have to do this."

On the second attempt, Magnus unlocked and opened the door. Frank followed him inside.

The hallway. A carpeted floor worn from the tread of feet. A small table with a cordless telephone nestled in its cradle. He picked it up, put it to his ear; the phone was dead. To the left, the stairway and its stained steps leading upstairs. Straight ahead was the kitchen, shrouded in dim shadows. To Frank's right was the living room. The door was closed.

Magnus headed to the kitchen, treading softly on the carpet and onto the linoleum. Frank followed him, more than willing to let Magnus take the lead.

There was nobody in the kitchen. The sink was brimming with dirty plates, stained mugs and stagnant water. Forks and spoons and knives encrusted with food and dried fluids formed a mound of skeletal metal upon the worktop.

The window above the sink showed them the back garden. Out there were the boys' bicycles and a trampoline. The window was smeared with grime and dirty fingerprints.

The house stank. When Frank took a deep breath he had to stop himself from gagging.

He grabbed a serrated bread-knife from the rack. Magnus eyed him, then the knife.

"Are you gonna kill my family with that?"

"I never said that. Just in case something happens. We don't know what's in here with us."

"My family are here."

"Where are they?"

Magnus turned and nodded back the way they had come. "They're in the living room."

When Magnus stepped forwards, Frank retreated from him.

* * *

The Magnus Heap of old was fading. He was becoming something else. He was changing.

I'll become a beautiful butterfly, he thought, and almost laughed.

He could hear Debbie's voice inside his head. No words, just a gentle humming. She sounded happy. But she hadn't been happy for a long, long time. Not since before the twins were born.

Magnus placed his right hand on the door handle, turned it slowly and pushed with his leading arm. Frank didn't move from the doorway. Magnus stepped into the room.

The sickly-sweet stench of blood and shit hit Magnus.

The room was dimly-lit. The curtains were pulled shut. Shapes and suggestions lurking and unmoving. The sofa and the two armchairs had been moved against the walls, clearing the centre of the room. The television was lying on its face, dead and useless and smashed. The natural light from the hallway brought a dull definition to the room. Magnus's eyes adjusted. There were soft things under his feet. Damp raggedy strips of newspaper and a mulch of mushy organic matter covered the floor. One of the boys' shoes. There were small bones amongst the litter and waste. Animal bones gnawed clean by little teeth to a gleaming shine.

Something moved on the far side of the room. He didn't react. Frank was at Magnus's shoulder, his breathing shallow and tense.

Magnus's family was waiting for him.

His sons, Grant and Adam, were crawling around in the filth, naked and covered in offal and a pale oily substance. They were tragically thin. They moved like animals. Their little faces were like dolls' faces, puffy and pale and tinged with a red bloom like rouge upon their cheeks. Their eyes shone. Their mouths shifted open, displaying their small teeth, which were like ivory. The boys coiled together, sniffing the air, and they swung their heads towards Magnus and Frank.

Were they grinning?

They hissed, and eyed Frank, and made to move towards him, their fingers extended into sharp hooks, their mouths curled back to show the teeth that would sink into his body and rip bits away.

Magnus stepped in front of Frank, held out his hands.

The boys halted, hissing. They began to mewl and whimper. They looked at Magnus, tilting their heads to one side. They approached him cautiously, sniffing at him, clicking sounds coming from their throats.

"It's okay, boys," Magnus said. "I won't hurt you."

The boys sniffed at Magnus's outstretched hands, licking his fingers tentatively, almost affectionately. It tickled. Magnus felt such a swelling of warmth and love for his boys that he nearly burst into tears. He looked down at them and smiled.

His boys looked up at him. Then they darted away from him, feet scrabbling and squelching on the waste-filled floor.

Behind them was their mother.

Magnus felt tears sting his eyes.

The boys scampered towards Debbie. Her clothes had been removed. She was a writhing mass of blubber and white skin. Her scalp was bare apart from a few wisps of hair. Her neck was a trunk of fat. Her wedding ring had vanished into blubbery fingers, of which the nails were long and dirty. Her legs were covered in lesions and sores and blisters that wept fluid. She was lying on her left side, facing the room, cooing softly as the boys knelt by her side making small yipping noises and patting their excited hands on the floor.

Debbie's breasts had sagged and drooped until they resembled empty water bladders. Punctured flaps of skin without a use. Her nipples were sore and red, blooming into leaking pustules. Her face was as he remembered it, save for the dried blood and scraps of meat around her mouth and down her chin. Around her were the scattered remains of four, maybe five, children; their bones stripped clean, yellow-white, and discarded. Leftovers. Mixed in with them were more animal bones and tufts of fur.

It was a nest.

Debbie had grown six large udders, which were hanging from her torso, pale and wrinkled above the matted, tangled patch of pubic hair. Her teets were weeping some sort of milk from the bloated tips. Tips that would slip into a mouth quite easily. The milk looked greasy, like warm ejaculate.

Magnus watched as his boys lowered their heads and started to feed from her udders. They were eager, biting down with their jaws hard enough to make Debbie whimper and moan. She quietened as the boys began to suck. They squirmed and mewled as they fed from their mother, their shrivelled genitals shivering and their mouths working quickly, their tongues lapping at any milk that missed their mouths. They gripped their mother's grub-like body.

Magnus felt their slowly-fading hunger and Debbie's maternal satisfaction. He heard her heartbeat, its slow rhythm; the blood swimming through her veins. He felt the swell and rush of her insides adapting to the plague. But she was still Debbie. She was still his wife. And she still loved him.

"I'm sorry for everything," Magnus whispered.

This was his family. He felt proud. He felt humbled.

This was his home.

Magnus couldn't help smiling.

CHAPTER SIXTY-FIVE

Magnus and Frank returned outside.

"I'm staying here," said Magnus.

The others looked at him. Frank was the only one who didn't look stunned. There was only acceptance in his eyes.

Joel looked hurt. "You can't leave us. We stay together. There might be a cure. We can get you help."

"I'm too far gone," Magnus said. "You can see that for yourselves. Look at me." He could feel the plague needling his insides, changing his chemistry and his thoughts.

"You don't know that," said Joel.

"There's not enough time, even if there is a cure. I'm changing. I'll be a danger to you. I'm contagious. I can feel it pulling at me now. I can feel it in my blood and in my brain."

Joel shook his head.

"I can smell everything under your skin," said Magnus. For a second, all he wanted to do was slaughter his friends and the little girl with them. He wanted to open her up and see what she was made of.

He had known Frank, Ralph and Joel since childhood, since they were able to wipe their own arses, but when he looked into their faces he felt an urge to kill them and drag their bodies back to the house so his family wouldn't go hungry.

There was an itching sensation behind his eyes. He looked down at his hands and they looked like a stranger's. His skin was damp and glistening, but not with sweat. His body throbbed. His teeth felt too big for his mouth. There was a growing darkness in his chest and it was spreading outwards, and when it reached his extremities and his brain, he would finally succumb and be transformed.

He looked at his friends and saw their insides; saw their beating hearts and their digestive systems working. He saw their blood.

"So this is it, then?" said Joel. "That's it? Just like that?"

"Yes." Magnus felt a twinge of hot pain across his back.

"We've come all this way, and that's it. You're done?"

"Yes, mate."

"This is madness."

"Magnus is right," said Frank. Joel shot him a glare. "And it's his choice. His family is in there, waiting for him. It's too late for a cure."

Magnus nodded.

"Frank," said Joel, "you can't be serious."

"Frank's right," said Ralph. "It's Magnus's choice. He doesn't have long left. If he stayed with us, we'd have to kill him eventually."

Joel was shaking his head. "No, no, no."

Magnus smiled ruefully and shrugged. "I guess this is goodbye, lads. I'll forgive you if you don't want to shake hands with me."

The others stayed where they were. Joel was crying silently. Ralph was staring at Magnus. Florence offered Magnus a little smile and it comforted him.

"The infected are everywhere," Magnus said. "There aren't many places left to run to. The light is fading, lads. Time is running out. We are dying out."

The thought of never seeing his mates again made his chest ache. Magnus wiped his mouth.

"See ya, mate," said Ralph. "Sorry it had to end like this."

"Me too."

Joel wiped his eyes. "Bye, Magnus."

Frank said, "Go and be with your family, mate. Take care of them. Maybe we'll all cross paths again one day."

"I hope not," said Magnus. "It wouldn't end well for any of us." He wiped his eyes. "I remember when we were kids and we used to spend our summer holidays playing football and cricket, building tree houses and bases in the woods, pretending we were in the army. I never thought those days would end. I thought they would last forever. Maybe our younger selves are still doing that right now, in another time. I wish we could go back there."

"Same here," said Frank. Ralph and Joel nodded.

"Now there is nothing to say, I suppose."

"We won't forget you, mate," said Frank.

"I hope I don't forget you lot either."

Thunder rumbled far away.

"I hope you find your families, lads," Magnus said. "Frank, I hope you find Catherine. Joel, I hope you find Anya. I hope you all get to safety. I hope you all survive."

The others nodded.

"Cheers, lads," Magnus said. "Thanks for everything."

He limped back to the house. By the time he walked inside and joined with his family, the old Magnus Heap was gone and a new one was born.

CHAPTER SIXTY-SIX

"So what do we do now?" asked Joel. "Where do we go?" He wrapped his arms around his chest.

Ralph swigged vodka. He swallowed then grimaced. "Fuck knows."

Frank said, "We could go back to my house."

"And then what?" Joel said.

"We figure something out."

"Anya and Catherine could be dead, Magnus is gone, and you want to figure something out?"

"You have a better suggestion?"

"We have to find help."

"Find help where?"

"I don't know. There might be other survivors somewhere. Maybe the army will find us."

Ralph grunted. "Keep on dreaming, Joel."

"Shut up, Ralph," said Joel. "You're drunk."

Ralph grinned and it wasn't nice. "Not yet. But I plan to be."

"This isn't helping," said Frank. "We need to decide what to do next."

Ralph said, "Might as well get drunk while we still can."

435

Frank ignored him. He was still reeling from the loss of Magnus. He couldn't believe he'd never see Magnus again.

Magnus was gone.

Frank missed him already; missed his sniffles and the way he chewed the inside of his mouth. Frank hoped Magnus was happy with his family in his new existence.

A great emptiness bloomed inside Frank when he thought of Catherine. He could not give up hope of finding her alive. If he did that he might as well sit down on the road and wait for something hungry to find him.

"We're fucked," said Joel. "What are we going to do? Are we going to just wander around the village all day? What if there're infected still around?"

"Calm down," said Frank.

"We're fucked."

"Stop it."

"Have a drink, lads," Ralph said.

They both ignored him. They were staring down the road. So was Florence.

"Don't want a drink?" said Ralph. "Fair enough. More for me."

Florence pointed ahead of them.

There were people gathering down the road, emerging from passageways, doorways and garden

twitching and snarling. Some of them were transformed beyond recognition. Some of them Frank did recognise. Some of them were his neighbours. His friends. People he once passed on the street. People he used to wave at as he drove by in his car on the way to work every morning. Those he used to get drunk with in the pub, enjoying a pint and a laugh and watching the football. He saw Jim Bottomley and his wife Emma, both growling through stained mouths, their clothes torn and dirty. He saw the Field brothers, Pete, Tom and Addy, snarling at one another over a severed arm that Tom was trying to eat. He saw Josh Fade, Luke Oliver, Tom Brister, AJ Carvell, Rich Pippin and Josh Wilkinson. They were deformed and pale, glistening skin and growing tumours on their shivering bodies. Josh Fade was wearing a white dressing gown tainted with yellow stains; it opened to reveal his pyjamas bulging with wet growths and tendrils. Tom Brister was on all fours, his jaws swollen and dripping, his fingers raking the road. They were staring at Frank and the others with a naked hunger. The last time he had seen Luke Oliver was the Sunday before last, when he'd gone to the local shop to buy a newspaper and had spoken to him outside; now Luke was crouching by a car gnawing on his own fingers. He saw Rosie Milton, a young girl who lived four doors down from his house and had been friends with Emily. She was shaking with hunger, her eyes drilling into his face. Her neck had extended, swelling with fluids and gases, and scythe-like appendages twitched and jabbed from her shoulders.

Some of the infected were naked and covered in blood.

Frank wondered with a wave of hot panic if Catherine was amongst the infected. If she was, he would kill her. He would kill her quickly.

They gathered as a pack, darkened limbs and torn skin. The Field brothers discarded the severed arm and regarded Frank's group. Gibbering mouths opened to reveal black tongues and chattering teeth. Twitching hands grasped the air; hands that were deformed into sharp points of bone and muscle. Palsied arms folded into themselves. The sound of growling grew louder within them, until it was all that could be heard.

There were other faces that he recognised. It was too painful to remember them as they had once been. They were monsters now.

"Oh shit," said Joel, backing away.

Ralph stopped drinking.

Florence grabbed Frank's hand.

The pack of infected broke into a run, and before Frank could turn and flee, they had already halved the distance between them.

Ralph threw the vodka bottle at the pack, and it hit one of the infected, knocking her down. Ralph turned and ran.

We're not going to make it, Frank thought.

They ran past Magnus's house.

Frank glanced back to see the infected within ten yards. Ralph was already flagging, breathing hard. Joel whimpered as he ran.

One of the infected reached for Ralph. Something wet and black emerged from its mouth.

Ralph looked at Frank, a final exchanged glance.

The infected thing let out a scream, reached out and snagged the back of Ralph's jacket.

Ralph cried out.

The back of the infected thing's head exploded.

CHAPTER SIXTY-SEVEN

Another infected went down. A bullet whirred past Frank's head, into the chasing pack. He turned.

There were two men standing on the road, five yards back, one with a rifle and the other with a shotgun.

The man with the rifle shouted, "Get down!"

Frank dragged Florence down with him. Ralph and Joel hit the road on their stomachs.

The two men opened fire. Frank hugged Florence, burying her face in his chest. The world around him became an explosion. He screamed and Florence screamed with him.

Frank screamed until his throat was raw.

Then there was silence. Frank raised his head. The smell of blood and smoke hung in the air.

The two men reloaded their weapons. The infected were littered all over the road, many of them still twitching. The road was red and mushy. Arms and legs lay at broken angles, twisted and smashed, ripped from bodies. Pulped remains. One of them, a woman with most of her face obliterated by buckshot, reached out to Frank as he rose. He stepped away from the infected woman. Her hand grasped at the air, her muffled grunts desperate and gasping. She opened her mouth and a dark green fluid slipped onto her chin.

He was glad he didn't recognise her.

The woman slumped upon the road. Her bleeding wounds lessened their flow as her heart finally stopped. Her eyes remained fixed on Frank.

Ralph and Joel got to their feet. They looked at the bodies on the road, struck with awe.

The men with the guns raised their gas masks.

The man with the rifle was old and limping. He was in his late sixties with a face like pale, creased leather and a grey beard. He was short and narrow. The other man was younger and red-bearded, with large eyes. He was tall and broad-shouldered. They reloaded their weapons.

The men stopped five yards from Frank. They eyed him warily.

The old man grinned. "Frank Hooper. I thought you were dead."

Frank nodded. "I thought you were too, Roland."

* * *

They walked to the edge of the village, where the houses gave way to fields. The distant cries of infected drifted through the air. The day was darkening, becoming colder. Frank was hungry and exhausted.

Roland Pratt was friends with Frank's parents. "Here we are. Mary should be waiting for us. We don't want to be outside when it gets dark."

The other man was Henry Pratt, Roland's nephew.

Roland knocked on the front door and waited. The lock clicked and the door opened. Mary Pratt greeted them with a nervous smile. She was a short, plump woman wearing a long dress and a stained, white apron. Her grey hair had been tied into a bun. Roland gave her a quick hug and entered the house. Frank and the others followed him. Henry locked the door, threw the bolt.

They were in a hallway. The only light was from candles flickering by the walls. The house smelled of old shoes and sweat. Frank had been here before when he was a teenager and had come here with his father. It suddenly felt strange that he hadn't visited the house since then.

"I thought I heard gunshots," Mary said. "I was worried."

Roland kissed her on the cheek. "No need to worry, dear. We encountered some of the corrupted ones. We made short work of them."

"Good," she said, smiling. "That's good."

"Mary, you remember Frank Hooper, don't you? John and Lucy's son."

"Yes, I do. I hope John and Lucy are safe in France," she said. "And Ralph Barrow and Joel Gosling. I remember all of you lads!" She looked at Florence. "And who's this pretty thing?"

Florence eyed her warily.

"Ah, shy, is she? Never mind. All little girls are shy."

"Hello, Mary," Frank said.

Ralph and Joel greeted her, too, offering polite smiles and nods.

Roland smiled. "We found them near Piece Lane, being chased by the demons. A whole pack of the bastards."

"Roland and Henry saved us," said Frank. "We were very lucky."

"Don't mention it," said Roland.

"You're all safe now," said Mary. "Safe and sound." She held her hands together and smiled. "Now, who wants tea and cake?"

* * *

Victoria sponge, buttered scones, and tea weakened with powdered milk. Frank stifled a burp and relaxed into the armchair. He was drowsy from the rich food. He was ready to burst. His stomach had shrunk.

Florence was eating her third scone. Crumbs stuck to the edges of her mouth. She was sitting on the floor next to Frank. Ralph and Joel were slumped on the sofa. Joel was rubbing his stomach with one hand, holding a mug of tea with the other. Ralph was devouring a fourth slice of cake. He was on his second cup of tea.

It was a brief, glorious respite. Frank savoured it.

Candlelight painted the living room. The curtains were closed over the wooden planks nailed over the windows. Roland and Mary were on the other side of the room, sipping from their own mugs of tea. Henry was leaning against the doorway, still holding his shotgun, staring at the floor.

Before Mary had served the food and drink, Frank had recounted their journey to their hosts, finishing with the loss of Magnus.

Mary, Roland, and Henry had listened in silence.

"Do you know what happened to my wife?" Frank asked.

"And Anya, my fiancée," said Joel. "She's missing."

Roland looked at Mary, then at the floor. A shadow passed over his face. "They're gone. They're all gone."

"Gone where?" asked Joel.

"Gone away," replied Mary. "All gone away."

"They were evacuated," said Roland.

It felt like worms were making a home in Frank's guts. "Evacuated?"

Mary said, "People turned into monsters. The demons roamed the streets, made it their playground. We stayed here while people died. After two days we went outside. Many of the demons were gone, and there were other survivors. Catherine and Anya were among them."

Frank wanted to smile but couldn't. Not yet. Not until he knew she was safe.

"Then the army arrived," said Roland. "They took most of the survivors away."

"Where did they take them?" asked Joel.

"There's a camp on the coast, apparently. Near Sidmouth. Apparently they're evacuating people from Britain."

"Why didn't you go? Frank asked.

Mary held Roland's hand. "We wanted to stay here, so we hid. This is our home. We'll never leave."

"We're safe here," said Roland. "We've got enough supplies for a long time. We don't need electricity. We've got the stove to cook with. We've always been self-sufficient. We're safer here than in some filthy camp, and we've got guns, just as importantly. We'd rather die in our home with our own ground under our feet."

"I can empathise with that," said Ralph.

Frank and Joel exchanged a look. Joel's eyes were wide, wet and glassy. But the relief was evident on his face and the stiffness had drained from his body. Frank felt like collapsing into a fit of hysterical laughter. He wanted to hug and squeeze Florence and tell her that she would see her adoptive mother very soon, and they would be a family together. And then things would get better. He wanted to believe that.

"It's the Devil," said Roland.

Frank looked at the old man.

Mary nodded her head, pursing her mouth.

"All of this," said Roland. "It's the Devil's work."

Ralph snorted.

"Don't be so cynical," said Mary. "The Devil's come up to see us, and he's spreading his evil, making people become demons. Making them kill and spread the evil to others."

"The Devil's out there," Roland added, raising one finger and gesturing outside. "He's walking upon the earth. He's recruiting for his unholy army and he wants our souls. Maybe we'll all meet him eventually. Maybe he'll come knocking on our door soon…"

A shiver passed through Frank. He felt stupid for being so easily spooked. He glanced at Ralph, and Ralph's grin was like scar tissue. It was a mocking grin. Ralph was shaking his head.

Frank willed him not to say anything.

"The Devil?" Ralph asked incredulously. "Bollocks. Utter bollocks."

"Why are you so doubtful?" asked Mary.

Ralph sighed. "So, if the Devil is really the cause of this plague…or evil, as you call it…where is God while all this happens? Is God ignoring us? Doesn't God care? Is God just watching while everybody dies?"

"I'm sorry about Ralph," Frank said to Mary and Roland. "He's an opinionated atheist."

Their faces were blank. But there was piousness in their eyes.

"I'm not an atheist," said Ralph.

"Then what are you?" Roland asked, and one corner of his mouth curled upwards. "Please tell us. We'd like to know what you are."

"I'm an anti-theist."

"What is that?" asked Mary.

"It means that not only do I not believe in your god, but I also find the idea of your god, and any other god, appalling. If he's real then why did he let my parents die? What did they do wrong? Were they demons? Were they possessed? Were they *evil*, like you said?"

Neither Mary nor Roland answered. Their eyes gleamed.

"That's enough," said Frank. He looked at Mary and Roland. "I'm very sorry about Ralph. I'm sorry if he's caused any offence."

Ralph was glaring at Frank. He could see him in his peripheral vision.

Roland and Mary smiled together.

"No offence taken, Frank," Roland said, his voice calm and soothing. "We understand that young Ralph is suffering the loss of his parents."

"Don't talk about me like I'm not here," said Ralph. "Don't talk down to me. Fuck off."

"And we sympathise with you, Ralph," said Mary. "Your mother and father were good people. They didn't deserve what happened to them. No one stricken by the evil deserves it."

"We're sorry if we upset you, Ralph," said Roland. "Please accept our apologies."

Ralph said nothing. He folded his arms and lowered his head to look at the floor.

* * *

Three hours later, and darkness pressed against the house, craving to be let in so it could swallow the candlelight. Florence was asleep. Frank, Joel and Ralph formed a circle on the living room floor sipping cups of Bovril that Mary had made for them. They were studying the map.

Mary and Roland hadn't taken Ralph's insulting behaviour personally. They were resolute in what they believed, and Frank couldn't help admiring them for it, even if he didn't agree with it.

"I miss Magnus," said Ralph.

"Yeah," said Joel. "Feels strange without him."

Frank nodded.

"We'll never see him again," said Ralph. "Except maybe in dreams and nightmares."

They drank. Florence muttered in her sleep.

"We'll leave in the morning," said Frank. "Find a car somewhere."

"It's a long journey," said Ralph. "What if the camp isn't there when we get there? What if everyone's gone?"

"Please don't say that," said Joel.

"It's a possibility," said Frank, scratching his face. "They might have already been evacuated from the country by the time we arrive."

"Do you really think it's just Britain that's been affected by the plague?" Joel asked.

"It's probably global," said Ralph.

"It's irrelevant," said Frank. The other men looked at him. "We'll cross that bridge when we come to it, okay?"

"And what about Florence?" Ralph asked him.

"What about her?"

"Have you thought about leaving her here with the Jesus freaks? Is it a good idea to bring her along with us, all the way to Sidmouth?"

"She's coming with us."

"She'll slow us down."

"No more than you will. She probably would be safer here, and I have considered leaving her with Roland and Mary, but I promised to look after her."

"You could let *her* decide," said Ralph.

"No. She's too young to make that decision. I know what's best for her."

Ralph stared at him. Frank looked away.

"I think we should get some sleep," said Joel. He yawned, stretched his arms. "Big day tomorrow."

"Sounds like we're going on a day trip to the seaside," said Ralph.

Frank smiled, finished his drink. "Joel's right. Time to get our heads down."

Just as they settled down on the living room floor, a deep roar came out of the night, resonating from somewhere in the village. The cry of something stalking in the darkness. Something walking the back roads.

Frank blew out the candle. He shut his eyes, feeling sick that Magnus was gone, but also exhilarated by the possibility of finding his wife tomorrow.

He would not sleep much tonight.

CHAPTER SIXTY-EIGHT

When Frank awoke in the morning he thought Magnus was in the room, skulking in the corner and sniffling. When he realised Magnus was gone, something within his chest shrivelled.

The others woke up around him. Ralph cleared his throat, then realised he couldn't spit it out, so he swallowed it. Joel was ashen-faced and lethargic, dark patches under his eyes. The line of his jaw was stark and his cheeks were sunken.

Florence looked frail, all bones and skin.

They breakfasted on biscuits and apples brought in by Mary. They sat in the living room while an early morning mist rolled down the streets. There was a sense of anticipation and expectation in the air.

And fear. Always fear.

* * *

Roland offered them his car as he, Mary and Henry had no intention of leaving the village. Frank accepted it gratefully.

They left the house not long after the sun broke the horizon, burned away the mist and threw the day's first shadows upon the ground. The cloud cover was sparse and light, but grey. Maybe there would be rain. The chill in the air sharpened itself against Frank's skin, cleared his nose and made his eyes water. His breath was white vapour.

Roland and Mary gave them some extra supplies, including a spare tank of petrol. Henry stood at the foot of the garden and watched the street, his shotgun at his hip. They packed the car – a Vauxhall Astra – in a hurry.

Ralph, Joel and Florence waited in the car.

"Goodbye, Frank," said Mary. She hugged him. Her body was soft and motherly against him. She gave him a kiss on the cheek. Frank blushed.

"I hope you find your loved ones," she said.

Roland shook his hand. "Stay safe. Good luck out there."

"Thanks for everything," Frank said.

"Don't be silly," said Mary. "We're glad to help."

"Go with God," Roland said.

Ralph coughed to suppress a laugh.

Frank got into the car then looked back at them through the rear window.

They waved. Florence waved back at them.

Ralph moved the car down the driveway. Henry was standing at the end of the driveway. Henry nodded at them. No smile. No expression.

"I hope the monsters don't get them," said Florence.

Frank smiled at her. "I'm sure they'll be fine."

The road ahead was silent and dead.

* * *

Back through the village. They passed Magnus's house, and they looked at it one last time, wondering if he was still in there with his family. They passed Frank's house, and Frank could not help looking at the windows, hoping he'd see Catherine's face peering out at them. They passed the still-burning devastation that had been Joel's house, and Joel ignored it with his head bowed.

No one spoke. The men said a silent goodbye to their home village. Frank wondered if they would ever return here and, when or if the time came, he would want to return.

The village was dead and rotting, and the silent houses were nothing more than memorials to the people who once lived here.

CHAPTER SIXTY-NINE

They passed through many more places that were wrecked and spoiled and burnt. Most of them were lifeless, save for the scattered and ragged groups of infected watching from their squalid holes. Some ran at the car as it passed, bolting from doorways and passageways, reaching for the car with fleshy hooks and stained claws. Gibbering and shambling scarecrow-like figures scrambled out of houses painted with splashes of red.

They saw bodies that had been thrown into pits. They saw heaps of corpses in a field, piled high, burnt and blackened and twisted. Hollowed out and jumbled together. Piles of things taken from nightmares.

Amongst the corpse-mounds were abandoned army vehicles.

A few miles on, Ralph stopped the car next to a field covered with stubbly grass pushing from the earth. There were two figures in the field, heading towards them. Madly-gangling silhouettes.

"What are you doing, Ralph?" asked Joel, glancing towards the approaching figures.

Ralph didn't answer. He stared at them. Every breath he took induced judders in his arms. His face was creased, lilywhite and angry. His eyes were seething moons, bloodshot and framed with shadows the colour of grave dirt. His mouth was a thin and narrow cleft. His temples pulsed. The skin tightened on his face until his cheekbones were pronounced and bulging.

"Ralph," said Frank. "Ralph, what're you doing?"

Ralph grabbed his baseball bat and got out. Before Frank could open his door, Ralph had already opened the gate to the field and was stomping towards the figures, his bat swaying in his hands.

"Wait here," Frank said to Joel and Florence. Then he was out of the car and running after Ralph.

Ralph was almost upon the skittering infected.

Frank broke into a run.

* * *

The inhuman, slick-faced mutations growled at Ralph. The first one, a woman who was naked except for a torn t-shirt stretched over warped arms and crooked shoulders, went at Ralph with hands formed into raking talons. She frothed and screamed, her eyes bleeding down her skeletal face.

Ralph swung his bat and hit her on her arms, breaking them with a sickening crack. She howled, but still came towards him, gibbering and crying. He went at her with such intensity and such rage that when he had finished with her, and his bat was dripping with red, she was nothing more than a shattered heap of wet bones upon the dirt.

The other infected, a man with needle-sharp black quills protruding from his back and a damp gurgling in his throat, leapt at Ralph. His face was malformed into a mask that looked like it was made of melted wax. His mouth parted in small gasps in which his tongue slithered through and tasted the sore skin around his lips.

Ralph smashed his head in. His skull bled onto the cold ground. His legs twitched and jerked. Ralph finished him without hesitation and then spat on his corpse.

Ralph turned to Frank and stared at him. Frank took a step back. Ralph's face was pallid and severe. His eyes bore the look of sickness.

"Are you okay?" Frank kept his voice as low he could.

Ralph exhaled through his mouth. "Am I okay? Good question. I'm fucking dandy, mate; thanks for asking."

"I'm sorry about your parents."

"They didn't deserve to die, Frank."

"I know."

"Then why did they?"

"I don't know."

Ralph's eyes reflected the grey world around him. "I had to kill my mum, Frank. She was infected. She killed and partially ate my dad. She had loved my dad. They had loved each other. And I had to fucking kill her like she was a diseased animal."

"I'm sorry," Frank said.

"It's not just my parents; it's Magnus as well. He's gone. He's one of them. What's happened to the world? What's happened to us? I want things to go back to what they were like before. Everything's fucked, mate."

"Let's go back to the car," said Frank.

"I hate them," said Ralph. "I want to kill them all. I don't want to stop until I've wiped them out."

"I don't think that's possible."

"Doesn't matter. We'll be dead by the end of the week."

"Don't say things like that."

"It's true."

"No, it's not. I made a promise to take care of Florence."

Ralph laughed bitterly and shook his head. "Of course, it comes back to the girl."

"What's that supposed to mean?"

"You know what I mean. The way you look at her. She looks like Emily, doesn't she?"

Frank didn't look at Ralph. "I don't understand what you're talking about."

"You think, somehow, that she's your daughter. I don't know how. But you're wrong. She's not your daughter. Your daughter is dead, Frank."

"Shut up," Frank said.

"She's dead. Emily's dead, Frank."

"Shut up."

"She's gone. Wake up. You're a fucking fool."

Silence. Frank's hands were shaking. They held eye contact, neither willing to look away first.

Then Ralph lowered his gaze to the ground, shame burning his face.

"Let's go back to the car," said Frank.

Ralph nodded. They didn't talk as they left the field.

CHAPTER SEVENTY

Joel was driving the car now and Ralph was sitting in the front seat next to him, staring out at the dull, washed-out world.

They wormed through South Somerset and into Devon. Speckles of rain patted against the windscreen, but the downpour that threatened didn't appear.

They were fifteen miles from Sidmouth, heading towards the coast. There were gulls drifting lazily in the air. They passed a burnt out truck with charred corpses spilling from its open back. Crumbling remains. A charcoal scarecrow was leaning against the truck, white teeth grinning, tufts of hair jutting from its scalp. Drifts of ash like ghosts.

There were no signs of life along this road. The silence and stillness of the empty earth. It was enough to make Joel's heart shrivel.

All he could think about was Anya. All he could think about was holding her, kissing her.

They rounded a corner and there was an army Humvee parked across the road, blocking their way. Three soldiers were standing next to it. One soldier held up his hand for Joel to stop. The others raised their rifles.

Joel stopped the car.

"I hope they're a welcoming party," said Frank.

* * *

The camp had been set up in the fields outside Sidmouth. It was a sprawling, stinking mess of mud, ramshackle tents, open latrines and just under a thousand refugees, according to the soldiers. The military was fighting the infected in the town, mopping up those still infesting the streets and buildings. The soldiers said that the army had incurred heavy losses all over the country and was heavily undermanned here. The remaining soldiers stationed at the camp had been dragged together from the surviving remnants of different units in the area.

The Humvee made its way down the hill towards the camp. The camp filled two fields. Tents in blocks and rows, like the regimental formations. A chain-link metal fence surrounded the entirety of the camp. Just beyond the northern side of the camp was an area of dark grey land. Plumes and drifts of smoke. The soldiers were burning something down there. Flickers of flame.

Florence had a look of wonder on her face.

"The camp's a shithole," said Private Underwood, a young man with dark skin and green eyes. He kept wiping his nose with the back of his hand. A boy with an assault rifle. "But it's better than trying to survive on the streets."

"Too right," said Corporal Graves, from the front passenger seat. He was a bull-necked, softly-spoken man. "The infected are everywhere. That place down there is paradise compared to some of the other emergency camps I've seen set up since the outbreak."

"What happened to the other camps?" asked Joel.

Graves hesitated. "Most of them are gone. Wiped out."

Soldiers patrolled the camp's perimeter. They watched the Humvee approach the front gates. Tired-looking men. They were ghosts. They were shades.

Private Bunce stopped the car. Graves spoke to one of the guards as another soldier confiscated their improvised weapons including Ralph's baseball bat.

Ralph complained, albeit quietly.

The Humvee was waved into the camp.

"Underwood's right," said Ralph. "It is a shithole."

Bunce parked the Humvee next to a portable cabin situated between two haggard shacks. A child was crying somewhere nearby. A dog was barking. Frank could smell wood smoke.

They exited the Humvee. Corporal Graves pointed towards the cabin. "You'll be registered in there. First, you'll all have to be checked for infection. Follow me."

Graves led them to another portable cabin. Inside were two middle-aged women playing Hungry Hippos on a rickety table. The women looked up, annoyed at being disturbed. One of them, grey-haired and plump, glared at Graves.

"More stragglers," she said. It wasn't a question.

Graves nodded. "Yeah. If you'd be so good as to check them for infection, Violet."

The woman eyed him, didn't move.

Graves sighed. "Please."

"That's better," she said, and stood. "Right, you lot take your clothes off. We're gonna take a look at ya." She glanced at the other woman, who had also risen to her feet. "Sandra, you take the girl in one of the cubicles. I'll check the men."

Sandra went to Florence and took her hand. Florence resisted, looked at Frank.

He nodded. "It'll be okay. Go with the nice lady."

"I ain't nice," said Sandra.

Florence whimpered. She snatched her hand from Sandra's and stepped back. "I don't wanna go."

466

Sandra glowered at her and sighed.

Frank went to Florence. He brushed a strand of hair from her forehead and put one hand on her shoulder. He smiled at her. "It'll be okay; we'll be out here. We're not going to leave you here, okay? I would never leave you here on your own."

Sandra rolled her eyes. "Oh, please…"

Florence looked at Frank, bottom lip quivering a little. She blinked. The faintest of nods. "Okay. You promise to stay here?"

"Yes, I promise."

"Okay."

Sandra led her into a cubicle and closed the blue plastic curtain behind them.

Violet looked at Graves. "You stay here, in case they're infected and something happens. One of the last survivors you lot brought in nearly tore my face off."

"It wasn't that bad, Violet," said Graves. "You do embellish, don't you?"

"I'll remember that when one of these fuckers bites me in the arse."

"It's big enough."

"Cheeky fucking squaddie."

Graves nodded, grinning.

"Okay, lads," Violet said, slipping on a pair of surgical gloves. "You lot seen *The Full Monty*? Strip off and let me see what you've got."

* * *

After being given the all-clear they had gone to the registration cabin. Inside was a greasy-haired man behind a desk cluttered with pens, stacks of paper and notebooks. He was called Simms. He noted their names in a register, writing with the methodical nature of a seasoned administrator who takes too much pleasure in numbers and pie charts.

Joel and Frank had asked about Anya and Catherine.

Simms regarded them with pale eyes. There was a yellow bruise on his chin. His glasses were held together by duct tape. His shirt was crumpled. His beard stuck to his lined face in wispy patches and clumps, black and white in colour.

Their names were on the register.

Joel almost cried when her name was read out.

"Where are they?" asked Frank.

"I'm not sure where your wife is, Mr. Hooper, but Mr. Gosling's fiancée is working as a nurse in the medical centre."

Joel swallowed. "The medical centre?"

Simms's face was blank. "It's a big tent about a hundred yards from here. You can't miss it."

Joel was already out of the door.

CHAPTER SEVENTY-ONE

Ralph followed Frank and Florence to the medical centre. Joel was ahead of them, struggling to keep his footing in the mud. He stopped at the entrance to the tent, lifted one of the canvas flaps and looked inside.

The others caught up with him.

Rows of beds, most of them occupied. Medics buzzed between the aisles. Volunteer nurses tended to patients. A soldier stood guard in a far corner, tiredness slackening his face. There was a desk in the nearest corner with a thin woman stationed behind it. Her hair was pulled back in a vicious ponytail. She looked up at Joel. Her eyes were dull and sleepy.

"Excuse me," said Joel, breathing hard from his run. "Is Anya Lewandowski here?"

"Who?" She was sucking on a sweet, rolling it around her mouth.

"Anya Lewandowski."

"Who are you?"

"I'm her fiancé. Where is she? Is she here?"

"She's just finished her shift."

"Where has she gone?" Joel's voice was watery and weak.

"I'm here, Joel," Anya said.

Joel turned. Anya was standing there. She said something under her breath in Polish. She smiled.

He threw his arms around her. Relief and amazement and reunion. Joel held her by the arms. They kissed deeply and slowly. Anya put her face against his chest as he nuzzled her blonde hair. He closed his eyes, rocked against her. She was crying.

Ralph watched them with envy burning in his stomach. And a little bit of hatred. He thought about his parents, their faces dwelling at the fringes of his mind, and tried to push them away. He didn't want to think about them. He wanted to feel anger, not grief. He could do something with anger. It felt like his eyes were heating up inside his head.

"Thank God I found you, Anya," said Joel. "I thought I'd never see you again." He gazed into her eyes.

"I thought you were dead," she said. Her words were muffled by tears. Joel wiped her eyes dry. "I can't believe you're here, all of you. I thought you were either killed or infected."

"We barely survived. You wouldn't believe some of the things I've seen. That we've *all* seen."

Anya looked at the others in turn. "Is Magnus not with you?"

No one spoke.

"Magnus is gone," said Joel, finally.

Anya nodded. Her face was sad and flushed pink, her mouth a thin crease. "Oh. Poor Magnus. I always thought he was a good man."

"Yes, he was," said Joel. "I miss him. We all miss him."

"But the rest of you made it," Anya said. She smiled at them, but the smile faltered at the corners of her mouth when she looked at Frank.

Frank looked at her. "Where is Catherine?"

Something changed in Anya's face.

"I'm sorry, Frank," Anya said, her voice low and trembling from her throat. "I'm sorry."

"Why are you sorry?"

* * *

Anya led them to the northern perimeter of the camp. Frank's legs were shaking cartilage and bone. He looked absently down at his feet as the ground sucked at him; his shoes were caked with mud. A creeping dread was filling his body.

The air smelled of rot and smoke, meat and ash.

Anya turned to him, apologetic and silent. Joel was next to her, and he was slack, pale and morose. Ralph and Florence looked past Frank, out to where the land was mutilated and burnt. The scorched earth where figures meandered.

Frank looked beyond the fence. He placed both hands against the wire. Something was unravelling slowly in his guts and he expected it to come spilling out of him in a slow, slick, slopping bundle. His eyes were stinging. He bit his tongue and wanted to taste his blood.

"I'm sorry, Frank," Anya said. He barely noticed her until she handed him Catherine's wedding ring. He snatched it from Anya's hand, holding it between his fingers.

"She's dead," he said, not believing the words he was saying.

"Yes, Frank," Anya said.

He stared at the ring. It was warm. His last piece of Catherine.

The smoke. The stench. The craters in the ground. Pits where the flames writhed like nesting serpents. Beyond the fence was where the corpses were taken; where the dead were put to rest.

Where Catherine had been put to rest.

Frank swallowed. "Catherine's out there." His voice was papery, the words swept away on the breeze.

Anya said, "The soldiers take the bodies out there to be burned in the pits. I wanted to give Catherine a proper burial, but the soldiers wouldn't let me. They said that every corpse had to be burned in the pits."

Frank watched the men push bodies into the ground. The men were masked and wearing boiler suits, boots and gloves. They were carrying spades and shovels. A mechanical digger punched into the earth and scooped up dirt, piled it into a mound as big as a house. Soldiers guarded the gravediggers, keeping watch upon the grey land.

The dead were piled up and dowsed with petrol. A man lit a match and tossed it into the pit. Flame took to life and roared. The smell of burning flesh.

A horrible, corrupting stench slithered into Frank and coiled around his spine, filling his lungs with black vines that would wrap themselves like twine around his organs. He thought of Catherine being thrown into a pit like a dead animal. Like a stray dog put to sleep and dumped. He thought of those men carrying her to the edge of the pit. Maybe the men had joked whilst doing so; maybe they had said a prayer; maybe they hadn't said a word. He thought of those men counting to three and adding her to a growing heap of cadavers. He thought of her body falling until it came to rest alongside the other dead, her limbs finding the shape of those around her, entwining with other dead limbs, becoming a patchwork of meat and bone and skin. Dead eyes staring at the sky. He thought of her face amongst the other dead faces, and if she had a peaceful look on her face as she was covered with petrol and set alight.

What had been her last thought? What had been the last thing to go through her mind before she died? Did she die wondering if her husband was dead? Did she die mourning him?

All this way to reach her, to find her…

He wondered what she looked like now; a charred, crooked and blistered thing.

Tears struggled down his face; he tasted them, bitter and pathetic. There was an emptiness spreading inside his stomach, gnawing at him with blunt teeth at his soft vulnerable places. A womb of darkness that was poison and anger and all things sickening. His heart was a hammer. His throat tightened until he was sure he would choke. His lungs were heavy and sodden like sacks of water weighed down with stones.

He turned to Anya. She met his gaze.

"How did it happen?" How did she die?"

Anya didn't look away. Her lips moved. No sound. She wiped at her glistening eyes.

"How did she die?!" Frank screamed. "How did it happen?"

"It was to save her from pain. A mercy."

"What?"

"It happened on our first day here." Anya paused, took a deep breath.

"Go on," said Frank, urging her.

"There was an attack. The monsters got into the camp, somehow. They caught her; two of them. They were…biting her. She was crying. Bleeding. The soldiers shot her to spare her suffering. They didn't have a choice."

He wiped his mouth. A vague sense of surrealism overcame him. He was hearing about how his wife died; he couldn't believe it. It had to be a mistake or a bad joke. A trick. Yeah, it had to be a trick. He eyed Anya, blinking away a dull pain in his eyes. He thought he could hear someone laughing at him.

"So that's it? That's how she died? Just like that?"

Anya muttered, "Yes." She looked away from him.

Frank's arms fell to his sides. Dead weight. He felt dizzy. His heart was palpitating. Insects crawled up his spine.

And then it all just faded away. Every single feeling. He lowered his head, stared at the ground, and closed his eyes.

Then someone was holding his hand.

He opened his eyes.

Florence was beside him, offering a porcelain, wan smile. Her skin was warm and soft in the cold air. He accepted her hand, tightening his own around her small fingers, and he tried to return her smile with all of his remaining will, but couldn't. He was exhausted and battered, like something dragged for miles over jagged rocks and sharpened stone.

He wanted to lie down. He wanted to shut everything out and curl up in a dark corner and forget all that had gone before. He was beaten.

There were gunshots.

Frank and the others looked beyond the fence. A small pack of infected was running towards the men working at the pits. Monsters inhabiting barely-human disguises. Men and women, lurching and malformed, hunched and twisted into nightmarish creations from the minds of dark dreamers.

The soldiers shot them down. They sprawled on the ground like beached marine life. Some of the soldiers approached the bodies, inspecting and prodding them with booted feet. They would be taken to the pits and thrown amongst the other bodies.

"More and more infected come each day," said Anya, her voice quiet. "More of them attack the camp each day. They sense us. They know we are here. They come in packs. Some come alone. Lonely ones who come here to die. But, soon, there will be a swarm of them, I think. Like an army."

"A swarm," said Ralph. "Fuck."

"Are more of them coming?" Joel asked.

Frank watched the soldiers collect the dead infected. "Let them come."

CHAPTER SEVENTY-TWO

The next few days passed slowly. Food and water rations were meagre. Every person stank of dirt, sweat and filth. The latrines overflowed, filling the camp with the rotten stench of human waste. More refugees arrived at the camp, exhausted and traumatised people with nowhere else to go. They huddled in small groups waiting for the soldiers and the volunteers to offer them aid. People were waiting to die, or waiting to be saved. Some didn't care, it seemed. Some of the people were broken, gently fading away without a struggle. They were broken long before they'd reached the camp.

Sparse packs of infected attacked the perimeter each night. The threat of them was constant. Every attack was repelled and the infected shot down like wild dogs.

More were on their way, said the rumours drifting around the stinking shelters and tents.

The refugees were the sheep and the soldiers were the shepherd dogs. The infected were the wolves. It rained every day. Puddles formed into large pools of dirty brown water. The ground became boggy as the

481

camp turned into a mud hole, like Glastonbury Festival in the old days. The fires in the corpse-pits still burned. People still died. Medical supplies were running low. People got sick and spent their days confined to the beds in the medical tent.

The refugees were told that the Royal Navy were sending ships to evacuate them. Devonport, the home of the navy's amphibious fleet, was overrun with infected. Gone. Wiped out.

The ships would arrive soon. Salvation was close, it seemed. It was hard to believe, and no one did believe except for the few still hoping and praying for deliverance.

Joel was one of those people.

Four days had passed. It was raining again, great droves of it lashing down, turning the ground into slurry. There was thunder far away. The wind blew cold and sharp. The wind had claws. Joel was hungry. He had only eaten half a chocolate bar all day. The light was already fading. He held Anya's hand as they walked back to their tent. He would never leave her again.

Joel pulled back the canvas flap.

The others were in the tent. Ralph and Florence were playing an improvised game of Snap. A married couple, Ross and Michelle, were huddled in one corner, silent with heads bowed. Stuart Lenkman, a professor of biology before the outbreak, was sitting on the ground staring at his hands. A single mother called Donna cradled her baby son in her arms, cooing to him as he cried. The baby always cried. Joel had forgotten the boy's name. And if he was honest he didn't care. There were other people here, and he didn't know their names. He didn't want to know.

He was so tired he could sleep standing up. His eyelids were drooping. He hadn't slept properly since they had left the holiday cottage. How long ago was that? Six days? A week? Ten days? Two weeks? Could have been a year and he wouldn't have been sure.

The inside of the tent was cramped. The constant poke of elbows and knees against his body. The smell of bad breath, farts, baby shit and body odour. Stale sweat and old socks. He could hear people whispering in the adjacent tent, even above the pattering drizzle, so close were the tents crammed together. More refugees arrived every day. Joel wondered when the soldiers would start turning people away.

"Where's Frank?" Joel asked.

Only Florence looked up. "He's gone for a walk."

"Again?"

"Yes."

He turned to Anya. "I'm going to find him, see if he's okay."

Anya nodded. "I'll stay here. I'm going to try to get some sleep." She kissed him.

Joel went back out into the rain.

* * *

Joel found Frank at the northern perimeter staring at the plague pits. His hood was raised over his head. He was statuesque. The rain was coming down harder, and the wind picked it up and blasted it into Joel's face. He wiped his face dry, tasted the rain in his mouth, on his tongue.

He looked at the sky and wondered if one of the giant sky-things was up there, watching the camp, waiting for the right time to descend and crush it and the poor bastards sheltering here.

Joel spat. Whatever those things were, they were not gods. They were not even fit to be compared to his God. His God was all-loving and merciful and kind.

But does He exist, Joel? asked a little voice secreted at the back of his head like an entrenched parasite. *Are you sure that He exists? Do you still believe in Him? I'm not sure you still do.*

"Piss off," he muttered.

Maybe your faith is wearing thin.

"Go fuck yourself."

We'll see about that.

He shook his head. The voice didn't go away, only faded in volume. He walked over to Frank, clearing his throat to let him know he was there. Frank didn't react.

Joel stood beside him, looking out through the fence as the breeze picked up drifts of ash and soot from the mass graves and made them into swarms that tainted the sky. It was desolation. No one was at the pits.

It was a wasteland, scorched and ruined. Poisoned.

"Hey, mate," said Joel.

"Hey." Frank's voice was quiet. His hands were in his pockets. Overhead, gulls and crows performed aerial duels over scraps of food and rubbish. If Joel closed his eyes and listened very, very carefully, he could hear the sea. He had always loved the sea, ever since his parents had taken him on daytrips to Weymouth and Seaton when he was a boy.

His parents were with God now. No suffering for them. No pain. For the first time since they had died, he was glad they were dead. He was glad for that maniac in the stolen Porsche who had run them off the road. He was glad they had died together.

He almost envied them.

"You alright, mate?" asked Joel.

"Yeah."

485

"We're worried about you."

"I'm fine."

"You're not."

"I don't care if you believe me."

Joel didn't reply. He hugged himself against the cold.

Frank said, "I want to go out there and see if I can find her."

Joel turned to him. Frank was staring at the pits.

"The soldiers won't let you go out there unless you're on grave-digging detail. You know that."

"I'll do that, then."

"I'm sorry about Catherine. I can't pretend to know what you're going through, but you've still got us. You've still got your mates. And Florence."

"Florence," Frank muttered.

"I remember you said to me that you promised to take care of Florence. You said to me that you would look after her."

"So what?"

"So, are you going to break your promise to her? I know what it's like to lose parents. Imagine what it's been like for her being a young girl. She needs you, Frank. You're her guardian."

Frank looked at Joel, shallow creases and lines in his face. A darkening beard. "When we left for your stag weekend, I didn't think I'd never see my wife again. She didn't even get a decent burial. She deserves to be honoured."

Joel said nothing.

Then Ralph appeared alongside Joel. He was shivering against the cold and rain.

The three men looked out towards the plague pits, and beyond that, the hills and fields.

If God exists, Joel, said the voice in his mind, *how come everything's falling apart? How come your friends' loved ones are dead? What did they do to deserve death? What did they do to endure such suffering? Where was God when they were suffering and dying? Shouldn't He have saved them? Shouldn't He save us all?*

Joel sighed.

If your God does exist, Joel, He's an utter cunt. And, deep down, you know this.

Joel looked out across the fields and thought he saw distant figures flitting between trees and hedgerows. Could have been his imagination; he was tired and his eyes ached.

"I haven't seen a plane or a helicopter for a while," said Ralph.

"That's a bad sign," Frank murmured.

"Is it?"

Ralph grimaced against the breeze pushing at his face. "Frank's right. Yesterday I heard from a bloke that Salisbury's been lost. The army were overrun. Don't know where he heard it from."

Frank closed his eyes. "The centre cannot hold."

Ralph looked at them. "Is this the end of the human race? Stuck here at this shitty camp? Maybe we're the last ones left, waiting for the monsters to close in. Maybe we're just treading water, getting tired, until we get swallowed up."

"Will the ships arrive?" asked Joel. "What do you think?"

Ralph grunted. "I think we're waiting to die here. I think we're alone. Nobody's coming to save us."

CHAPTER SEVENTY-THREE

The days and nights clouded together and it was cold all the time. Hunger was something that kept Ralph awake at night. He thought of his parents often, especially his mother. Her face, her awful mouth and her nightmare eyes, made a nest in his mind. He considered leaving the camp and travelling beyond the perimeter, past the soldiers and into the ruined country to find something to kill. Despite his quick temper, he had never felt the urge to kill anyone or anything, but now he was being consumed by it. The urge made his heart palpitate and his mouth go dry. Made his teeth itch until he could barely sit still.

Maybe he'd go home, where he belonged, and give his parents a decent burial. Put them in the ground. Maybe he'd just build a funeral pyre for them. Yeah. Burn the dead. Fire purifies.

He wondered if he would be buried or cremated or left to rot as sustenance for the rodents, the insects and the birds.

Ralph was huddled in one corner of the tent, his arms wrapped around his chest. The cold air he pulled into his mouth made his gums ache and thrum.

His breath stank of sewage. He tongued the gap where one of his front teeth had once been. It was spongy and raw, tasted of copper.

There were gunshots at the perimeter. The wailing cries of the infected. Guttural sounds echoing through the night. Strangled, insane shrills scraped from bleeding throats. It was enough to send a man insane. He shivered. It was a cosmic terror; something alien that didn't care for him or any other human. Something beyond the understanding of humanity. Something that couldn't be reasoned with, because the plague only wished to infect and multiply.

And when there was nobody left to infect...

The gunfire stopped. Raised voices. Then silence again.

Ralph decided to stay. He would help his mates. Help them survive.

He would stay with them until the end.

* * *

Morning. No colour in the world. Everything bleached and drained.

"The ships are coming!" Joel and Anya burst into the tent, hope and exhaustion across their faces.

"What?" asked Frank. He and Florence were playing Snap. Florence had won the last five games.

Joel got his breath back. "One of the soldiers said the ships are coming."

"To Sidmouth," said Anya. "Very soon."

"How soon?" Ralph was watching from his claimed corner, chewing on a stale granola bar. It had the texture of cardboard.

Joel smiled, showing dirty teeth. "Today."

* * *

Word of the ships' arrival spread around the camp. The ships were waiting just off the coast. The refugees were told that requisitioned buses were coming to transport them to Sidmouth, which had finally been cleared of most of its infected population.

For the first time in a while people spoke with a renewed sense of hope and purpose. Some couples even rutted in their tents in celebration.

An old man and his elderly wife wept and embraced.

Some started to sing songs in celebration.

People began to talk about salvation.

Ralph thought they were fools.

CHAPTER SEVENTY-FOUR

The refugees massed at the front of the camp. The large gates were kept closed and the soldiers manned the perimeter as they had done before. The air was cloying and turgid. So many different and terrible smells. The ground was sticky, clinging onto those standing upon it. Some people were caked in mud. Children sniffled and watched the adults with glassy, expectant eyes. They were so close to being rescued from this diseased isle. No one wanted to be left behind. Apprehension and anxiety flitted through the crowd like the creeping arms of a silent mist.

Some people stood in silence, but a few outspoken men, determined and a little too proud, advocated walking the few miles to Sidmouth. But they were overruled by the soldiers; it would be too dangerous on foot.

Some people complained, but quickly fell silent when a coach crested the hill and started down the road towards the camp.

Then people were cheering.

Frank was jostled by the warm, musty bodies around him. He kept hold of Florence.

There were only five coaches. Each coach could hold probably fifty to sixty people. Not enough to carry all of the refugees. The rest of the crowd realised this just as he did.

The crowd surged. Bodies pressed him on all sides. Joel was hugging Anya, keeping her close to him. Florence whimpered and then she was drowned out by the collective roar of the crowd. A man was asking if they'd be left behind. A woman asked if more coaches were coming. The pulse of the crowd quickened, people slipping in the mud, and some were knocked down, battered by errant legs and feet. Someone screamed.

A gunshot.

The crowd fell silent.

"Please stay calm!" a sergeant said, raising his hands. "There is no need to panic."

"Where's the rest of the coaches?" asked a fat man near the front of the crowd.

The sergeant hesitated then looked to the officer in charge of the camp, Captain Shaw, who was watching the coaches descend the hill.

Shaw turned to the crowd. He was a tall and morose man, black haired and dark-skinned. Eyes like dark stone fetched from the earth. "Everyone will be evacuated, I promise you. I have been told by my superiors that there are more transports arriving soon. There's no need to worry. Salvation is here."

He wasn't lying. Frank could tell. But Shaw's superiors might have lied to him, for all he knew.

The coaches halted outside the front gates. They were being driven by soldiers, haggard and exhausted-looking. The sides of the coaches were streaked and smeared with blood, grime and mud. Frank wondered if the coaches had enough fuel to reach Sidmouth.

He held Florence's hand and offered her a crooked smile.

* * *

The first coach had been filled, packed tight, the refugees weighing it down as it left the camp.

Frank and the others were near the front of the crowd. He was confident they'd be on the next coach when it was ready to receive them. He breathed in, breathed out, tried to keep his heart steady. Florence was jittery beside him.

"Are we going to France? Or an island?" she asked, large eyes peering up at him.

His mouth felt dry and cracked, like a desiccated corpse's leathery skin. "Maybe, Florence. We'll find out when we get on the ships."

"Okay."

Frank looked at Ralph and nodded. Ralph returned the gesture. Joel and Anya were struggling to stay on their feet as the crowd swayed and flowed.

"Keep together," Frank said. "No matter what." He looked down at Florence. He wished Catherine was here with them. He wished she was here to hold his hand.

His insides were cold, and he missed her enough to offer his own heart for her return. But he had to push away his grief and deal with it later. Now, he had to help Florence.

The second coach was slowly filled with refugees. The soldiers checked the lines of people to keep them in order. Belongings were left behind. All they could take was what they were wearing.

Frank and the others missed the cut off point for the second coach.

"At least we'll get a decent seat on the next one," Ralph said sourly.

"Hopefully," said Frank.

Then there was gunfire. A woman screamed. Frank looked to the east side of the camp.

"What's that sound?" asked Florence.

Frank lowered his head to look at her. "What sound?"

But then he heard it, and so did everybody else.

A roaring. A screaming. A wailing. The tremor of the ground from a thousand footfalls.

"What is that?" asked Joel.

The horizon was filled with an enormous writhing swarm of infected. Sprouting tendrils and baying mouths. Mangled faces with too many teeth. Abominations. Travesties and twitching wretches. So many of them. More than a thousand. More than two thousand. More than three thousand.

Enough to wipe the refugees from the earth.

The soldiers opened fire upon the swarm, but the infected still came forward, their numbers barely affected by the hail of gunfire meeting them. The infected surged down the hill and nothing could stop them.

The refugees panicked, bolted for the buses. The gates were wrenched open. People were trampled and left as easy pickings for the infected. The coaches were swamped by the rush of desperate, terrified people.

The swarm of monsters was upon the refugees. Blood and meat. Screams and pleas for mercy.

The infected tore through crowd.

CHAPTER SEVENTY-FIVE

No one spoke on the coach. Frank was staring out the window. The blood on his face was not his own and still wet. Florence was on his lap, silent. Ralph was sitting next to them, his head bowed. Joel and Anya were seated across the aisle. A few people were crying and sobbing quietly. A woman at the front of the coach was wailing, mourning her husband who'd been left behind.

There were many empty seats.

Only two of the remaining four coaches had escaped. The other two had been left behind, overrun by the infected. Hundreds of refugees left behind to die or be assimilated into the swarm.

Frank was still shaking.

The infected had poured down the hill towards the camp. A wave of gnashing mouths and rending claws. The swarm had emitted a collective scream and crashed against the crowd of refugees. The soldiers who stood and fought fell quickly, overwhelmed by the sheer number of infected. Other soldiers turned and boarded the coaches, abandoning the people they were supposed to protect.

Screams had filled the air.

Frank had managed to board one of the coaches, carrying Florence in his arms, Ralph and Joel and Anya right behind him. They were among the last on the coach before it pulled away from the camp, shrieking infected hanging from it trying to get at the people inside. More infected had been crushed by the coach's large wheels, snapping and cracking like wet twigs.

Frank had looked back at the camp as they drove away. The image of what he'd seen was branded into his mind. Only a fraction of the refugees had managed to escape, he estimated. He shook his head, tried not to believe it.

How many had been left behind?

They were approaching Sidmouth. Houses appeared alongside the road, dead and empty. Piles of bodies stacked in a field.

He put his hand in his jacket pocket, felt for Catherine's wedding band. He was relieved it was still there. He looked at his own ring; it was loose on his finger.

The coach entered Sidmouth.

* * *

500

Through the town, towards the beach. Gutted buildings and smoke. Shattered windows. Frank saw a little girl's bicycle lying by the pavement, its front wheel buckled. Cars had been pushed to the sides of the road to allow the coaches through.

Gulls swooped overhead and drifted over the roofs.

The army had cleaned out this town.

The two coaches reached the shorefront. Coaches and buses from other camps and rescue centres had already arrived here. Beyond the seawall, the beach was covered with refugees, crammed together and waiting to be rescued. Frank was reminded of holidays in Spain where the beaches were packed with sunbathers and tourists. There were thousands of people here, stretched along the beach for a mile. A desperate, exhausted mass of humanity. The thrum and drone of chatter and moaning and shouting. Some people were injured; on crutches or being carried on stretchers. Medics tended to those needing help. Soldiers patrolled the beach. There weren't many soldiers left.

And beyond the beach was the sea, tempestuous and broiling; dark and uncaring. Waves fell against the shore. Some people were even stood in the shallows, the water up to their knees, so desperate were they to escape.

The tide was low.

Frank counted four Royal Navy ships were out there, as close to the shore as they could come without beaching themselves in the shallows. Landing craft were ferrying people straight from the beach to the ships. But the turn-around was slow and torturous. It would take hours – maybe a full day – to evacuate the refugees.

It could all fall apart so easily, Frank thought, as he and the others were herded from the coach to the edge of the beach.

"It'll take ages to evacuate us all," said Joel. He squeezed Anya's hand.

"We'll have to wait," said Frank. "No other choice. At least we have some time before it gets dark."

"I'd like to be out of here before nightfall," said Joel. "Anyone fancy swimming out there?"

"That'd be pointless," said Frank. "And probably suicidal. You'd drown in that water. And there's no guarantee the ships would let you on if you made it out there. They could even shoot you."

"Can the infected swim?" asked Joel.

"I hope not," said Frank.

"We'll be okay," Anya said.

Ralph looked out to sea. "Now we just have to wait. Fucking great."

They had been waiting for over three hours without food, water and shelter from the elements. The landing craft from the ships constantly went back and forth delivering people to the safety of the waiting ships, but the beach was still packed with bodies. Soldiers deterred desperate refugees from diving into the water and swimming from the shore.

The smell of dead fish, brine and seaweed filled the air, carried upon the wind sweeping at the huddled masses. The waves pawed at the shore, frothing and churning. A few small fires had been started, scattered along the beach like small beacons. People gathered around them, warming their hands and faces. But most of the refugees were left in the cold.

Frank and the others were sitting in a small circle, shielding one another from the wind. Damp sand under their feet; granules of it danced in the cold sea breeze, invading their eyes and mouths, and sticking to clothes and skin.

"You think we'll ever come back?" asked Anya.

"Not sure I want to," said Joel. "The country is dead."

Ralph scooped a handful of sand and then let it fall between his fingers. "If the whole world's been hit by the plague, then it doesn't really matter where we go."

Joel shook his head. "There must be somewhere safe…"

"There is, somewhere," said Frank, mindful of Florence next to him. "The navy will find somewhere safe."

"I hope so," said Joel.

Ralph muttered, "I'm not getting my hopes up." He looked at the others and there was something dead behind his eyes. It unsettled Frank. "This is the end of the world, isn't it? What will happen to us once we get to safety? Will we be running and hiding every day for the rest of our lives?"

No one answered. Ralph was right, but what else could they do? Give up? Frank couldn't give up while Florence was still alive.

"These are the last days," said Ralph. "And this is the last plague. I'm glad I'm not religious, because I'd be shitting myself right now."

"What do you mean?" Joel asked him.

"Think about it. If you're a believer in God and Jesus Christ, how does that fit in to all of this? How could God let this happen?"

"I don't think it's that simple," said Joel.

"Really?" said Ralph. "Surely it is that simple? All of these people around us, these refugees who were just ordinary people not even a fortnight ago, with lives and jobs. Families. Birthday parties. Roast dinners on Sundays. Hangovers. Bank accounts and mortgages. Loans and bills. That Monday morning feeling at work. Remember the mundaneness of the old world, and remember it well, because it's gone forever, my friends. All gone. And God hasn't lifted a finger to help us."

Joel was shaking his head. He stared at Ralph until Ralph looked away. Anya touched Joel on the shoulder and he turned to her and accepted her head on his shoulder.

Ralph started picking his teeth.

Frank looked up and saw the soldiers glancing nervously at the road leading into the town.

Something cold and wet bristled in his stomach.

"I'm hungry," said Florence.

"So am I," Frank told her. "We'll have something to eat when we get on the ship."

She clutched her belly. "Okay."

He smiled at her and the corners of his mouth hurt.

A terrible shriek rose from within the town. It rippled through the crowded beach.

Ralph took his finger out of his mouth.

"Oh shit," said Joel.

The infected streamed out of the streets. The swarm from the camp had arrived. Victims of the plague and those recently welcomed to the swarm.

The soldiers opened fire.

CHAPTER SEVENTY-SIX

The crowd turned towards the sea. Frank grabbed hold of Florence. Bodies rushed around them. Joel and Anya gripped each other, desperate not to be separated. Ralph was moving with the tide of people, towards the water. The fires were trampled and extinguished by so many feet. Ashes and cinders flitted in the air.

Many people were fleeing into the water, attempting to swim to the ships.

Frank glanced back. The infected were being shredded by suppressing fire. Grenades detonated with sharp concussions, throwing infected bodies into the air and slicing the swarm with hot shrapnel. Bodies fell and lay twitching; others were ripped apart by automatic fire. Death-screams and gurgles from torn throats.

But the infected were still coming, pouring through the streets.

There were not enough soldiers to hold them back.

The refugees stampeded towards the shore. The landing craft hadn't returned yet. Frank was terrified that they wouldn't return at all. People were screaming, shouting, wailing, crying. The soldiers at the shore who'd been organising the loading of refugees onto the landing craft were trying to hold the people back from the water. Men and women fell down in the shallows. Some were trampled. Others drowned in less than a foot of water. There was red in the surf. One of the soldiers fired his rifle into the air, but to no effect on the refugees, who simply engulfed him. Parents carried their children to the water's edge. A few refugees had thrown themselves into the sea, attempting to swim to safety. Some people had been knocked down on the beach and were now crawling towards the shore on their hands and feet. Some were lying prone, dead or unconscious.

Frank stumbled, knocked from all sides by flailing arms and elbows. A hand struck him in the face and he reeled away, stunned, but still holding Florence. He would not let go of her. They were in the middle of the crowd. Frank couldn't see the water past the scrum of bodies. A woman was screaming next to his face, deafening him temporarily.

The ground was trembling underneath him.

Behind him the infected were coming forward under withering fire. Machine guns opened up, ripping into their ranks. Frank wondered how much more ammunition the soldiers had left.

"The boats are coming back!" someone in front of him shouted. The crowd broiled. Utter confusion and chaos. The light dimmed. Frank couldn't move; he and Florence were hemmed in tight. She was crying. He kissed the top of her head said that everything would be okay.

More gunfire from the water's edge. Were the soldiers firing upon the refugees? Frank glanced at Joel, Anya and Ralph. He dug his feet into the sand and pushed forwards, struggling through the bodies, determined to get to the water. An elbow clocked him in his right eye and his vision swayed. Behind him he could hear the others following his lead. Ralph was shouting.

Frank stumbled forwards. Cold water up to his ankles like metal encasing his skin. He could hear the landing craft approaching. People begging for help. The soldiers were shouting.

The gunfire behind him lessened. The soldiers were falling to the infected. And then there were screams from the back of the crowd. The infected were amongst them, ripping and tearing. People collided with one another, fell down, were crushed. Bones snapped. Bodies left helpless on the sand. People collapsed, peeled and emptied like treats.

He had to get to the landing craft.

Bullets shot through the crowd. A man's head became red mist and splinters of bone. Another man was caught in the shoulder, and he went down and was trampled, broken and cracked open.

Frank kept hold of Florence. He clung to her so tight that she whimpered. Looking back, he saw people being dragged down, swamped by the rampaging infected. Their screams didn't last long.

He saw a woman, coated in fluids, her arms like scythes. Bony spines had erupted from her back. She had lost most of her hair, and her knees were bending the wrong way. She was removing a man's throat with her puckered mouth. And there were others, their gaping mouths delivering the most awful of sounds, like newborn things being pulled from primordial mud. Hungry mouths. The hungriest mouths. Wet grimaces that could have been smiles. Sharp-toothed things with shivery breath, their eyes loose and grey within their sockets. Engorged growths consuming faces, and limbs melding together. Naked, lurid bodies.

There was an infected man with eyes and mouths on his naked back, and the mouths were opening and closing, sensing prey and movement, something they could batten upon, something to suckle and drain.

There was a bloated, wheezing figure, neither man nor woman, but something in-between. Its sightless eyes were vestigial, distractions from the rest of its slippery, greased form.

People were falling.

Frank was pushed one way then the other. He tripped, fell, managed to land on his back. He was kicked in the back of the head. Things blurred. Florence was screaming. He saw dead bodies on the ground, and the infected battening upon them. More infected were coming, chattering and shrilling. He couldn't see Joel or Anya or Ralph. Florence knelt by him and helped him up. He stood, picked her up again. An infected man barrelled towards him, mouth lined with teeth growing over his lips. His hands were raking claws. Things squirmed underneath his skin. Frank dodged him at the last moment, and the man jumped upon a screaming woman and ripped at her face until her eyes were gone and her skin was hanging like a sloughed mask.

Frank looked around, breathing hard. There were injured on the ground, their hands clutched to bleeding wounds and bite marks. A man was having what appeared to be a seizure. He was becoming infected, his skin paling and his flesh shifting on his bones, which were snapping and reforming until the seizure passed and he flipped onto all fours, snapping

511

his mouth at the air. His eyes filled with scarlet and black, and he leapt away into the crowd.

Hot blood sprayed Frank from a teenage boy who fell with an infected man's dark tendrils puncturing his throat.

Frank put his head down, held Florence tightly, and shoulder-barged through the crowd. He glimpsed wet mouths and squirming tongues flicking outwards. Horrid, malformed faces shrieking and covered in blood. There was a severed arm on the ground, still with a wristwatch. People were dragged back up the beach, clawing at the sand.

He saw a blond-haired girl ravaged by two infected men. They pulled at her and she came apart easily like tender well-cooked meat slipping from the bone. An old woman, bleeding from her stomach, crawled on her hands and knees, reaching out to Frank, until a girl with a serrated mouth, moving like an insect, with fleshy vestigial limbs emerging from her torso, pulled the old woman towards her. Frank watched. The infected girl's limbs developed clawed fingers and began pulling apart the old woman's mouth until her face tore with a sound like ripping fabric. Then some kind of dangling stinger emerged from the girl's torso and slid between the old woman's legs. The stinger began to thrust, moving slickly and deep. The girl's body sagged and she let out a soft moan, both tortured and pleasurable. The old woman bucked and writhed, her hands flailing vainly at her assailant until the life drained out of her and she went still as the infected girl violated her.

This all happened in the space of five seconds.

Frank turned away and vomited onto his shoes.

Florence was screaming.

Frank turned back and held the girl.

A man stood before them, his clothes torn and his body shaking. His mouth stretched wide and a glistening proboscis emerged from between his teeth. Frank stepped back. The proboscis probed the air. A clear fluid dripped from its tip and its sheath pulled back like a foreskin revealing a pink, thin appendage with a sharp, wriggling point.

The man lunged at them.

Florence cried out.

The man's head exploded and he collapsed.

Ralph walked over to the man and stepped on the still-wriggling proboscis until it was crushed beneath his foot and leaked white fluid onto the sand. He was holding a pistol. Army-issue. He looked at Frank and nodded.

"Where did you get that gun from?" Frank asked.

"Belonged to a soldier. He didn't need it anymore."

Frank tightened his grip on Florence's hand.

Ralph put a bullet through a growling woman's face as she lunged at him. Then he turned back to them. "Follow me."

CHAPTER SEVENTY-SEVEN

The infected man opened his stinking mouth and snapped his teeth towards Anya. She recoiled, stumbling. The man let forth a growling roar and the fleshy needles on his face quivered. A dark fluid dripped from his eyes.

Joel smashed him in the face with a rock he'd found on the sand. The infected man fell to his knees, clutching his face with one gnarled hand.

Joel brought the rock down on the man's head. The man slumped on his back as his shattered skull leaked a putrescent liquid onto the sand. Joel discarded the rock, grabbed Anya and ran for the shore, pushing people out of the way. He saw one of the landing craft straight ahead. Navy crewmen were loading people onto it, and there were Royal Marines alongside them, shooting any infected that got too close. Other craft were getting swamped by the desperate refugees. One craft was a heaving mass of bodies, infected and uninfected, the marines lying dead in the surf.

Some of the craft were leaving. Joel pulled Anya with him, bursting into a sprint.

A young boy bolted towards them, his body festering with coiled tentacles and rupturing tumours. Joel and Anya halted as the boy blocked their path. The boy wailed through a contorted mouth. His head split open into teeth-lined halves and a nest of trembling wormlike feelers rose from within his cranium like snakes from a charmer's pot. The feelers, each one of them approximately three feet in length, possessed clusters of tiny sucking mouths upon their forms, dilating at the close proximity of prey. Joel and Anya backed away, and the boy-thing followed. Pale, milk-white spider-legs grew from the boy's flanks and came to rest on the ground lifting him from his original height and supporting him in his new form.

Joel put himself between Anya and the boy-creature. People were running past them. The infected boy reared up and wailed a terrifying and painful sound and came towards Joel and Anya.

Then Joel did something he never thought he would have done.

A middle-aged, chubby man stumbled next to them, and Joel pushed the man towards the boy-thing. The man screamed and looked at Joel with an expression of undiluted terror and fear.

"I'm sorry," said Joel, but the man didn't hear him.

The boy reeled the man in and wrapped dripping tentacles around his body. The man begged to be released. The boy pinned him on the sand.

The man screamed again.

The boy's feelers elongated from within his head and clamped upon the man's face. The man wriggled and squirmed, clawing at the feelers as they drilled into his eyes, his mouth, and the soft tissue of his cheeks and chin.

The man stopped moving. The feelers detached, then retreated, leaving only a skull and a few scraps of skin and muscle.

Joel and Anya ran for the shore. The craft was almost full, getting ready to leave.

"Wait for us!" Joel shouted.

One of the marines turned and fired at them. They both screamed, then glanced back to see a bloated woman collapsing onto the sand behind them, a red wound where her face had been.

"Quickly," the marine said. He shot two more infected advancing towards them.

Joel pushed Anya onwards. His legs felt like they were on fire. One last push. All he could hear was the screams of the infected.

The marines pulled them on board over the lowered ramp, and they collapsed among the other refugees who had made it. Many of them were crying

517

and sobbing; others were in stunned, traumatised silence.

Joel turned back to the beach. He couldn't see Ralph, Frank or Florence. The shoreline was a field of slaughter. Blood stained the sand and made the water red. Body parts floated in the water. Most of the craft were leaving. So many people left behind. The majority of the refugees still on the beach were either dead or too badly injured to move. Arms and legs torn away. Severe mutilations. Grisly mounds of meat still alive and begging for mercy. Packs of the infected were feeding.

Gunshots down the beach, where a few marines were holding off the infected until their craft could escape. There were bodies everywhere. He saw infected children scavenging on warm remains and sucking the marrow from snapped bones.

Monsters stalked the beach.

"Let's go," said one of the marines.

"You can't leave yet," said Joel. "My friends are still out there."

"Sorry, mate. It's too late. Too dangerous to stay."

"Look!" said Anya, pointing to their left.

Frank, Florence and Ralph were running towards them, weaving between scavenging infected and wounded refugees. Ralph raised his hands. He had a pistol.

A pack of infected were behind them.

"Come on!" Joel shouted.

They splashed through the surf towards the craft. Ralph turned and shot two infected.

They kept running.

"Move faster!" Joel said.

They were ten yards from the craft when something came out of the water and battened upon Frank.

CHAPTER SEVENTY-EIGHT

Frank went down and dropped Florence. She fell into the water with him. She reached out for him and screamed. Frank looked at her once before he was dragged into the water. The creature had hold of him and there was a sharp pain in his stomach. He saw its face, and the sight of it almost stopped his heart. He took in mouthfuls of saltwater and it filled his lungs.

The pale thing had once been human, emaciated and twitching, its eyes like black marbles surrounded by bleeding cysts pricked with tiny teeth. The ragged remains of a white shirt clung to its form. It was still wearing a red tie. It leered at him with a wound of a mouth and lifted him out of the sea. He vomited water, sucked in air, his eyes stinging. Cold fingers gripped him. His stomach was bleeding. The creature's teeth were stained red. It roared at him and he smelled its fetid, warm breath. Rot and mould and something worse.

Ralph shot it in the face. The creature dropped Frank. Ralph pulled him up. The other infected were closing in.

Frank turned to Florence. "Go! Get on the boat!"

Florence hesitated.

"Go!"

Then Joel was running back to them, kicking his legs through the water. He scooped her up, but she resisted him, flailing her arms.

Agony bolted through Frank's body. The wound on his stomach was deep. He was losing blood steadily. Ralph was beside him. He looked dazed and pale. There was a red slash on his neck; the edges of the wound were already turning black.

They looked at each other. They both understood. Then they turned to Joel and Florence.

Joel was crying. He nodded.

"Get out of here," said Ralph.

Joel said nothing. Florence had stopped fighting him. She was shivering and soaking wet, her red hair plastered to her head.

"I can't leave you both here," Joel said. "You can't stay here."

Ralph raised his pistol, aimed it at Joel. "Go."

"Get Florence off the beach," said Frank. "Get to Anya."

Joel looked at them, his face slack and unbelieving and his mouth open. He glanced at the pistol.

Ralph's arm was shaking. "You have to go, mate. No time."

Joel nodded, turned and ran back to the craft with Florence.

Frank watched them climb aboard the craft. Anya took hold of the girl and hugged her. They turned to Frank and Ralph.

Frank waved. He had done all he could. He had done his best. They would live. They would survive.

Ralph turned back to the pursuing infected. He fired the pistol until it clicked empty. One infected man remained from the pack. Ralph let the man come to him. Ralph pistol-whipped the man in the face until he went down, and then dropped the pistol so he could gouge out the man's eyes with his thumbs. The deformed man raked at Ralph's body with hooked claws until he went limp in Ralph's hands and floated away, face-down and half-submerged in the water.

Frank went to Ralph and helped him to his feet in the surf. Ralph's hands were raw and weeping, the skin torn into maggot-white flaps and clefts. He was bleeding into the water.

They both turned to watch the last of the landing craft leave.

They staggered onto the beach, supporting each other. Both of them were losing blood. The monsters left them alone.

Ralph nodded and tried to smile. "I can feel it inside me. I don't feel like myself."

"Me neither," said Frank.

The cries of the dying echoed across the blood-soaked beach. Offal and bones were scattered. They walked past a little girl peeling a man's lips from his mouth. She paused to grin at them.

Groups of feeding infected had gathered along the beach, snaffling up piles of slick remains. They fed slowly and calmly. There was an infected man in a straitjacket, stumbling around in circles, his face a torn ruin. Black tentacles had burst through the straitjacket and were wavering around him. He was laughing.

There were many deformities and mutations. Faces with too many eyes. Bony, pale figures stumbling around clutching pieces of sopping flesh. Infected meat that glistened like succulent jelly, quivering and dividing and forming pincers, vermiform tentacles and black maws. Vaginal mouths parted to show such sharp teeth. Bodies were slipped free from their skin and consumed by ravenous appetites.

The beach was full of meat.

Frank and Ralph watched them feed. They made no attempt to harm the infected. They turned back to the sea and the ships out there waiting for the evacuated refugees. The lucky ones.

"I'm glad they made it," said Frank.

"Joel and Anya will take care of Florence," Ralph said. "You did the right thing, mate. You saved the little girl, and you got us here. You gave us a chance of survival."

Frank didn't answer. He looked out towards the ships, and he wondered where they would go.

Maybe they were just delaying the inevitable.

"Extinction level event," said Ralph, as though he had heard Frank's thoughts.

Frank nodded.

There were flashes of light from the ships. He didn't realise what this meant until the shells detonated around them. The world became a roaring of explosions and blinding light. The groups of feeding infected were smashed into wet mulch. The naval guns hammered at the shore, sending up great billows of sand, scarring the ground and obliterating those still on the beach. Shrapnel flew, decapitating the infected and shredding bodies into pulp. No sound but the boom of the guns and the shells hitting the ground. Frank couldn't hear himself scream. He and Ralph tried to stagger from the beach. A shell landed nearby, engulfing them in plumes of sand and dirt. The ground shook. They fell down. The scream of the shells overhead. Boom and crash. The earth shaking, coming apart, tearing and ripping. The smell of fire and burnt meat.

Frank looked up at the darkening sky, the taste of blood in his mouth. He felt the pain of the infected as they were destroyed.

The screaming world became oblivion.

CHAPTER SEVENTY-NINE

The landing craft moved towards the waiting ships. The escaped refugees were silent, vacant eyed and exhausted. Florence was sitting with her head on Anya's chest while Anya stroked her hair and hushed whispered words of comfort to her. Joel rested his arms on the side of the craft, staring at the beach they had escaped. The horizon was stained with smoke. The beach was a ruin of scars and craters. Great Britain was gone. England was gone. He would never return.

What about Europe and the rest of the world?

Joel wiped his eyes. "We made it."

"Not all of us," said Florence.

"I hope Ralph and Frank died quickly," Joel said. "I hope they're not alive and infected."

"Nobody could've survived on the beach," said Anya.

Joel took out his crucifix and extended his arm until his hand was over the side. The sea was protean and tempting, abyssal and dark. He lowered the crucifix towards the water.

Joel's hand flinched.

The waves crashed.

EPILOGUE

Frank awoke and watched the sky until his eyes stung. He was tired and his bones were heavy.

He sat up. His lungs ached with a cancerous pain. His inhaler was gone. He spat on the sand. His spit was bloody and glistening. His body was intact. The wound in his stomach itched and burned. He'd lost a lot of blood.

He was dying, and he knew this.

He looked around. Human remains littered the beach. The ground had been churned and torn. Craters and gouges in the earth.

There was something beside him.

Ralph.

"I'm sorry, mate," said Frank. His voice was weak and slurred.

Ralph had been spread around. Shrapnel had ripped most of him into sloppy little bits. The rest of him was a smear upon the sand.

Frank stood over his Ralph's remains and said a silent farewell to his friend. Then he turned towards the horizon. The ships were gone. There was only the sea. The waves were growing tall and violent.

There was a storm coming.

He hoped the storm wiped the land clean.

Frank walked from the beach, heading inland. His heartbeat was slow and loud. He stumbled on rubbery legs. Sweat beaded on his skin. He passed through Sidmouth. The infected he encountered left him alone. He was one of them, of course. His body, even as it was weakening and dying, was changing. His skin was getting paler, almost translucent. The cries of the gulls were the screams of tortured men.

He thought of Florence, and was grateful she had escaped. She was safe. Joel and Anya were safe. It was some consolation.

He realised how stupid he'd been to think Florence was his daughter. To think she was Emily.

She could have been his daughter, in a different life.

But he was only a man and there was only one life. And if he lived, he would become something else. He walked back to the camp, thinking of Catherine. He would be with her again. He would find her.

The camp was ruined. The two coaches left behind had been smashed and battered. Bodies on the ground. Crows picked over the cadavers. Frank could smell the rot and slaughter still in the air.

There were still some infected here; the stragglers and those too weak to walk away. Wretched specimens being absorbed by the mud and filth.

Captain Shaw was sitting on the ground against a scrum of corpses, staring at the skin peeling from his hands. His bones had changed and shifted so that his body was an ill-fitting sack over them. He wheezed and groaned. He had paled to ivory. His eyes were red-rimmed and haunted. He sagged like a pile of old clothes.

Shaw's naked stomach had birthed a colony of red writhing cilia. A yolky substance dripped from the corners of his mouth. Small, wet spikes were emerging from his scalp, like a crown of thorns.

Shaw looked at Frank and whimpered for mercy.

Frank took a pistol from a dead soldier's hand. He went over to Shaw and shot him in the head. Shaw's body quivered once then fell still. Frank dropped the pistol.

There was movement out by the edge of the camp towards the north side where the pits had been carved into the earth.

A little girl, red-haired and pale. It wasn't Florence.

It was Emily.

Frank smiled.

She beckoned to him.

Frank went to her.

As he approached Emily she turned and started towards the pits, glancing back at him. He followed. She led him to the pits. He thought he could hear her voice inside his head. Emily halted by one of the pits and looked down. Then she turned back to him. She smiled again. She pointed into the pit.

He looked into the earth. When he looked back at Emily, she had vanished.

Frank went down into the pit, amongst the scorched remains. He fell to his knees. He searched the pile of bodies as thunder roared overhead. He searched while his heartbeat counted down the time he had left, as his blood leaked from his body and he grew weaker.

Darkness closed in around him. He sensed Emily nearby, watching him. He remembered his friends and the world that was now lost.

I am still Frank Hooper, and I will die as a man, not a monster.

When he found what was left of his wife, in the midst of warped limbs and eyeless faces, he curled his body beside her and wrapped himself around her bones. Trace of red in her blackened hair. Her skull grinned, pleased to see him. Her spindly fingers brushed against his skin. She accepted him, welcomed him into her embrace as he produced her wedding band from his pocket and slipped it onto her ring finger. He put his mouth to hers. His lips opened. Her scent was smoke and old things. She tasted of ashes.

He closed his eyes.

His final thoughts ran through his mind.

Humanity was a dying flame, its passing barely noted by an unsympathetic, indifferent universe. The Earth would have new masters. The constellations would still burn and species greater than Man would emerge to grow and die in the dark reaches of the cosmos.

Frank went to sleep, content in his heart that he would never wake up.

www.richwhawkins.blogspot.com

www.crowdedquarantine.co.uk